THE GOLDEN MILE TO MURDER

Recent Titles by Sally Spencer from Severn House

THE DARK LADY

DEATH OF A CAVE DWELLER

MURDER AT SWANN'S LAKE

THE PARADISE JOB

THE SALTON KILLINGS

THE SILENT LAND

THE GOLDEN MILE
TO MURDER

Sally Spencer

This first world edition published in Great Britain 2001 by
SEVERN HOUSE PUBLISHERS LTD of
9–15 High Street, Sutton, Surrey SM1 1DF.
This first world edition published in the USA 2001 by
SEVERN HOUSE PUBLISHERS INC of
595 Madison Avenue, New York, N.Y. 10022.

British Library Cataloguing in Publication Data

Spencer, Sally, 1949
    The golden mile to murder
    1.   Woodend, Chief Inspector (Fictitious character) - Fiction
    2.   Police - Fiction
    3.   Blackpool (England) - Fiction
    4.   Detective and mystery stories
    I.   Title
    823.9'14 [F]

    ISBN 0-7278-5710-X

Typeset by Palimpsest Book Production Ltd.,
Polmont, Stirlingshire, Scotland.
Printed and bound in Great Britain by
MPG Books Ltd., Bodmin, Cornwall.

Acknowledgements

Thanks are due to the people of Blackpool who helped me with background to this book, especially the staff of the Central Library. As always, I am grateful to my webmaster, Luis de Avendano, for all his splendid work in maintaining my website – www.arrakis.es/~sspencer.

Author's Note

This book contains many real locations and buildings, though some of them appear under different names. The characters and events who populate them, however, are entirely products of my imagination.

One

B ehind them shone the bright lights of Blackpool, ahead of them lay the darkness of the Irish Sea. The iron struts of the Central Pier were above their heads and under them was the warm, friable sand. Perfect, Derek Thomson thought. Bloody perfect!

He turned to the girl sitting next to him. 'Happy?' he asked.

The girl shrugged awkwardly. 'I'm all right, I suppose,' she admitted. 'But isn't it time we were gettin' back?'

Derek forced himself to laugh, as if the very notion were preposterous. 'Gettin' back?' he repeated. 'But it's only half-past ten, Mavis.'

'I know, but me dad always says—'

'Your dad isn't here,' the boy reminded her. 'Your mam neither, for that matter.'

It was true – gloriously true. Though they had taken some convincing, both their sets of parents had finally agreed they could go on holiday together – or at least Mavis's had agreed she could go with a bunch of her mates, while his mam and dad had let him off the leash with some lads from the factory.

'Me mam warned me to be careful,' Mavis said.

I'll bet she did! Derek thought. Whenever he went round to their house, he felt Ma White watching him like a hawk, as if she suspected that within this shy, bumbling boy, a secret sex fiend was lurking. It wasn't like that at all. He loved Mavis. He really did. Hadn't he been going out with her for nearly a year? Wouldn't he probably end up marrying her? But he was still only nineteen, and until he finished his apprenticeship, in another two years, there was no chance of them getting wed.

1

And was he expected to wait that long before he satisfied his ever-stronger urges? Was he to be content with the occasional unsatisfactory fumble outside the youth club until he had served his time and become a craftsman like his dad? That might have suited the older people, but this was the start of the 1960s, and it was old-fashioned to wait.

'I think I should be goin',' Mavis said. 'The other girls'll be wonderin' where I am.'

'They'll *know* where you are,' Derek said. 'An' I bet they're wishin' they were here in your place.'

'What? With you?' Mavis asked, a hint of jealousy and suspicion suddenly evident in her voice.

'No, not with me,' Derek said hastily. 'With some lad who cared about them like I care about you.' He lowered his voice a little. 'An' I *do* care about you.'

'I know you do.'

'I care about you, an' I want to go all the way with you.'

Mavis shifted slightly away from him. 'Nice girls don't do that.'

'Nice girls don't *sleep around*,' he countered. 'But if they're with somebody they love, somebody they're goin' to spend the rest of their lives with . . .'

He let the sentence trail off, leaving her to fill in the rest of the details herself.

'We could get married now, instead of waitin',' she suggested.

'Your mam an' dad would never allow it. An' even if they would, I don't want to spend the first few years of our married life in their back bedroom, listenin' to your dad snorin' all night long. I want to do things properly. When we tie the knot, it'll be to move into a house of our own. But you see, I can't wait that long. I've got these . . . urges.'

'If you really loved me, you'd wait.'

'It's because I really love you that I *can't* wait.'

She fell unnaturally quiet, and he wondered if he had gone too far – pushed her too hard. He was almost on the point of telling her he was sorry for making the suggestion and begging her to forgive him when she said, 'All right.'

'All right?' he repeated, hardly able to believe his luck.

'But you will be gentle with me, won't you?'

'Of course I will,' he assured her, though since what was about to happen was almost as big a mystery to him as it was to her, he was not entirely sure what being gentle entailed.

'I won't get pregnant, will I?' Mavis asked.

'No, of course you won't. I've taken precautions.'

She giggled. 'You mean you've got a packet of them things from the barber's?'

'That's right.'

'Well, you'd better put one on, then, hadn't you?'

He recalled all the Sunday afternoon conversations he'd had with his brother, Fred, when the older lad had come back from one of his heavy lunchtime drinking session at the pub.

'You have to be careful with birds,' Fred had told him, as they lay sprawled across the beds in the room they shared. 'Thing is, they want it, but they don't want it at the same time, if you see what I mean.'

'I don't think I do.'

'They might quite fancy the *idea*, but it's the whatjamecallit – the reality – that puts 'em off. So you have to keep the reality at bay until it's too late.'

'An' how do I do that?'

'Well, for starters, don't stand in front of 'em while you're slidin' the rubber on your John Thomas. Do it in the lavvy.'

But there was no lavvy under this pier.

Derek climbed to his feet. 'What's the matter?' Mavis asked. 'Have I said somethin' to put you off?'

'No. I just thought I'd better go an' make sure that there's nobody else around.'

'That's a good idea,' the girl agreed.

He walked away from her, towards the sea. The pier rested on cast-iron pillars, and between their bases ran thick reinforcing bars, so that every few yards he was forced to take a high step. It was going to happen! he told himself. His little Mavis was actually going to allow him to put his thing in her – like a proper grown-up.

He reached into his pocket and took out the packet of

prophylactics which he had bought – after much hesitation and embarrassment – a few days earlier. He extracted one, lifted the tin foil wrapper to his mouth, and gently bit along the edge. Experience would have taught him to stand still while he performed such a delicate task, but instead he kept on walking and, his mind on the wrapper, he misjudged the position of the next reinforcement bar. He felt his ankle slam into the bar, and a split second later he was flying forward. Too late, he put his arms in front of him to break his fall, and his chest hit the sand with a heavy thud.

Lying there, gasping, he assessed his situation. He was winded, though not too badly. The rubber had flown out of his hand, but he still had two more in the packet – and nobody did it more than twice in a night, did they? What really had him bothered was that his right hand had landed on something hard and sticky. He wondered what it could be. Had a dog crapped on one of the rocks, or was his hand resting in some drunk's vomit?

He gingerly removed the hand from whatever the sticky substance was, and felt his fingers brush against something which stuck out above the gunge – a triangular outcrop which could almost have been a nose. He raised his head and gazed in horror at the black shape which lay in front of him. At one end of it was the round bit which his hand had explored. At the other end, there was what were undoubtedly a pair of feet pointing up to the sky.

All thoughts of carnal knowledge disappeared from his mind. Derek pulled himself up into a crouching position – and emptied the contents of his stomach out on to the sand in front of him.

Two

It felt strange to be in Whitebridge again after over twenty years away, Charlie Woodend thought as he made his way down Cathedral Street. Very strange indeed. It was in this town that he'd signed up to fight Hitler back in 1939, a course of action which had led him to the burning deserts of North Africa and from there to the D-Day landings and the horrors of the Nazi death camps. It was true he'd been back a number of times since then, but it had always somehow seemed as if he were a visitor, rather than someone coming home. Well, now it *was* to be home again. The new job – which had been thrust on him rather than sought – had ensured that.

Woodend looked around him. The old covered market was still doing thriving business. The tripe shops – something you never saw down South – still offered delicacies such as pigs' trotters. And every time you breathed in, you still filled your nostrils with the smell of malt and hops from the town's three breweries. Yet there had been changes, too. There was much more traffic than there had been when he was a lad. People dressed differently, too. Clogs had been the preferred footwear before the war, and many women had still worn dark woollen shawls. Now the folk who passed him were brightly dressed and almost indistinguishable from the Londoners he'd grown used to living amongst over the previous fifteen years. So perhaps you never really *could* go back, he thought – because *back* wasn't there any longer.

He came to a halt in front of a large red sandstone building. It had arched windows which seemed to glare disapprovingly down at the street, and over the door a stone mason – probably long dead by now – had carved the words 'Whitebridge Police Headquarters' in stern gothic lettering.

You'll be seein' a lot of this place, Charlie, Woodend told himself.

A balding sergeant with a well-clipped moustache was standing behind the duty desk. He gave Woodend's hairy sports coat and cavalry twill trousers the once over, then said indifferently, 'Can I help you, sir?'

Woodend nodded. 'I'm the new DCI.'

A look of surprise came to the sergeant's placid face. 'You're Chief Inspector Woodend, are you?' he asked dubiously.

'That's right,' Woodend agreed.

He was not surprised that the sergeant was surprised – most people would have expected a senior officer like him to appear in a suit. Aye, well, lounge suits had never been his style, and the bobbies in Whitebridge were just going to have to get used to that.

'If you'd like to show me to my office, an' then get somebody to give me the guided tour –' he suggested.

'Of course, sir,' the sergeant replied. 'Just as soon as you've had your meetin' with Chief Superintendent Ainsworth.'

'What! He wants to see me right away?'

'That's right,' the sergeant agreed. 'Said you were to report to him the minute you turned up.'

The door, like all the others in the building, was painted institutional chocolate brown. Woodend knocked, waited for the barked command to enter, then turned the handle. His first impression of the office he stepped into was one of neatness. Neat rug, perfectly aligned to the walls. Neat notice-board, all the messages squared and with a drawing pin in each corner. Neat desk, holding only a telephone, one in-tray and one out-tray, and an onyx ashtray.

He turned his attention to the man sitting behind the desk. Ainsworth had greying hair, suspicious brown eyes and the florid complexion of someone who either drank too much or got angry very easily. His new boss was older than he was himself, Woodend guessed – but only by a couple of years.

Ainsworth stood up, revealing the fact that he was only

a little over the minimum requirement for the force. 'Chief Inspector Woodend?' he asked, in a dry, tight voice.

'That's right, sir.'

The DCS shook Woodend's hand and waved him to a chair.

'When I heard you were called Ainsworth, I imagined you were a local lad,' Woodend said. 'But you're not, are you, sir?'

'No,' Ainsworth replied. 'I'm originally from Kent.' He scowled. 'Any objection to that?'

'Not really,' Woodend said. 'It's just that the reason I came up here in the first place was to get away from you Southern buggers.' He grinned, to show he was joking. 'No offence meant, sir.'

Ainsworth did not return his smile. Instead he reached into his drawer and produced a sheaf of papers.

'You didn't come up here to get away from southerners, Chief Inspector,' he said. 'You came because the Yard didn't want you, and because my chief constable – for reasons best known to himself – did.' He flicked through the papers in front of him, and selected the one he wanted. 'You were in the army, I see.'

'Aye, it seemed like a good idea, what with a war goin' on an' everythin',' Woodend replied.

'But you never rose above the rank of sergeant.'

'No.'

'And why was that? Were you never offered promotion?' Ainsworth asked, a slight sneer playing on his lips.

'Oh, I was offered it, but becomin' an officer would have meant leavin' my lads, an' I'd grown quite attached to them.'

'I was a major by the time the war ended,' Ainsworth said, making the statement seem almost like a challenge.

'Good for you,' Woodend said. 'Did you see much action, sir?'

'Wars aren't just won by the death-and-glory boys, you know,' Ainsworth replied. 'An army marches on its stomach, as the old saying goes.'

'That's true enough,' Woodend agreed, displaying uncharacteristic tact.

Ainsworth gave him a searching stare, and then returned to his notes. 'I've been reviewing your recent cases, Mr Woodend, and I have to tell you that your usual methods of investigation simply will not be tolerated here,' he said.

'How do you mean, sir?'

'This is a thoroughly modern police force. When we investigate a murder, we do it using the crime centre we have established in this station as our base of operations. That idea does not seem to find favour with you.'

He paused, giving the new man a chance to speak, but Woodend said nothing.

'Some of your recent investigations have been conducted from, among other places, a country hotel, a public house and – I still find this hard to believe – the social club office in which a victim actually met his end.'

'I like to be close to the scene of the crime,' Woodend explained. 'You learn a lot more cloggin' it round the area the victim lived in than you ever would sittin' on your backside in some crime centre.'

Ainsworth frowned again. 'There is no longer room for amateurism in the police force, Chief Inspector,' he said. 'We must run the business of investigating crime like any other business – with the senior management making the executive decisions and the lower ranks carrying out the work on the ground.'

'I'm not sure I could operate in that way,' Woodend said.

'You don't have any choice in the matter,' Ainsworth told him harshly. 'Not as long as you're serving under me.' He lit a cigarette, but did not offer Woodend the packet. 'Where are you living, Chief Inspector?'

'I've got a room at the Saracen's Arms. It's only temporary, of course. My wife's comin' up in a couple of days, and then we'll start lookin' for a hou—'

'I asked where you are living at the moment, not for an account of your domestic arrangements,' Ainsworth said. 'Not that that really matters, anyway, because you'll be going out of town.'

'I beg your pardon, sir?'

'Last night, a body was discovered under the Central Pier at

Blackpool – a man, with his face badly battered. He has since been identified as Detective Inspector William Davies.'

Woodend whistled softly.

'Exactly!' Ainsworth agreed. 'The chief constable feels – and I agree with him – that, given the nature of the case, it would be best to take the investigation out of the hands of the local force. You are the only one of my senior men not currently involved in any investigation, so you've drawn the short straw.'

'But I've only just arrived,' Woodend protested. 'I haven't got my bearings yet. My sergeant isn't even here.'

Ainsworth raised a quizzical eyebrow. 'Your sergeant?' he repeated.

'I mean, Inspector Rutter,' Woodend corrected himself.

He was still having trouble thinking of Bob Rutter as an inspector, even though he had been the one responsible for getting Rutter the promotion.

'You have already been assigned a new sergeant,' Ainsworth told him. 'You will be working with Sergeant Paniatowski.'

'Polish, is he?' Woodend asked.

A thin smile came to the Chief Superintendent's lips – Woodend wondered what had caused it.

'With a name like that, I would assume the sergeant is Polish, yes,' Ainsworth said, still enjoying his private joke. He stubbed his cigarette in the ashtray and immediately emptied it into the bin. 'That's all, Chief Inspector. The Blackpool police will have a briefing file ready for you when you get there.'

Woodend was almost at the door when Ainsworth said, 'There is one more thing, Chief Inspector.'

'Yes, sir?'

'I told you earlier I don't like the way you seem to work, but even without that there'd already have been a black spot against your name.'

'Is that right?' Woodend asked. 'An' why would that be, sir?'

'Because I don't like having some burnt-out Scotland Yard bobby dumped on me whether I want him or not. So take warning, Mr Woodend. I'll be watching you carefully, and if you step out of line by so much as a fraction of an inch, I'll have you back pounding the beat before you can say "disciplinary board".'

Woodend forced a grin to his face. 'Thank you for your confidence, sir,' he said.

The police canteen was a long thin room – badly in need of a fresh coat of paint – and was located at the back of the station. The counter stood close to the door. Behind it were two thick-legged, middle-aged women wearing hairnets, one lethargically buttering bread, the other filling the tea urn from a brown enamel kettle. Between the counter and the far wall were perhaps a dozen Formica-topped tables. Most of the officers in the canteen were in uniform, but there was one young man in street clothes sitting alone at a table and reading the *Daily Herald*.

Woodend gave him the once-over. Age around twenty-five. Thick black hair. Strong jaw. The same sort of determined aura around him as Bob Rutter had. He'd do very well once he'd been properly trained, the Chief Inspector decided.

Woodend walked over to the young man's table. 'Sergeant Paniatowski?' he asked.

A puzzled expression came to the other man's face. 'Sergeant Paniatowski?' he repeated. Then he laughed. 'Me – Paniatowski? You've got completely the wrong end of the stick, mate.' He pointed with his right index finger. 'That's Sergeant Panties sitting over by the window.'

Woodend's gaze followed the pointing finger, and suddenly he realised what Chief Superintendent Ainsworth's private joke had been all about.

Polish, is he? Woodend had asked.

Well, the sergeant might or might not be Polish, but the blonde with the firm bosom who was sitting next to the window was definitely not a *he*.

Three

It was a pleasantly warm morning and the holidaymakers were out in droves. Groups of mill girls, their curlered hair covered with cowboy hats bearing the legend 'Kiss Me Quick', made their way along the promenade, laughing and screaming at the tops of their voices. Gangs of young men sprawling on benches watched the girls appreciatively as they passed, then turned their attention to the new tattoos which had seemed such a good idea after five or six pints of bitter, but had now begun to itch. There were mothers pushing baby trolleys, and older children struggling to eat sticky candyfloss. The air was filled with the smell of brine, frying fish and cheap scent. The cream and green trams rattled hurriedly and importantly by. Paper Union Jacks were already being stuck in sand castles on the beach. This was Blackpool in the summer – and as far as the people out on the street were concerned, they were in the entertainment capital of the world.

The two men in dark suits sitting at a wooden table outside Dutton's 'Oh Be Joyful' Tavern did not seem to be sharing in the holiday spirit. The older of the pair was about forty-five and had a large nose and bushy eyebrows which were already turning grey. He was staring across the promenade and out to sea – as if he were expecting the answer to all his problems to appear suddenly on the horizon. The second man had just celebrated his thirtieth birthday, but had the sort of youthful features which ensured that most people took him for much younger. He did not seem to share his superior's fascination with the water, and instead occupied himself with studying the half-empty pint glass in front of him – and wondering just exactly what this meeting was to be all about.

Apparently giving up hope that his ship would ever come in, the older man – Chief Inspector Turner of the Blackpool police – turned to the younger man, Detective Sergeant Hanson, and said, 'I don't like it, Frank.'

'Don't like what, sir?' Hanson replied.

'I don't like the fact that "Punch" Davies' murder is being investigated by somebody from outside.'

Hanson frowned. 'Why's that, sir? Murder's not exactly our speciality, and from what I've heard of this Chief Inspector Woodend, he's a very experienced officer.'

'I was on the team Woodend put together to investigate that fishmonger's murder in Clitheroe a few years back,' Turner told him. 'You don't really know the meaning of the term "bloody-minded" until you've worked with Cloggin'-it Charlie. He's stubborn, unreasonable, relentless – and possibly the best policeman it's ever been my privilege to work with.'

'Well, then, what's the problem?' Hanson asked. 'Billy was a bloody good governor to me. I miss him already, and what I want most in the world is to catch whoever topped him. That's what we *all* want, isn't it? So why should we object when they send us a top-flight bobby to handle the case?'

Turner sighed. 'The problem is, Cloggin'-it Charlie may just be a bit *too* good,' he explained. 'He could uncover things that a lesser man wouldn't even notice.'

'I might be being thick, but I think you'll have to spell it out for me a bit more clearly, I'm afraid, sir,' Hanson said.

'I went round to see Billy's widow, Edna, this morning,' Turner told him.

'How is she, sir?'

'She's putting on a brave front, though I imagine she's absolutely devastated. But she has at least got one consolation. And do you know what that is?'

'No, sir.'

'That her husband was a first-class officer, and died as much a hero as any soldier who was killed in the last war.'

'And so he did,' Hanson said, sounding indignant even at the possibility that anyone could even consider thinking otherwise. 'I don't know what case he was working on when he died, but it's obvious to me that whatever it was, he was getting so close to cracking it that the villains had him killed.'

'That's one way of looking at it,' Turner agreed.

'And what's the other way?'

Turner hesitated for a second. 'There have been rumours buzzing around the station,' he said. 'No, not even that. There've been the merest *hints* of rumours. Have you heard any of them?'

'No, sir.'

Turner sighed again. 'There's just the two of us here, son, and this conversation is strictly off the record. So stop pissing about and open up for me.'

Hanson shrugged awkwardly. 'I may have got a little bit of the buzz,' he admitted, 'but I didn't pay attention to it.'

'What if those rumours are true?' Turner demanded. 'What if Punch really was up to what they say he was up to? If that comes to light, it'll leave the Blackpool force with its reputation tarnished, and Edna Davies will be forced to face the fact that she never really knew the man she'd been married to all those years.'

'I hadn't thought of it like that before,' Hanson admitted. 'But you're right – there's no question about that. So what do we do about it? Try and get Mr Woodend off the case?'

Turner shook his head. 'That wouldn't work,' he said. 'Dick Ainsworth's the head of CID for this county, and once that bastard's made his mind up about something, there's no changing it.'

'Well, then . . .'

'So we're going to have to content ourselves with just minimising the damage.'

'And what would that entail, sir?' Hanson asked, sounding as if he were not entirely happy with the way the conversation was going.

Turner placed an avuncular hand on the sergeant's shoulder. 'Charlie Woodend's not a man for tackling any investigation mob-handed,' he said, 'but he will need at least one man on his team with some local knowledge. I'm going to suggest that that man is you. It will be your job to give the chief inspector all the help he needs in solving the murder – you're quite right about everybody on the force wanting the bugger who killed Punch caught – but you'll also be there to steer him away from any of the grey areas we'd much rather he didn't go into. Do you understand what I'm saying, Sergeant Hanson? Am I making myself completely clear?'

The younger detective thought about it for a few moments. 'Yes, I think so, sir,' he said finally.

'And you'll do it?'

Hanson nodded. 'Whatever else may or may not have been true about Mr Davies, he was a bloody good feller to work for, and I'd like to see him buried with honour.'

Turner turned his gaze back towards the sea again. A breeze had blown up and the fluffy blue-grey waves were considerably higher than they'd been a few minutes earlier.

Everything changes, he thought. The weather. The seasons. The way people look – and what they expect out of life. If the rumours were true, then Punch Davies had certainly changed from the earnest young bobby he'd been a few years earlier into a different kind of man entirely. But then wasn't what he'd been through with his kid enough to change *anybody*? Well, whatever had happened had happened, and Punch was dead. Sergeant Hanson wanted to see him buried with honour, and so did everybody else. So what would be the *point* in raking up the muck now?

Four

W oodend sat at a corner table in the saloon bar of the Rising Sun, his gaze fixed vaguely on the women's toilet into which Monika Paniatowski had vanished as soon as they'd reached the pub. He took a reflective sip of his pint of Thwaites' Best Bitter. Being back in a place where they served decent ale should have put him in seventh heaven, he thought. Yet he was feeling far from happy. He'd expected his new boss – if Ainsworth was at like all the other bosses he'd ever worked for – to become antagonistic towards him over the course of time. But from the very beginning of their relationship? That was not good. And he didn't like being sent out on a case before he'd got his bearings – especially a case which was made all the more delicate by the fact that it involved another bobby.

Then there was his new sergeant to consider. He'd never had a female as his bagman – maybe he should call her bag*woman* – before, and he was still not sure what complications that might lead to. The fact that she was a woman had already started to modify his behaviour – if Bob Rutter had been with him, he'd have been sitting in the public bar now; with Paniatowski by his side he had felt obliged to plump for the lounge.

The toilet door swung open, and Paniatowski came out. Woodend took a closer look at the woman he would be spending much of his time with. Her blonde hair was short – almost severe. She had deep blue eyes which looked as if they could be quick to show her anger and a jaw which was firm, without being masculine. Overall, he decided, she could be said to be a pretty woman, though her nose was a little too large and her lips a little too thick to make her quite 'English pretty'.

She noticed him watching her, and he instinctively turned away. Another difference between the sexes, he thought. A man would have assumed – quite rightly – that his new boss was assessing his character, whereas, from the look on her face, it was obvious that Paniatowski already had him marked down as a lecher.

'I'm sorry I've been so long, sir,' the sergeant said, sitting down as far as was possible from him, given the limitations of a small, circular table.

Woodend bit back the comment that she *had* been a long time – but then women usually were – and said, 'That's all right. I never feel lonely when I'm in the company of a pint of Thwaites Best Bitter. What are you havin'?'

'I'd like a vodka, please.'

'You think they'll have an exotic drink like that in an ordinary pub like this one?'

'I know they will. I'm a regular. They stock it 'specially for me.'

Woodend nodded. He should have expected that, he thought – Monika Paniatowski looked like the kind of woman who knew what she wanted and made sure she got it.

As the Chief Inspector stood up and walked over to the bar, Monika found herself going over her first impressions of him. He was a big feller, she thought – broad as well as tall. His hair was light brown, but unlike most of the men in Whitebridge, he didn't use Brylcreem, so it looked quite unruly. His mouth was wide, and his jaw square without being brutish. He looked like a nice man. But then Arthur Jones – who she never had been able to bring herself to call 'Dad' – had looked like a nice man, too. And so had most of the officers down at the cop shop.

Woodend returned with a double vodka and a fresh pint for himself. 'You must be a bloody good detective,' he said disarmingly, as he sat down.

'What makes you think that?'

'Just before we left the station, I was lookin' over your record.'

'And . . . ?'

'An' the number of people you've managed to rub up the

wrong way is quite impressive – even by my high standard of bloody-mindedness.'

Not that every one of her superior officers who'd filed a report on her had been critical, Woodend reminded himself. There'd been one in particular who, before his transfer from the area, had consistently presented her in a positive light – had seemed, in fact, to go out of his way to protect her. The Chief Inspector wondered what the man's motives had been – and whether that was going to be just one complication he'd have to deal with when they reached Blackpool.

'So the way I see it is this,' he continued. 'If you have a natural talent for gettin' up your bosses' noses an' still managed to get promotion, you *have* to be bloody good.'

'I am good,' Paniatowski said. 'I'm the best detective sergeant in Lancashire.'

'The best detective sergeant? Or the best *woman* detective sergeant?'

'There is only *one* woman detective sergeant.'

Woodend grinned. 'I rather thought that might be the case,' he admitted. He took a generous sip of his pint. 'Since we're goin' to be workin' together, I think it's about time I started layin' down some ground rules. Don't you agree, lass?'

Lass! Paniatowski thought angrily. The first step to sweetheart, bird, judy and totty!

'You can cut that out for a start,' Woodend said firmly.

'Cut what out, sir?'

'Lookin' so disapprovin'. Doin' an impression of a hen's backside with your lips. If you'd been a feller, I'd have called you "lad". Since you're a woman, I called you "lass". Don't go readin' anythin' into it.'

'I'd much prefer it if you'd call me "Sergeant", sir.'

Woodend shook his head wonderingly. 'All right, have it your way, *Sergeant*. First off, I expect the men on my team – the *people* on my team – to work bloody hard. Round the clock, if that's what's called for. Secondly, I expect them to use their own initiative an' not come runnin' to me to get their noses wiped every five minutes. An' thirdly, I expect them to put up with my bad moods – just as I've had to put up with the bad moods of *my* bosses on the way up. Understood?'

'Yes, sir,' said Paniatowski, woodenly.

'Now the other side of the coin is that I'm more interested in catchin' criminals than I am in impressin' men with pips on the shoulders of their uniforms,' Woodend continued. 'Which means that if you make a breakthrough in an investigation, I won't start pretendin' it was my idea all along – unlike some buggers I could mention. My last sergeant got promoted up to inspector in record time. Did you know that?'

'No, sir, I didn't.'

'An' you could follow in his footsteps – if you play your cards right.'

He sounded decent, Paniatowski thought. He sounded fair. They all did in the beginning. But the night would come when he'd had too much to drink and he'd let his hand rest on her shoulder, then begin an artful journey down towards her breasts.

And if she resisted – as she would – he'd just repeat all the taunts she'd heard a thousand times before.

Come on, Monika, it's only a bit of fun!
What's the matter? Don't you like men?
You could do yourself a bit of good by being nice to me.

Either that or – for all he'd just said – the jobs he'd give her would be ones which were considered suitable for *women* police officers rather than *real* ones. Oh, she'd seen it all before.

'You've still got your doubts about me, haven't you, Sergeant?' Woodend asked.

Paniatowski looked straight into her new boss's eyes, and noticed for the first time how dark – almost black – they were.

'If I do have reservations, sir, can you really blame me?' she asked.

Woodend shook his head. 'No, I suppose not. It can't be easy bein' the only female detective sergeant in Lancashire.' He drained the remains of his pint. 'Would you like to know why I think Chief Superintendent Ainsworth has put the two of us together?'

Paniatowski thought about it for a second, and then nodded.

'It's because I'm my own man, an' you're your own woman,' Woodend told her. 'It's not an easy path to follow – it means we've got to be twice as good as anybody else just to stay even – but it's the path we've both chosen.'

'Are you saying that Mr Ainsworth assigned me to you because he thinks we'll make an excellent team?' Paniatowski asked.

Woodend shook his head. 'No, sergeant. I'm sayin' he put us together because no other bugger really wants to work with either of us.'

Five

The black police Humber made its way along the A59, skirting old mill towns and passing through lushly green countryside which never failed to surprise visitors from the South with their preconceptions of what the black industrial North looked like.

Had he been on his own, Woodend would have automatically sat next to the driver, but since he had WDS Paniatowski with him, the chief inspector had chosen to travel in the back. Even before the car left Whitebridge, Woodend realised this was a mistake. There was plenty of room in the rear seat of the Humber, but Paniatowski pressed her body firmly against her door, leaving a large – uncomfortably obvious – gap between them.

What was going through her mind? Woodend wondered. Did she really imagine he'd make a pass at her under the watchful eye of the driver? In fact, why should she imagine he'd make a pass at her at all? Oh, he'd had his chances in his time – Liz Poole, the mature and gorgeous landlady of the George and Dragon, whose daughter had been involved in the Salton case, came immediately to mind – but he'd always resisted them. And having turned down Liz, he certainly wasn't to chance his arm with a slip of a girl like Paniatowski.

He lit up a Capstan Full Strength and took a thoughtful drag. The trouble with Paniatowski was that she was an unknown quantity – and he wasn't sure yet whether this was because she was a woman, or because she was a Pole, or due to something else entirely. All of which was going to add extra difficulties to the investigation – which was exactly why that bastard Detective Chief Superintendent Ainsworth had assigned her to him!

'I always used to come to Blackpool for me holidays when I was a lad,' Woodend said.

'Is that right, sir?' Paniatowski asked – neutrally, disinterestedly.

'Aye,' Woodend said, already slipping into the golden glow which was the memories of his childhood. 'An' it wasn't just the Woodend family. All the mills were closed down for Wakes Week, an' the *whole town* ended up in Blackpool.'

He remembered it clearly as if it were only yesterday. There'd been no Saturday lie-in on the first day of the holidays. The family had got up early, so that Mam could cook them a decent breakfast before they'd started out. And almost before they'd finished eating it, they'd hear the noise of an engine purring outside. The sound of a taxi – the only one they'd ever consider taking between one summer holiday and the next. Pure magic!

That was when the holiday really started – when they climbed into that big cab and he felt the leather seat pressing against the backs of his bare knees. The excitement had mounted by the time they'd reached the bus station, and he saw all the hundreds of other voyagers waiting to get on the charabancs – fathers in their best suits, mothers in floral-print dresses, children with small cardboard suitcases of their own.

It hadn't been a long trip – no more than fifty miles – but in those days it had seemed like an epic journey. There'd even been a stop at a pub called The Half-Way House, which couldn't really have been halfway for *everyone* who travelled to Blackpool, where the men would have their first pint of the day and the women and kids would order cups of tea and cakes.

It was after the stop that things really reached fever pitch. All the children – and many of the adults – would gaze into the distance, hoping to be the first one to spot Blackpool Tower.

The tower! A tapering cast-iron structure pointing to the sky, which served no purpose other than to announce that Blackpool existed. It had been built a few years later than the Eiffel Tower, was only half the size and, instead of spreading its legs majestically across the Champ de Mars, it rose – beanpole-like – out of the Woolworths Building. A poor relation to the French model, in fact. But that it was inferior to the other tower didn't matter to the kids on the bus – even if they'd heard of Paris. They spent fifty-one weeks a year in dark towns of huddled stone terraced houses, and they knew – with an absolute conviction – that Blackpool was the greatest place in the world. The enchanted kingdom. Fairyland.

A great cheer always rose up when the Tower was sighted, and from then on, until the charabanc finally came to a halt in the coach park, the children would be nervously twisting and turning in their seats.

A taxi had been the only way to get to the coach station in their home towns, but it was not the way that visitors journeyed from the bus to their boarding houses in Blackpool. As they stepped down from the bus, they were mobbed by dozens of local kids pushing wheeled vehicles which had once formed parts of prams and delivery bicycles. The family luggage would be loaded up on to one of these unlikely contraptions, then the Woodends – or the Ramsbottoms or the Battersbys – would follow behind the truck, savouring the sea air and relishing the thought of a whole week of freedom.

'Of course, it was different in them days,' Woodend said. 'For instance, now, you all eat the same meal at the same time, but when I was a kid, the mams did the shoppin', an' the landlady cooked a different meal for every family. There was one coal miner from Sunderland, I remember, who used to polish off six or seven pork chops at a sittin'. Nobody seems to have the appetite for that kind of eatin' now. I expect it was the war – live on rations for a few years an' your stomach's bound to shrink.'

'The British have no idea what it's like to be really hungry,' Paniatowski said, so softly she could almost have been speaking to herself.

'What was that, lass?'

'Nothing, sir.'

'So I was imaginin' it, was I? Come on, I hate it when people won't say what's on their minds.'

Paniatowski sighed. 'The British have no idea what it's like to be really hungry,' she repeated.

'But you do?'

'For five years – under Hitler – we were slowly starving to death in Warsaw. And after that, when my mother and I fled the city to escape the Russians, it was even worse. If I ever did have a decent meal before I came to England, then I certainly don't remember it.' Monika Paniatowski paused – as if embarrassed at having been forced to reveal something of herself to the big chief inspector – then glanced out of the window. 'There is your tower, sir,' she continued.

So it was. And despite all the years which had passed since he'd last seen it – despite the changes he'd gone through in that time – Woodend felt just a twinge of that unbridled joy he'd experienced as a child.

There were chief inspectors who would have sat in their offices and had their visitors shown in to them, but Turner was waiting in the corridor to welcome the two arrivals from headquarters. A nice touch, Woodend thought, as they shook hands. A very nice touch indeed.

Having greeted his fellow chief inspector, Turner immediately shifted his attention to Paniatowski. 'Hello, Monika,' he said warmly. 'How are you keeping?'

'I'm fine, sir,' the sergeant replied.

And Woodend noticed that, for once, Paniatowski seemed to have given up playing the Ice Maiden.

Turner led them into his office, and gestured to them to sit down.

'I was wonderin' if you were the feller I thought you were,' Woodend said, as he lowered himself into one of the visitors' chairs. 'An' now I see that you are.'

Turner looked puzzled. 'I beg your pardon, si— I mean, Charlie.'

Woodend grinned. 'Aye, you're right, there's no need to "sir" me now,' he said. 'While I've been standin' still halfway up the promotion ladder, just lookin' at the view, you've been climbin' it like a mountain goat. An' good luck to you.'

'I wasn't sure you'd remember me,' Turner said.

'What? Not remember the sergeant who found the adjustable spanner which finally led us to the plumber?' Woodend shook his head. 'No, when a man's sweated blood for me, I don't forget. I knew you were him the second I saw you, but until you spoke to my assistant here I wasn't sure whether you were the Inspector Turner who'd written such nice things in her records while he was based in Whitebridge.'

'I . . . yes, that's me,' Turner said, noticing that Paniatowski, who was now sitting in other visitors' chair, was starting to blush.

'Well, it's nice to start with an "in", even if it is only through the good offices of my sergeant,' Woodend said pleasantly.

'You'll want briefing about the murder,' Turner suggested.

'Indeed I will,' Woodend agreed. 'But before we get on to that, why don't you paint me a bit of a picture of what it's like bein' a bobby in this place?'

'All right,' Turner agreed. 'We get a lot of visitors, s— Charlie, but in most respects Blackpool is essentially a small town with typically small-town crime.'

'A fair number of pickpockets, I'd imagine.'

'Yes, plenty of them. And there's some prostitution, though not a lot. We have our share of drunken holidaymakers – especially when they've just arrived or are about to leave; and a fair amount of vandalism.'

'But no murders?'

'We get the odd heat-of-the-moment killing, but none of the really deep mysteries like the ones you'll be used to working on.'

'Until now,' Woodend pointed out. 'Tell me about the dead man – this Inspector Davies.'

'Pu— Billy put his heart and soul into his work. Everybody thought very highly of him.'

'You weren't goin' to call him Billy, were you?'

'I beg your pardon?'

'You were goin' to call him "Pug" or somethin' like that.'

'Punch,' Turner admitted. 'That was his nickname. Though nobody called it him to his face.'

'Punch,' Woodend repeated thoughtfully. 'Why'd he get that name? Handy with his fists, was he? Not averse to havin' the prisoners he was interrogatin' accidentally fall down a couple of flights of stairs?'

'It was nothing like that,' Turner assured him. 'The lads called him Punch after the puppet, and his wife – Edna – has always been Judy to them.'

'Now why is that?' Woodend wondered.

Turner shrugged uncomfortably. 'It's only three years since I was transferred here from Whitebridge. When I arrived at the station he was already saddled with the nickname. You know how it is – nobody can remember where the names come from, but once they're there, they tend to stick.'

'So you've no complaints about Davies?'

'None at all. He was never going to be what you might call a "great" bobby, but you couldn't fault his commitment to the job. You've only to look at his arrest record.'

The words had come out far too pat, Woodend thought, almost as if they'd been rehearsed. Now why would that be?

'So what was his problem?' he asked.

'His problem?' Turner repeated, as if he had no idea what the other man was talking about.

'Bit too fond of the sauce, was he?'

'He didn't drink at all.'

'What? Never?' Woodend exclaimed, as if the idea were inconceivable to him.

'Not as long as I've been here.'

'Gamblin', then?'

'The odd flutter on big races like the Grand National, but always well within his means. If he'd been in debt, I'm sure that Edna would have told me about it when I went round to see her.'

'Women?'

'Billy would never have so much as looked at another woman. He was devoted to Edna.'

'Punch always says how much he loves Judy – but it doesn't stop him beatin' her to death,' Woodend pointed out dryly.

'There's no evidence that Billy ever mistreated his wife,'

Turner said, and though he was obviously trying to avoid it, he couldn't stop himself glancing concernedly at Monika Paniatowski.

'There very rarely is any evidence of maltreatment,' Woodend told him. 'Not the least because the wife in the case often proves the most reluctant of witnesses. Still, you don't see it as a strong possibility, an' I'm prepared to take your word – for the moment.'

Out of the corner of his eye, he saw that Paniatowski's hands were gripping the arms of her chair very tightly – so tightly that her knuckles were turning white. He wondered why that might be – but knew that now was not the time to go into it.

Woodend lit up a Capstan Full Strength. 'Let's get down to practical details, shall we? Where are me an' my sergeant stayin'?'

'We've booked you rooms at a boarding house,' Turner said, almost apologetically. 'I'm afraid it's nothing like as grand as one of the better hotels like the Metropol, but at this time of year—'

'Where is it?' Woodend interrupted.

'Just south of the Central Pier.'

'Then it'll do fine.'

'We've also assigned you a murder room. Actually, it's the police basement, but we've cleaned out all the rubbish, and the Post Office assure us they'll have installed at least four telephone lines by tomorrow morning.'

'I can't talk on four phones at once,' Woodend told him.

'No, but your team will need them.'

'Team? What team?'

'I've assigned you a detective sergeant – Frank Hanson's his name, he's an excellent man – and three detective constables. When you want to use the uniformed branch, you've only to put in a request.'

'Bloody hell, why would I need *any* detectives?' Woodend asked. 'I've only just arrived here. Until I've clogged it around a bit, I'll have no idea what kind of help I'm goin' to need. Why don't you put your lads on some other job? Don't tell me you couldn't use them somewhere else.

There's not a police force in the whole country that isn't short-handed.'

Turner looked at Paniatowski again, but this time there was awkwardness, rather than concern, on his face. 'I . . . er . . .' he said.

'Would you excuse us for a few minutes, Sergeant?' Woodend said.

Paniatowski nodded, rose to her feet and left the room. When she'd closed the door behind her, Woodend said, 'Let's cut through the crap, shall we? Tell me what's goin' on here.'

Turner shifted uncomfortably in his seat. 'I'd love to have my lads working through our own backlog,' he confessed, 'but, unfortunately, I didn't have any choice but to assign them to you.'

'Come again?' Woodend said.

'Orders from HQ. I've been told to give you a room and put at least four men at your disposal.'

'That order would come directly from DCS Ainsworth, would it?' Woodend asked.

'It's got his dabs all over it,' Turner acknowledged.

Woodend's eyes narrowed. 'Tell me the rest.'

Turner coughed. 'As far as I remember the wording of the order, it said I was to submit periodic reports on how well you were using the resources that I'd allocated to you,' he said.

'In other words, if I'm solvin' this murder on my own, as far as Ainsworth's concerned I'll be buggerin' things up,' Woodend said. 'Whereas, if I'm runnin' the men under me around like blue-arsed flies – but gettin' nowhere – I'll be judged to be doin' a good job.'

'Reading between the lines, I'd say that's a pretty fair assessment,' Turner admitted.

'An' how do you stand on all this?' Woodend demanded.

'I'm not sure I'm quite following you, si— Charlie.'

'Are you for me? Or are you against me?'

'I learned a lot from working with you over in Clitheroe,' Turner said. 'Your methods might not come out of the standard police manuals, exactly, but there's no doubt that they work. I

27

admire you as a policeman. We could do with more like you, in my opinion.'

Very nice – but not unqualified. 'On the other hand –' Woodend said, giving Turner an opening.

'On the other hand, I've got my sights set on being an assistant chief constable before I retire,' Turner admitted. 'And you don't achieve that ambition by crossing a man who's two steps further up the ladder than you are.'

'So would you care to spell it out for me?'

'I'm prepared to give you more rope than Mr Ainsworth would probably be happy with,' Turner said. 'On the other hand, I'm not willing to put my own neck in the noose just to spare yours.'

'Thanks for bein' so honest with me,' Woodend said. 'Well, that about covers everythin', doesn't it?'

'I believe so,' Turner agreed, standing up. 'So if you'd like me to introduce you to your team –'

'That can wait for later,' Woodend told him.

'Later?'

'Aye. Before you introduce me to these four poor buggers who've been foisted on me, I think I'd like to wear out a bit of shoe-leather cloggin' it up an' down the Golden Mile.'

The woman making her way along the promenade was wearing a flowing black skirt and a garishly embroidered jacket. On her head was a red kerchief, and hanging from her ears were a pair of heavy gold earrings. There was other evidence of gold about her person, too – bracelets, rings and chains. It was not that she particularly liked gold jewellery – as a matter of fact she considered it rather vulgar – but it was what the punters expected her to wear, and she supposed it was as good an investment as putting the money in the bank.

She had reached her kiosk – her place of business. It stood on a corner, next to a newly opened bingo hall. She stopped for a moment and listened to the caller shouting out the numbers.

'Eighty-eight – two fat ladies. Twenty-two, two little ducks, quack, quack. Twenty-one, key to the door.'

Now that really *was* mumbo-jumbo, she thought.

Her booth was painted with the same traditional swirling pattern as had appeared on so many horse-drawn caravans in the past, and the sign over the door read, 'Gypsy Elizabeth Rose. The only genuine Romany on the Golden Mile.' More than a dozen photographs hung from the wall – each one featuring Elizabeth Rose standing next to a celebrity who was doing a summer season in Blackpool. The punters liked that.

Elizabeth Rose unlocked the door, stepped into the booth, and slid behind her consulting table. It would probably be a few minutes before the first customer turned up, so there was time for her to smoke a cigarette if she wished. And she did wish – but she didn't dare take the risk of being spotted with a Players' Navy Cut between her lips. Gypsies were not supposed to smoke. Gypsies were not supposed to do anything that normal people did. Ah, but if only those 'normal' people could see her when the season was over – holidaying on the Isle of Capri. No red kerchief then. No bangles. She dressed as smartly as a countess and spoke an elegant English unhedged with ominous warnings and dark predictions.

Neither of her lives could be called a fake, she thought as she reached for the gin bottle which rested against the leg of the table. She really was that sophisticated woman in Capri. And she really was an authentic gypsy who could sometimes see into the future when she was in Blackpool. She hadn't foreseen the death of Detective Inspector Punch Davies, though. And perhaps she should have, because it hadn't needed psychic powers to divine that the course he was heading on was almost bound to lead to tragedy.

As she lifted the gin bottle to her mouth, she noted that her hands were trembling. And why shouldn't they be? Hadn't she got a right to be afraid when she was almost certain she knew who had murdered the policeman? Wasn't she entitled to shake when she examined her own predicament and saw that Davies' death had set off a trap which now gripped her in its iron jaws?

Six

The area under the Central Pier where DI Davies had been found was roped off and guarded by three young constables, but on either side of the ropes – and for as far as the eye could see – the beach was filled with canvas deckchairs. Woodend let his gaze rove over the thousands of people who had chosen to spend their time on the beach. It was a hot day, and some of the men had taken off their jackets and even loosened their ties, but few had gone so far as to remove their sleeveless pullovers. Further away, down at the edge of the sea, a group of young women had tucked the hems of their dresses into the bottom of their knickers, and were tentatively paddling in the water. It could have been a scene from his own childhood, the chief inspector thought.

'That's where the body was found,' DCI Turner said, pointing to a strip of sand between two of the pier's cast-iron supports.

'But was that where he was *killed*?' Woodend asked.

'It seems likely.'

'You can't be sure?'

'The tide was just going out. If there'd been any signs of a struggle the sea would have washed them away. But if Punch was killed somewhere else, how did the murderer get his body under the pier? He couldn't very well drag it along the prom, now could he? There'd have been too many people about.'

'Perhaps he brought it along the sands,' Monika Paniatowski suggested.

Turner shook his head. 'He'd have been spotted by someone on the promenade, Monika, and whoever saw him would have been bound to report it. No one has.'

'He could have been brought by boat,' Paniatowski said.

'What would have been the point of that?' Woodend asked. 'If the killer had gone so far as to load the body into a boat, why not simply dump it in the sea?'

'Perhaps because he wanted it to be found.'

It was possible, Woodend thought, but not likely. The most obvious explanation was probably the accurate one: that Davies had been killed where he'd been found. Woodend closed his eyes – a trick he'd learned helped him to concentrate his mind. There were two explanations for Davies being under the pier, he reasoned. The first was that he'd been following someone, the second that he'd gone there for a meeting.

'What sort of case was Inspector Davies workin' on the day he died?' he asked Turner.

'As far as I remember, he was running three investigations.'

'An' they were –?'

'A suspected car-theft ring, a series of cat burglaries in Poulton-le-Fylde, and a hit-and-run case in Fleetwood.'

None of which seemed to have any connection with the Golden Mile, Woodend thought – not that he could rule out that possibility altogether. He noticed a stall selling seafood further down the sands, and reached into his pocket for some change.

'Just nip down there an' get us a ration of Morecambe Bay prawns, will you, lass?' he asked Paniatowski, holding out the money to her.

Paniatowski gazed down at the hand as if the sight of it offended her, then, slowly and reluctantly, took the coins and headed off towards the stall.

Woodend waited until she was out of earshot, then turned to Turner and said, 'I'm tryin' to give that lass plenty of slack, Ron, but I'm findin' it bloody hard work. She's as brittle as treacle toffee, you know – an' not half as sweet.'

'She's not had it easy,' Turner said.

'I can see it might be hard work bein' a woman in a man's world,' Woodend conceded, 'but she's goin' to have to come to terms with that if she wants to be successful. An' she's goin' to have to learn to recognise it when people are on her side.'

'When I say she hasn't had it easy, I'm not talking about the ragging she's had since she's joined the police,' Turner told him. 'I'm talking about before.'

'Go on,' Woodend said.

'Before I was transferred here, I'd spent my entire working life in Whitebridge. I knew her family at the time Monika was growing up.'

'And –?'

'Her stepfather was a Whitebridge lad called Arthur Jones. He met Monika's mum in Berlin in 1945. She and Monika were refugees running away from the Russians, and Jones was part of the Allied army of occupation. In a way, it's a good thing Jones married Blanca Paniatowski, because if he hadn't, she and Monika would have been shipped back to Poland with the hundreds of thousands of other refugees.'

'In what way *wasn't* it a good thing?' Woodend asked.

'I'm coming to that. Jones had what you might call "expectations" when he brought his new family back to Whitebridge. You see, though he'd started out as a private in '39, by the time the war ended, he'd risen through the ranks to captain. Well, that's a common enough story. It wasn't *too* difficult to get a field promotion if you were halfway competent and managed to dodge the German bullets.'

Woodend – who had both dodged more bullets than he cared to remember *and* turned down a commission twice – grinned. 'So what happened to Captain Jones when he returned home?' he asked.

'Like I said, he had expectations. He'd developed tastes above his station in the army, and he thought he could continue to live the same privileged life in Lancashire. It didn't take long for reality to sink in. There weren't enough fancy jobs to go round in Whitebridge, and from having a personal valet and an officers' mess where he could drink with gentlemen, he found himself back in the mill, just as if the war had never happened.'

'It turned him bitter?' Woodend suggested.

'It turned him to *pints* of bitter,' Turner said. 'Eight or nine a night – with whisky chasers to follow. Now there's some men who can take their drink without getting nasty, but Arthur Jones wasn't one of them. If he was in a bad mood, he took it out on his wife and stepdaughter.'

'Knocked them about, did he?'

'We could never prove it,' Turner said. 'The mother always came up with a reasonable explanation for the bruises, and however much pressure we put on her, she refused to press charges.'

No wonder Monika had tensed up when they were discussing wife beating earlier, Woodend thought. It would have been odd if she hadn't.

'I expect Blanca thought that however bad life was with Jones, she'd be even worse off without him,' Turner continued. He clenched his fists into tight, angry balls. 'Oh, I'd really have liked to nail the bastard.'

'There's somethin' else – beside the beatin's – isn't there?' Woodend guessed.

Turner nodded gravely. 'I'm sure the mother never believed this, or she couldn't have stayed with Jones however bad the alternative was –' he lowered his voice even though there was no one close enough to hear – 'but it's my belief that her stepfather didn't just hurt Monika – I think he interfered with her. You know . . . sexually.'

Woodend found himself thinking of his own daughter, Annie, as he always did when he was working on cases which involved kids. If anyone ever dared so much as touch her . . .

'So you see the point about Monika?' Turner asked. 'She's had a lot to put up with.'

'Aye, well, maybe I'll have to give her even more rope than I have already,' Woodend said. 'But unless she learns to keep her anger under control – or at least channel it – she's never goin' to get anywhere in the force.'

'She's made sergeant already,' Turner pointed out.

'An' how much of that did she owe to you – the bobby who felt sorry for her when she was a helpless kid?' Woodend wondered.

Turner almost blushed. 'She's a good officer,' he said. 'I wouldn't have helped her otherwise.'

Paniatowski had returned from the seafood stall carrying a cardboard tray in her hand. 'Here's your prawns, sir,' she said, her voice expressionless as she held them out to Woodend.

'They're not for me,' Woodend told her. 'They're for all of us. Take a couple, Sergeant.'

'No, thank you, sir.'

'Bring you out in a rash, do they?'

'No, but –'

'Then take a couple. You'll soon learn that when you're working with me, you grab a snack whenever you get the chance.'

With another show of reluctance, the sergeant picked out a prawn and, conscious that Woodend's eyes were still on her, popped it into her mouth.

'That's the advantage of bein' the underling,' Woodend told her. 'You might have to do the fetchin' and carryin', but if there's a price to pay, it's not usually you that pays it.'

He wasn't just talking about the prawns, Monika sensed – he was laying out what he saw as a working relationship.

Woodend offered the prawns to Turner. The local man took a couple of them, then said, 'Now that you've seen where the body was found, shall I take you to your digs?'

'Not too far from the scene of the crime, are they?' Woodend asked.

'No, as a matter of fact, you can see them from here,' Turner replied. He pointed across the sands, over the sea wall and along the promenade. 'That's it – The Sea View.'

Woodend's gaze followed the direction of the pointing finger. The hotel was one of a block of dressed-stone four-storied hotels, all of which had bay windows jutting out slightly over their small front yards.

'Sea View,' he said reflectively. 'That's an original name.'

'If you'd prefer somewhere else –' Turner began.

'Nay,' Woodend interrupted. 'You've worked with me before, Ron. You should know that all I want from my digs is a bed I can lay my head on for five or six hours a day – if

34

I'm lucky. The Sea View will do me an' Sergeant Paniatowski here just fine.'

'Well, would you like to go across there now and settle in?' Turner suggested.

'No. Why waste the best part of the day?' Woodend replied. 'Have our luggage sent up there, an' tell the landlady not to expect us for tea. Or supper, either – if there's one provided.'

Turner nodded. 'All right. I'll arrange that. And what would you like us to do next?'

'I wouldn't expect *you* to do anythin',' Woodend told him. 'You've got quite enough on your hands without shepherdin' us around.'

'So what will you and Monika be doing next?'

'If the car's still available, I thought me an' Sergeant Paniatowski might just go an' see the grievin' widow.'

Seven

The Ford Zephyr crossed the promenade and headed into the centre of Blackpool. For the first quarter of a mile it passed virtually nothing but boarding houses, bingo halls and souvenir shops, but beyond that it began to penetrate the solid, respectable suburbs where the all-year-round residents of Blackpool lived.

Sitting in the back of the car, Woodend turned carefully towards his new assistant, well aware that the Zephyr was less spacious than a Humber and that, however much he tried, it was almost impossible to avoid his leg touching hers.

'You could be very useful at this interview, Sergeant,' he said.

'Any reason in particular you should say that, sir?' asked Paniatowski, the reluctant errand-girl, still not willing to give an inch.

'In case you haven't noticed, you're a woman,' Woodend replied. 'An' it's highly likely that Punch Davies' widow is a woman, too. So there's a good chance you'll notice somethin' I'll miss.'

The remark seemed to antagonise Paniatowski further. 'It's not important that I'm a woman,' she said.

'Then what *is* important?'

'That I'm a trained police officer, sir, just like you are.'

'Is that what you really think?' Woodend asked. 'That it's the *trainin'* which makes a good bobby?'

'Essentially. Yes.'

If he'd been dealing with a man, Woodend thought, he'd probably have tapped the lad's knee as he made his next point. But he couldn't do that with Paniatowski.

'It's not like that, lass,' he told her. 'I wouldn't say that what you've been taught counts for nothin' in an investigation, but you can't build a proper house if there aren't any decent foundations to start with.'

'I'm not sure I know what you mean, sir.'

Woodend sighed and wondered how his literary hero, Charles Dickens, would have explained it.

'Good police officers – *really* good police officers – are born with certain qualities,' he said, 'an' all the trainin' does is to refine those qualities into somethin' *better*.'

'Are you telling me that all policemen should be like you?' Paniatowski asked aggressively.

'No,' Woodend replied, forcing his voice to stay level and reasonable. 'An' if you don't mind me sayin' so, Sergeant, you're completely missin' the point. There's plenty of room for differences. In fact, they're essential. If two bobbies see somethin' – *anythin' at all* – in exactly the same way, then it's a waste of time them workin' together. It's the differences which make a team good or bad – an' I want us to be a good team.'

The driver pulled up at the curb before Paniatowski had time to reply. 'This is the place, sir,' he said.

Woodend looked out of the window. They had stopped in front of a row of largish terraced houses.

'Is she expectin' us?' Woodend asked.

'Yes, sir. We rang her from the station.'

The chief inspector extracted his bulk from the car, taking pains as he did so not to brush against his sergeant. Once on the pavement, he stopped to take a look around. The row of houses was in good condition. They all had neat lace curtains, recently painted doors and an uninterrupted view of Stanley Park, with its cricket ground, putting green and rose gardens. Nice, very nice. But not anything like *too* nice – not the sort of area Woodend would have been surprised to find a detective inspector living in.

'What are we looking for, sir?' asked Paniatowski, joining him on the pavement.

That was better, Woodend thought. Much better. She was

finally starting to chuck her prejudices out of the window and use her brain.

'A murder turns a family inside out,' he said. 'You have to expect that. But what we're lookin' for is somethin' that wasn't quite right even *before* the victim met his end.'

'Won't that be hard to isolate?' Paniatowski asked.

'Almost impossible,' Woodend agreed. 'But it's what's expected of us – that's why we get such fat wage packets at the end of the week.'

The crazy-paving path was weed-free, the borders each side of it neatly trimmed. Woodend walked up to the front door and pressed the bell.

The woman who answered the ring was wearing an old floral dress. 'Mrs Davies?' the chief inspector asked.

'That's right.'

Detective Inspector William Davies had been thirty-five when he'd met his end, and Woodend had been expecting his wife would look roughly the same age. She didn't – and the Chief Inspector tried to work out why. It wasn't just that her blonde hair had begun to fade, or that her upper arms – clearly visible in her short-sleeved frock – had begun to put on weight. There were deep lines around her blue eyes and small mouth – lines which, if she really was thirty-five, she should not have earned for at least another ten years.

She wasn't wearing make-up, either. That – to most people – would have been perfectly understandable. After all, you couldn't expect someone in mourning to make that kind of effort. But Woodend had talked to dozens of recent widows in his time on the force, and knew that the majority of them – either from habit or to have something to hold on to – usually made at least a token effort to be presentable.

A discreet cough from Paniatowski reminded him it was his turn to speak again.

'I'm Chief Inspector Woodend and this is Sergeant—' he began.

'I've been expecting you,' the woman interrupted. 'Follow me.'

She led the two police officers down a carpeted hallway into a lounge which contained two modern easy chairs with skeletal wooden arms, a sofa in the same style, a radiogram, a cocktail cabinet and a television. Thoroughly conventional, Woodend thought. Exactly what he would have expected.

'Won't you sit down?' Mrs Davies said.

Woodend lowered himself into one of the easy chairs. Paniatowski took the sofa.

'You have a very nice house,' Paniatowski said.

Mrs Davies crossed her arms and hugged her shoulders tightly. 'Billy was a good provider,' she said. 'It was only right that he should come home to a bit of comfort.'

'Was he often at home?' Woodend asked.

The widow shook her head. 'He worked very hard. He gave his job almost everything he had. But he always called to tell me when he was going to be late.'

'What about the night he was killed?' Woodend asked. 'Was he workin'?'

'Not exactly.'

'What do you mean by that, exactly?'

'He officially came off duty at six. But he rang me at about four o'clock – before I'd started to get his tea ready – to say he was going to be late.'

'Did he give any reason for it?'

'He said he had some paperwork to catch up on.'

'That would mean he intended to stay on at the station?'

'I suppose so.'

'So how did he come to end up under the Central Pier?' Woodend asked. He paused. 'I'm sorry to have to put things so bluntly. I know it must be painful.'

'I'm . . . I was . . . a policeman's wife,' Mrs Davies said. 'I know what has to be done. In answer to your question, Mr Woodend, I've no idea what Billy was doing anywhere near the Central Pier.'

'As far as you know, was he havin' any problems at work?'

Mrs Davies hesitated for a second, then said, 'Not generally. But I think something's been preying on his mind for the last few weeks.'

'Did he mention anythin' specific?'

'No,' Mrs Davies admitted. 'Billy wasn't one to talk about his work. But I was still his wife, and I *knew* that something wasn't quite right.'

'Is there anythin' else you think I ought to know?' Woodend coaxed.

'Nothing comes to mind,' Mrs Davies said firmly.

Either the widow had no more to say, or she was unwilling, for the moment, to say it. There seemed no point in prolonging the interview. Woodend stood up, and was just about to hold out his hand to her and produce some conventional soothing platitude when he noticed the silver-framed photograph on the mantelpiece.

It was a picture of two children – a boy and a girl – standing in what was probably the Davieses' back garden. The boy was about eight and, obviously conscious of the camera, had a wide grin on his face. The girl was perhaps two years younger than her brother. Her expression was blank, and her eyes were empty.

'That's Peter and Susan,' Mrs Davies said, noticing that Woodend was examining the picture. 'I've sent Peter to stay with his auntie until after Billy's funeral.'

'And Susan?' Woodend asked, before he could stop himself.

Mrs Davies' face clenched in an emotional agony Woodend could only dimly begin to comprehend. 'Susan's . . . Susan's in a special boarding school,' she gasped. 'I tried to look after her myself, but I couldn't. *Everybody* said I couldn't.'

Woodend had not even seen Paniatowski rise from her seat, but suddenly the sergeant had her arms wrapped around the widow and was cooing softly into her ear.

'That's all right, Mrs Davies. Don't try to hold it in, Mrs Davies.'

The widow didn't. Instead she buried her head in the other woman's shoulder, and began sobbing in earnest. With her right hand, Paniatowski gestured to Woodend that he should leave. The chief inspector needed no such urging. Cursing himself for his insensitivity – for not immediately grasping the meaning of the blank expression on the girl's face – he tiptoed quietly down the hallway and out of the house.

Mrs Davies took one last sip from her cup, and placed it back on its saucer. 'It was very kind of you to make the tea,' she said.

Paniatowski smiled. 'It was the least I could do after that boss of mine put his size nine clodhopper in it,' she said. 'Are you feeling a bit better now?'

'Much better,' Mrs Davies said. 'I know I shouldn't get so upset – and most of the time I don't – but then there comes a moment now and again when it's all too much.'

Paniatowski reached across and stroked her hand. 'I know,' she said soothingly.

As soon as the sergeant had released her hand, Mrs Davies stood up. 'Well, I can't stand around here moping all day,' she said. 'Widow or not – daughter in a special school or not – there's still the housework to be done.'

'You're sure you're all right?' Paniatowski persisted.

'Perfectly fine.'

'In that case, could I ask you a favour?'

'What?'

'When we were standing outside, I couldn't help noticing your bedroom curtains. I'm almost certain they'd be perfect for my flat, but if I could just have a closer look –'

Mrs Davies forced a weak smile to her lips. 'Of course. If you'd just follow me.'

She led the sergeant up the stairs and into the main bedroom. Paniatowski walked straight over to the window. She could see a group of lads playing football in Stanley Park, and noticed that, below her on the pavement, Woodend was striding up and down and puffing energetically on a Capstan Full Strength.

The sergeant ran the curtain material through her finger and thumb. 'Very nice,' she said. She lifted the curtain and saw it had been machine-hemmed. 'I don't suppose you've got a spare bit of this material, have you?'

'There should be some in my sewing basket downstairs,' Mrs Davies told her. 'Let's go and see.'

'I . . . er . . . Would you mind if while you're looking, I just use your toilet?' Paniatowski asked. 'Only, it's that time of the month, and you know how often you've got to go when you've got your period.'

Mrs Davies nodded. 'I certainly do,' she agreed. 'Take your time. I'll see you in the lounge.'

As Paniatowski followed Mrs Davies out of the room, she took a quick look around her, and what she saw pretty much confirmed the suspicion she'd had since Mrs Davies had said that her sewing things were *downstairs*.

Woodend was waiting next to the car, his third cigarette since he had left the house clamped between his lips.

Paniatowski smiled. 'Smart thinking, sir,' she said as she approached him.

Woodend took a deep drag of his cigarette. 'I beg your pardon?'

'It was smart to pretend to be a typical, insensitive man. That made you into an enemy, but me into an ally – and that bought me another fifteen minutes in the house. That was your intention when you put on the show, wasn't it, sir – to buy me more time?'

'Did you learn anythin' useful while you were in there?' Woodend asked, avoiding answering his sergeant's question.

'Oh, I think so,' Paniatowski said with confidence. 'Mrs Davies keeps her sewing machine downstairs.'

'Now that is a revelation!' Woodend said sarcastically.

'Yes, it is,' Paniatowski said, quite serious. 'How many bedrooms would you say these houses have, sir?'

'Four?' Woodend guessed.

'That's right,' Paniatowski agreed. 'Now in most houses, that would mean one for each of the kids – even if one kid was in a special school and only came home for the holidays – one for the parents, and one that the wife would use as her sewing and ironing room. Only that isn't the case in the Davies household.'

'You seem to know a lot about it,' Woodend said uneasily.

'I told her I was interested in her bedroom curtains, and

asked if I could take a closer look at them. Then, when we were just about to go downstairs again, I pretended I needed to use the bathroom, so she'd leave me alone.'

'Bloody hell, lass, you can't go lookin' around people's houses without the proper search warrant!' Woodend exploded.

'She invited us into the house, and invited me upstairs. I might have looked around, but I didn't touch anything. I don't think I've broken any laws, have I, sir?'

'No,' Woodend conceded reluctantly. 'Probably not. So what did you discover on your little only-slightly-illegal search?'

'Like I said, I went into the main bedroom first, on the pretext of examining the curtains. It's a very feminine room – all soft furnishings and bright colours. The next door up the hallway is obviously the boy's room, with model aeroplanes hanging from the ceiling and pictures of footballers stuck up on the walls. You know the sort of thing I mean?'

'Yes,' Woodend agreed. 'I know the sort of thing you mean.'

'The third bedroom's the girl's. But it's the fourth that's the interesting one. That's where I would have expected to find Mrs Davies' sewing machine if I hadn't already known better. Instead I found a single bed – made up – and a battered wardrobe. When I opened the wardrobe—'

'I thought you said you hadn't touched anythin'.'

'Hardly anything. When I opened the wardrobe, I discovered it contained jackets and suits. You know what this means, don't you, sir?'

'It means that the Davieses no longer shared a bed,' Woodend said.

'Exactly. And wasn't that worth finding out?'

'Maybe,' Woodend admitted. His eyes narrowed. 'Tell me, Sergeant, when you threw your arms around Mrs Davies like that, was it already in your mind to try and talk your way upstairs?'

'No. But when I thought about it – when I saw how you'd deliberately created the opportunity for me – it seemed too good a chance to miss.'

Did she really believe he'd done it deliberately, Woodend wondered – or was she just putting the onus of the search on him? If it were the former, she was more naïve than her record would indicate. If it were the latter, she was playing just the sort of game of running rings around her boss as he remembered playing when he was an ambitious DS himself. Whichever the case, this young woman would need watching.

Eight

S ergeant Frank Hanson sat facing the three detective constables who formed the rest of the team, and puffed
listlessly on a Woodbine.

The room in which they were meeting – the basement
of Blackpool Central Police Station – had for years been
nothing more than a dumping ground for things it was easier
to store than to sort through. Since the murder, however, the
old bicycles, damaged traffic signs and cardboard boxes full
of mouldy reports had all been cleared out, to be replaced by
a long table, a blackboard and several gun-metal desks.

Out of chaos had been created the nerve centre of a major
criminal investigation, Hanson thought cynically. It was a
pity then, that the new nerve centre still smelled like a
junk room.

'Where the bloody hell did you say Mr Woodend had gone,
Sarge?' asked one of the detective constables, DC Brock, a
thickset young man with a bullet-shaped head.

'To see "Judy" Davies, Badger,' Hanson replied.

'An' while he's pissin' about doin' that, we're left sittin'
here on our arses instead of bein' on the streets lookin' for
the killer.'

'It's apparently the way Mr Woodend usually works,'
Hanson said mildly. 'First he gets a feeling for the scene of
the crime, and *then* he decides what direction the investigation's
going to take.'

He was trying to sound reassuring – it was a necessary
prerequisite for a murder team that they had confidence in
the man who would be leading them – but he did not feel very
reassured himself. Chief Inspector Turner had told him that he

should keep a tight rein on Woodend, and already, after only an hour or so in the town, the ex-Scotland Yard man had gone off on his own bat. Of course, it was highly unlikely he'd learn anything damaging from 'Judy' Davies. Living out by Stanley Park – a couple of miles away – she would never have heard any of the ugly rumours which had been buzzing around the cop shop. But still . . .

'We don't need anybody from headquarters stickin' their oar in,' said another of the constables – a slightly overweight ginger-haired officer who went by the name of Eric Stone.

'You don't think so?' Hanson asked.

'No, I don't. We're the ones with the local knowledge, aren't we? We could handle this on our own.'

'So who did it?' Hanson asked, as if he really was expecting an answer.

'Who did what?'

'Who killed "Punch" Davies?'

'I don't know,' the ginger-haired constable admitted.

'But you know how to find out, do you? You have a plan for conducting the investigation?'

Stone shrugged. 'I'm only a DC, Sarge. I haven't got the experience yet. But there's men here who have – men like DCI Turner.'

Hanson stubbed out his Woodbine in a battered tin ashtray.

'DCI Turner is a good boss to work for,' he said, 'and though he's only been here a couple of years, he already knows Blackpool like the back of his hand. But if you want to talk about experience, how much experience do you think Mr Turner has had in leading murder inquiries?'

'I don't know, Sarge.'

'Well,' Hanson said patiently, 'he won't have led one *before* he got promoted, will he? And as soon as his promotion came through, he was transferred here, so he'll only have dealt with domestics. Mr Woodend, on the other hand, must have handled a couple of dozen serious cases while he was at the Yard. Bearing all that in mind, don't you think he might be just a little bit useful?'

'What about *her*?' the bullet-headed DC Brock asked.

There was no need to enquire who the 'her' in question was. '*What* about her?' Hanson countered.

'Why's *she* on the case? She doesn't have either the experience or the local knowledge.'

Hanson reached into his pocket for his cigarettes. 'Have you got something against women officers, Badger?' he asked.

Brock shrugged. 'They're all right for lookin' after missin' children and brewin' up, but they've no place in a murder investigation.'

'She's Mr Woodend's bagman. Nothing more and nothing less,' Hanson reminded him. 'You should know by now what a bagman's job is. She'll be running his errands while we do the real detective work around here. And I'm sure even you, Badger, can have no objection to a woman running errands.'

The other two constables chuckled, and even Brock allowed a smile to come to his lips.

'No. I've no objection to that,' he agreed. The smile twisted, and acquired a lascivious edge. 'I might even be able to think of a few little jobs that she can do for me.'

Someone – a woman – coughed, and the four detectives turned to see Sergeant Paniatowski standing in the doorway.

'How long have you been there?' Hanson asked.

'I've just arrived,' Paniatowski told him – though none of the men were sure whether she was telling the truth or not.

'And where's Mr Woodend?' Hanson asked. 'He'll be along in a minute, will he?'

Paniatowski shook her head. 'He's walking back.'

'All the way from Stanley Park?'

'No, he came most of the way by car. It's only the last bit he's doing on foot.'

Hanson remembered his conversation with DCI Turner earlier in the day, and felt his stomach churn over. 'Where did you drop him off?' he asked.

'Just near the Tower.'

At the northern end of the Golden Mile, Hanson thought – right in the middle of the area on which the rumours about Punch Davies had been centred. Bloody hell fire!

*　　*　　*

47

It had been towards the end of the nineteenth century that Blackpool Borough Council had passed legislation to ban most traders from the beach, thus leaving more room for holidaymakers. But the traders had not wanted to lose their lucrative businesses, and the holidaymakers – while appreciating the extra lounging space – still wanted the services the traders offered. The solution had been simple. The traders had hauled their barrows and stalls off the sands, crossed the promenade, and set up shop again in the front gardens of sea-front hotels. The traders were happy their businesses continued, the buyers were happy to still be able to buy, the hotel owners were happy with the unexpected extra source of revenue – and the Golden Mile was born.

The Mile ran from the Tower to the Central Pier and was rightly considered by just about everyone to be the heart of the town. There were garishly painted amusement arcades here, full of one-armed bandits which greedily gobbled up the pennies and occasionally condescended to spit out a shilling's worth of change in return. There were bright-red 'What the Butler Saw' machines, over which pimpled youths bent, licking their lips as they cranked the handles and their eyes devoured flickering black-and-white pictures of half-naked women. A dozen or more small shops offered cartoon postcards of huge women in bathing costumes with crabs firmly affixed to the rears, and blondes with improbable bosoms and silk-stocking legs. Photographs could be developed here, and all the equipment necessary for making sandcastles purchased. Anyone with a shilling in his pocket could go and see 'The Sensational Severed Living Hands of Patma' or 'Tanya, the Tattooed Girl'. Anyone with an urge to gamble could sit in for a game of bingo.

Grand, Woodend thought, as he weaved his way through the crowd, sniffing the fried onion at hamburger stalls and the tart smell of vinegar which drifted over from the whelks. Absolutely grand! Yet something was missing – something which would have enhanced his pleasure was simply not there. And then he realised what that something was. He felt incomplete working on a case without Bob Rutter by his side.

He imagined the conversation they would have had:

'Now this is what you call a holiday resort, Bob,' he could hear himself saying. 'Take Brighton, which all you southerners seem to think is so bloody marvellous. It's only got one buggerin' little pier, hasn't it – whereas Blackpool now, Blackpool's got *three*.'

And no doubt Rutter would have smiled in his slightly superior grammar-school-boy way and replied, 'But it hasn't quite got the *style* of somewhere like Brighton, has it, sir?'

No, it bloody hadn't! But it had got a style all of its own, and he would have made quite sure Rutter understood that.

He couldn't imagine ever talking to Monika Paniatowski in the same light-hearted way. Perhaps that was his failure – or perhaps it was hers – but whatever the reason, he felt he had lost something valuable when he had lost Bob Rutter as his bagman.

Woodend came to a halt in front of a small, open-fronted shop which was sandwiched between two gaudy amusement arcades and had a sign over it announcing that it sold 'The World Famous Blackpool Rock'.

The chief inspector ran his eyes over shelf upon shelf of lurid pink tubes wrapped in cellophane, and felt the sticky-sweet taste of childhood gently oozing into his mouth.

'Take some sticks home for the kids?' suggested the shop-keeper, a middle-aged man with a slight cast in his left eye.

In point of fact, I was almost on the point of buyin' one or two sticks for myself, Woodend thought.

But aloud, he said, 'A couple of years ago I might have, but I'm sure my daughter thinks she's far too grown-up for that kind of thing now.'

The man with the squint shrugged his shoulders fatalistically. 'You're not very brown,' he commented. 'Just startin' your holiday, are you?'

He'd never have been asked the question if it had been the promenade at Brighton he'd been wandering along, Woodend thought. That was the difference between the North and the South – southerners minded their own business, but in the North they regarded *everybody's* business as their own.

'I'm not on holiday at all, as it happens,' he said. 'I'm workin'.'

A southerner, even if it he *had* raised the first question, would have let the matter rest there, but the rock seller said, 'Oh aye, an' what kind of business are you in?'

'I'm a bobby,' Woodend told him. 'From Whitebridge.'

'The big city, hey? Well, there can only be one reason you're down here, can't there?'

'Can there? An' what might that be?'

'You're here to find out who killed poor Mr Davies, aren't you?'

Poor Mr Davies, Woodend repeated to himself. 'Did you know Inspector Davies at all?' he asked.

'Not what you might call well – but well enough. I had a break-in a couple of years back – I'd been stupid enough to leave some cash in the shop overnight – an' it was Inspector Davies, Sergeant Davies as he was then, who investigated it.'

'What was your impression of him?'

'Very favourable. He was my kind of bobby.'

'An' what kind of bobby is that?'

'He seemed serious about his job. Like he really cared about catchin' the feller who'd robbed me. Like he wouldn't sleep at night if he didn't get a result. You don't mind payin' your taxes when you know the money's goin' to make up the wages of people like Mr Davies.'

'An' did he actually catch the robber?'

'He did. Got him for a string of other burglaries along the front as well. Of course, the bugger denied it – well, they always do, don't they? – but Mr Davies assured me he was the man, right enough.' He sighed. 'It's a pity they have to promote men like him, isn't it?'

'Why do you say that?' Woodend wondered.

'Well, they lose touch with the ordinary people, don't they? After the robbery, Sergeant Davies often used to drop round to check that everythin' was all right, an' have a bit of a chat. But that stopped once he got made up. I don't want to suggest he got snobbish or anythin',' the shopkeeper added hastily, 'I just think he was so busy with his new responsibilities that he didn't have the time to stop an' talk any more.'

'So you hadn't seen him recently?'

'Not to speak to.'

'But you did *see* him,' Woodend persisted.

'Just walkin' past, like. He'd wave to me, but he'd never come over.'

'An' how often would that be?'

'Difficult to say for sure. There was a long while after he got promoted when we didn't see him round here *at all*, but lately he seemed to have been poppin' up every other day.'

'Is that right?' Woodend said thoughtfully.

Tommy Bolton was having THE DREAM again. That was what he always thought of it as when he woke up – THE DREAM. In capital letters. This time, he'd decide later, it was worse than it had ever been. The things he touched seemed so solid, the smell of the night air was so agonisingly realistic. And though he did not know he was dreaming, he knew that he was still only about a quarter of the way through a terrible and terrifying sequence of events – and that there was nothing he could do but stay with them until the end.

It was the loud knock on his dressing-room door that saved him from his own subconscious.

'On in ten minutes, Mr Bolton!'

Bolton opened his eyes. When he'd fallen asleep on the couch, he'd been fully stretched out, but at some time during the course of THE DREAM, he'd raised his knees, so that now he was almost in a foetal position.

It's a wonder I didn't go arse over tip, and end on the bloody floor, he thought as he swung his body off the couch.

He walked over to his dressing table and examined himself in the mirror. His eyes were red from sleep and booze, but the audience would think that was make-up – a part of the act which had made Tommy 'Now Where Was I?' Bolton popular up and down the country. He was *so* popular, in fact, that he had finally received the ultimate accolade – being booked to top the bill for an entire summer season in Blackpool, the mecca of entertainment. And not just in any old theatre, he reminded himself. Not in some backstreet show with a load of old has-beens – but on the Central Pier, supported by a host of rising stars.

He lit a cigarette, and looked at his reflection again. Who would ever have thought that little Sid Dawkins, the rag-and-bone man's son from Moss Side, would turn into Tommy Bolton, a man who already owned a detached bungalow in Lytham St Anne's outright, and had a bank account which was steadily climbing towards five figures.

'Why did you have to bugger it up?' he asked his reflection angrily. 'You were sitting pretty. Why couldn't you just take a little more care?'

Because, he supposed, when everybody around you told you that you were the king of the world, you started to believe them. So that excused one mistake.

But *two*?

The second mistake had been so incredibly stupid that however much he tried to convince himself otherwise – and he'd tried very hard indeed – he knew that he had no one to blame but himself.

There was another knock on the door. 'On in five minutes, Mr Bolton.'

The comedian from Moss Side adopted a comical, bemused expression. 'Now where was I?' he asked the mirror. 'Oh yes, I was telling you about my Aunt Gladys, and how she came to lose her knickers on a day trip to Skegness.'

Nine

Woodend looked around the long Formica table at the team which had been assembled to work under his supervision. Sitting closest to him was Sergeant Hanson. Woodend approved of the intelligent grey eyes and serious expression which looked back at him – an expression which suggested Hanson was a conscientious bobby who knew his own patch. Next to Hanson was the bullet-headed Constable Brock, and Woodend got a distinct feeling that this wasn't a man he'd like to meet in a dark alley. From the opposite side of the table, Constable Stone looked expressionlessly back at him, his sandy hair and slightly rounded face making him seem like a big lazy ginger tomcat. Constable Eliot, sitting next to Stone, had a fresh, young face, but from the frown on his unlined forehead he was obviously deeply troubled by something or other. Finally, at the far end of the table, Sergeant Paniatowski sat in splendid isolation.

It was not necessarily the team he would have chosen for himself, Woodend thought – in fact, most of the time he preferred to work with no team at all – but he supposed he was stuck with them and there was nothing he could do about it.

'How far has the investigation progressed so far?' he asked Sergeant Hanson.

'Hardly at all,' the local sergeant admitted. 'We've questioned people who might have been on the prom at the time of the murder, but everybody claims to have seen nothing. We've sent Mr Davies' clothes up to Whitebridge for forensic examination, and we're still waiting for the results. We should have the autopsy reports sometime in the morning.'

'No facts, then,' Woodend said. 'Does anybody have any theories?'

'The general belief around the station is that Mr Davies was killed by someone he was investigating. Either that or by somebody he'd locked away in the past and who was still harbouring a grudge.'

'Let's talk about his case load,' Woodend suggested. 'He was workin' on three investigations at the time of his death, wasn't he?'

'That's right, sir. A car-theft ring, the Poulton-le-Fylde cat burglaries and the hit-and-run in Fleetwood. But in the first two of those, he was merely the supervising officer. The men actually conducting the cases were both sergeants.'

'Were you one of them?' Woodend asked.

Hanson shook his head. 'No sir. I worked with Mr Davies a lot in the past, and I probably would have been on one of the teams if I'd been here when they were set up – but I've only just come back off leave.'

Woodend closed his eyes for a second, as if he were absorbing all this new information. 'What strikes you about the *type* of cases Mr Davies was involved in?' he asked, when he'd opened them again.

'That they were a pretty mixed bag?' Hanson suggested.

'Yes, they were – but you're missin' the point.' Woodend turned his attention to the woman sitting at the very end of the table. 'Do you have any suggestions, Sergeant?'

'They were the sorts of crimes which could have been committed in any medium-sized town, sir,' Monika Paniatowski said.

'Exactly!' Woodend agreed. 'But this isn't just *any* medium-sized town. In fact, it isn't one town at all. There are two Blackpools. There's the one that runs from the promenade to no more than six or seven streets back – the Blackpool that the holidaymakers know an' love. An' there's the other one, where Inspector Davies – an' probably most of you lot – live. Different places – different sorts of crime. An' the crimes Mr Davies was investigatin' belong to your part of town. Holidaymakers have nothin' to do with car theft, because they arrive by coach or train. And they're not likely to have their televisions nicked from them in Blackpool, because they haven't brought them with them. We're talkin' *resident* crime here.'

'True,' Hanson agreed, 'but I don't see why—'

'So if he'd been topped in one of the areas where he was conductin' his investigations, your theory that he was killed by some criminal who was scared of bein' collared by him might make sense. But – for God's sake – he was killed on the Golden Mile.'

'I don't see the difficulty there, sir,' Hanson said. 'Maybe the killer had been following Mr Davies for some time, and the first chance he got to strike was when the DI went under the Central Pier.'

'An' just what business did he have goin' under the Central Pier in the first place?' Woodend demanded.

'Maybe he just wanted to look at the sea, sir,' the baby-faced DC Eliot suggested.

'You mean he might have felt a sudden impulse to breathe in the air – blow the cobwebs away?'

'Something like that, sir.'

'That theory might hold water if it was a one-off,' Woodend conceded. 'But you do know that Mr Davies has been spendin' quite a lot of his free time on the Golden Mile, don't you?'

The four local men exchanged uneasy, questioning glances, then Hanson said, 'No, sir. We didn't know that.'

'Well, you bloody well should have!' Woodend told him. 'So now we're left with a big question, an' it's this: if all Mr Davies' investigations were concerned with residential crime, what was he doin' visitin' the Golden Mile so often?'

'Maybe he went there to relax?' DC Brock suggested.

'Not a chance,' Woodend said. 'When people want to relax, they go lookin' for a change. Now if he'd been spendin' his free time in the Lake District or the Forest of Bowland, I could understand it. But the Golden Mile? Never.'

'With respect, sir, I don't think you can simply dismiss the theory that he—' Hanson began.

'When did you last pay a visit to the Golden Mile on anythin' other than business?' Woodend interrupted.

'That's different, sir,' Hanson said. 'I've got my prize racing pigeons to consider.'

'An' didn't Mr Davies have any hobbies?'

'I believe he flew model aeroplanes, sir,' Constable Stone volunteered. 'He was county champion one year.'

'Well, there you are then,' Woodend said triumphantly. 'Obviously, his visits to the Golden Mile had somethin' to do with police business. Does any of you have any idea what that police business might be?' The four local bobbies shook their heads. 'Then we'd better find out, hadn't we?' Woodend continued. 'I want you lot coverin' every inch of the Mile. I want to know how often he was there, who he talked to, and what he talked to them about. Sergeant Hanson will co-ordinate.'

Sitting at the far end of the table, Paniatowski felt her hackles rising. *She* was his sergeant. She should have been doing the co-ordinating. But then, of course, Sergeant Hanson was a man, and she was only a *woman*. It was to be expected that, whatever impression Woodend had attempted to create of being egalitarian earlier, he would eventually show his true colours and put Hanson in charge.

'There's one more thing,' Woodend continued. 'I'll be coverin' the same ground you are.' He caught the frown on Hanson's face. 'Anythin' wrong with that, Sergeant?'

Hanson shrugged uncomfortably. 'I suppose not, sir. It's just that most of the senior officers I've worked with tend to leave the job on the streets to their men and concentrate on the bigger picture.'

'Or to put it another way, you don't like the idea of me checkin' up on you?' Woodend said.

'There's that as well, sir,' Hanson admitted.

Woodend nodded understandingly. 'I can see how it might worry you,' he conceded. 'But you've got the wrong end of the stick again. I always trust the men who are workin' for me – at least until they give me a reason not to – so you won't have me breathin' down your necks. But I'll still be

doing what I do best – which is buildin' up the big picture
by lookin' at the small details myself.' He checked his watch.
'It's just about tea time. You lads grab somethin' to eat, then
hit the streets. I'll expect your preliminary reports first thing
in the mornin'.'

The four Blackpool men and Paniatowski rose to their feet.
'Not you, Monika,' Woodend told his new sergeant. 'I've got
somethin' else in mind to keep you busy.'

I'm sure you have, Paniatowski thought bitterly. Tea has to
be made, doesn't it? Reports have to be typed, don't they? I
should have anticipated this.

Woodend waited until the rest of the team had left the room,
then said, 'What I want you to do, Sergeant, is investigate
Inspector Davies' investigations.'

It sounded better than brewing up, Paniatowski thought –
but was it anything other than a way of keeping her away from
the main thrust of the case?

'What do you hope to achieve from that, sir?' she asked,
trying to keep her voice level.

'Maybe nothin',' Woodend admitted. 'But while I'm startin'
to think that Davies' death is tied in with somethin' on the
Golden Mile, it's just possible that the local lads are right, an'
it's connected with one of his other cases.'

'If it's just a *possibility*, why aren't you letting the local
men handle it and using me in the main inquiry?' Paniatowski
asked, the anger now clearly evident in her tone.

Woodend sighed. 'Blackpool Tower's a bloody big buildin',
isn't it?' he asked.

'Yes, sir,' Paniatowski agreed, mystified.

'We first spotted it when we were miles away. Yet once you
get into the town itself, it's an entirely different matter. You
can be a few hundred yards away from it an' yet you *can't*
see it, because you're at street level an' the other buildin's are
blockin' your view. Do you see what I'm gettin' at?'

'Sometimes you're too close to a thing to see it properly,'
Paniatowski said.

'Exactly. I could put Sergeant Hanson on that side of the
investigation, but he'd be on familiar territory, and *because* it

was familiar, he might start takin' things for granted that he shouldn't be takin' for granted at all. That's why I'd rather use one of my own people.'

One of his own people. Paniatowski ran the phrase through her mind. She didn't feel like one of his people. If the truth be told, apart from the period she had worked under Mr Turner in Whitebridge, she had not felt like one of *anybody's* people since she'd joined the police force.

Sergeant Hanson sat at a table in Yates's Wine Lodge, facing the other three local detectives. He let his gaze move from Brock to Stone, and from Stone to Eliot.

'What I'm about to say comes straight from Chief Inspector Turner,' he told them. 'Mr Woodend's the senior officer on this case, which means that you're working for him – but nothing goes to him without it passing through me first. Is that clear?'

The three constables nodded.

'And whenever we have a brainstorming session with Cloggin'-it Charlie like we had earlier, you leave all the talking to me,' Hanson continued.

Eliot looked troubled. 'But what if he asks one of us a direct question?' he asked.

'Think of him like you'd think of an unfriendly brief asking you an awkward question in the witness box,' Hanson advised. 'Appear to be co-operating, but give as little away as possible.'

'I don't want to do anything which will damage my career,' Eliot said.

'Then you'll play it the way I've told you to,' Hanson countered. 'Listen, whether he finds Billy's killer or not, Mr Woodend will be gone in a few weeks. But Mr Turner won't be. Get on the wrong side of him and you'll be back directing traffic. And you'll stay directing traffic for as long as you're on the force.' He sighed. 'Look, we're in a difficult situation here. We want to find Punch's killer, right enough, but at the same time we want to protect the inspector's reputation – and that of the force.'

'Maybe there's no need to do that,' Eliot said hopefully. 'Maybe all the rumours floating around about him aren't true. I don't believe them, for one.'

Hanson shook his head slowly – almost despairingly – from side to side. 'You don't believe them,' he repeated. 'I've said that I don't believe them either. So have Stone and Brock. It's the natural thing to do when one of your colleagues comes under attack. But let's be honest, at least within *this part* of the team. Whatever we say – however much we might defend Punch – I think we all know, deep down inside ourselves, that the rumours are spot on.'

Ten

The interior of the Sea View Private Hotel was exactly as Woodend had pictured it would be. Beyond the entrance was a hallway just large enough for the polished wooden table which held the guest register and the brass gong used to announce meals. The door to the dining-room lay to the right, the stairs to the left. The narrow corridor running along the side of the stairs had a sign pinned to the wall which announced it was 'Private', and presumably led to the kitchen and staff quarters.

The woman who had admitted Woodend and Paniatowski into this peaceful haven announced that she was the landlady, Mrs Bowyer. She was tiny – almost bird-like – but compensated for her slight frame with a hard gaze which could easily slice its way through thick copper piping. In other words, Woodend thought, she was a typical example of the kind of seaside landlady he remembered from his family's holidays before the war.

'I was expectin' *two* policemen,' she said accusingly. 'That's what the young bobby who came round to book the rooms told me.'

Both her tone and her expression suggested that she suspected there was more to all this than met the eye – that she would not be the least surprised if she had been caught up in a vast conspiracy involving the whole of the Lancashire Constabulary, the sole aim of which was to allow the man in the hairy sports jacket to slake the fires of his burning lust on his young blonde companion.

'*Two* policemen,' she repeated.

'You were told to expect two police *officers*,' Woodend

60

responded. 'And here we are – Chief Inspector Woodend and Detective Sergeant Paniatowski.'

'Are you sure that's who you are?' Mrs Bowyer asked, the clear implication being that detective chief inspectors should dress better than Woodend did, and that as for Paniatowski, well, women simply had no business being detective sergeants.

'We can show you our warrant cards if that will make you happier,' Woodend suggested.

Mrs Bowyer sniffed disapprovingly, but bowed to the inevitable. 'No, that won't be necessary,' she said. 'If you'll wait here for a minute, I'll go an' check what rooms I've put you in.'

As she retreated down the narrow corridor, Woodend chuckled to himself. What a breed apart these landladies really were, he thought. Unlike most people, the thought of having a senior police officer under their roof did not intimidate them. If the Queen herself turned up and asked for a room, they'd probably want to know why Her Majesty hadn't booked in advance and remind her that a deposit would be required.

'I'm goin' to take a wander when I've unpacked my case,' Woodend said to his new sergeant. 'Want to come with me?'

'No, thank you, sir. I think I'll stay in and wash my hair.'

Woodend suppressed a grin. *I'm staying in and washing my hair.* How many lads had he known in his youth who'd been given that excuse, when what the girl giving it really meant was: 'I'd rather go out with a gorilla than go out with you.'

A new thought struck him, and he felt his good humour evaporate. Had Paniatowski really imagined that he was asking her out on some kind of date? Her previous behaviour suggested that she probably had. How was he ever going to get through to her? How would he ever convince her that the only sort of close relationship he wanted with his new sergeant was the sort he'd had with Bob Rutter?

The landlady returned. 'If you'd like to follow me,' she said, mounting the stairs.

On the first landing was a long, narrow corridor. 'Down here,' the landlady said, but when both Woodend and Paniatowski started to follow her, she quickly added, 'No, not you, madam. Just the gentleman.'

Most of the doors along the corridor were closed, but two of them, right next to one another, were open, and inside Woodend could see freshly made beds. The landlady had been planning to put the two police officers in adjacent rooms, he thought – but that was before she had realised one of them was a woman.

'That's your room,' Mrs Bowyer said, pointing to the second of the open doors. 'The toilet and bathroom are at the end of the corridor. There's hot water between seven-thirty and nine-thirty, then again between seven and nine in the evenin'. Breakfast is at eight, dinner at twelve and tea at five-thirty. Guests are asked to refrain from smokin' in bed. Thank you.'

'Thank you,' Woodend replied, but Mrs Bowyer was already on her way to shepherd Paniatowski to a part of the house where she would be safe from his evil clutches.

Woodend threw his battered carpet bag on to the bed, watched it sink into the lumpy mattress, then lit up a Capstan Full Strength. If it weren't for sex rearing its ugly head all over the place, his job would be a lot easier, he thought. But then, remembering how often the sexual element had played a part in the cases he'd investigated, he realised that without it he probably wouldn't have a job at all.

Eleven

The Gay Paree Theatre stood on a street corner halfway down the Golden Mile. It was shaped like an upended domino, and had a rickety platform jutting out from it at about six feet above ground level. For most of the time, the double doors at the end of the platform were closed and the platform was empty, but as the evening wore on – and the children were safely tucked up in bed – the place came to life.

There were two people on the platform at that moment – a man and a woman. The man, dressed in a cheap, flashy suit, was standing. The woman, a brassy blonde woman in a peach-coloured beach robe – and who knew what else, *if anything*, underneath? – was sitting on a chair next to him. On the pavement below stood a couple of dozen men and a few couples. The single men showed marked signs of interest in what was going on. The ones with their wives or girlfriends were doing their best to feign a lazy indifference.

The man on the platform held up a crudely made and crudely painted black wooden box.

'And now, before your very eyes, ladies and gentlemen, I will perform an incredible feat of magic,' he said.

But none of the men were looking at him, because the brassy blonde had just – slowly and deliberately – crossed her legs.

'I put the box over my partner's head, like so,' the man continued.

He slid the box in place. The front of it projected out at least six or eight inches past the blonde's face, so that its edge was poised over her bosom.

'And now,' the man said, producing a long-bladed knife, 'I will insert this dangerous weapon right into the box – so

63

far that it will come out on the other side. This is a piece of magic, ladies and gentlemen, which calls for the utmost concentration – and I would be grateful if you would maintain complete silence until it is finished.'

Woodend, standing in the middle of the pack below, shook his head in wonder.

Complete silence?

With the trams thundering past on the other side of the road?

With the noise of the amusement arcade to their left and the amplified shouts of the bingo callers on the other?

Or perhaps the 'magician' just meant the complete silence of the people standing in front of the platform. If that was his aim, then he should have no problem achieving it – because the brassy blonde had just shifted position again, revealing even more of her legs to the watchers below.

The man on the platform inserted the knife into a slot in the box, and, just as he had promised, the tip appeared out of the other side. With a little less than a flourish, he lifted the flap on the front of the box. The knife had indeed gone all the way through, and the brassy blonde's head had completely disappeared. Or at least, it would *seem* to have disappeared to any onlooker with such a poor sense of perspective that he failed to grasp the fact that the box had a false bottom about a third of the way down its length.

The man closed the front flap again, pulled out the knife and removed the box from the blonde woman's head. There was no applause. Nor had he probably expected any. The whole 'show' – such as it was – had been nothing more than an excuse for exhibiting a semi-naked woman on an open-air platform.

'What a spectacular show we've got waiting inside for you, ladies and gentlemen,' the man continued. 'See Helga, the sex slave of a vicious Berlin night-club owner. Drugged and beaten, Helga was forced to perform acts of incredible depravity every night in front of a group of slavering German businessmen. Now she is free of her humiliation at last, and you can see her – live – on this very stage.' He paused to let his words sink in. 'Ladies and gentlemen, I don't know how much longer the Blackpool Watch Committee is going to allow this daring show to go on,' he continued. 'The police could close it down tomorrow morning.'

Woodend grinned to himself. There would be no Helga, the drugged sex slave, inside. The 'entertainment' offered would be almost innocent, staying strictly within the limits imposed by the obscenity laws. Still, it was amusing to listen to such a good line in patter.

'Yes, only at the Gay Paree Theatre, Blackpool, can you see the show that has shocked the whole of Europe,' the barker continued. 'Don't miss what might be your last opportunity.'

Had Detective Inspector Punch Davies stood before this platform on one of his still-unexplained trips along the Golden Mile? Woodend wondered. And after the barker had finished his patter, had Davies walked up the wooden steps to the platform, crossed it and entered the Gay Paree Theatre?

'You'd pay ten pounds to see a show like this in London,' the barker told the small crowd below. 'But how much will it cost you tonight? Not ten pounds. Not five pounds. Not even *one* pound. All I'm asked you to part with, ladies and gentlemen, is five shillings. A miserable five bob for the erotic thrill of a lifetime.'

After one more flash of thigh, the brassy blonde stood up and walked slinkily back into the theatre. 'Follow me,' her walk seemed to saying. 'Follow me and get some of the titillation your frumpy wives will never give you at home.'

'Come on, ladies and gentlemen,' the barker exhorted. 'Don't be holding back.'

A group of three lads – it was always easier to do something slightly risqué in a group – began to climb the steps.

'That's the spirit,' the barker encouraged them. 'Only five bob? For a show like this? We must be mad!'

Young men were looking at their girlfriends, their expressions suggesting that *they* weren't bothered one way or the other, but if the *girl* wanted to see it, then it might be a bit of a laugh. Two of the couples followed the initial group of lads up the stairs, the rest drifted away.

'Come on, gentlemen,' the barker cajoled the single men

still standing below. 'You'll have a good time – and I promise you that I won't tell your wives you've been here.'

Woodend felt in his pocket for a couple of convenient half-crown coins.

Standing at the window of her hotel room, Monika Paniatowski watched the waves break against the shore and thought about her first sight of the sea.

She had been just eleven years old at the time, and had been standing with her mother and Arthur Jones on the dock at Calais.

'See that?' Jones had asked Monika and her mother, pointing across the water. 'That's England, that is. The White Cliffs of Dover. In a few hours we'll be over there ourselves, at the start of our wonderful new life.'

And Monika had taken him at his word – had actually believed that just by crossing a stretch of water, she could magically find happiness. That belief in the possibility of happiness was still there, somewhere deep inside her – but she had long ago abandoned the idea that it could be attained just by wishing for it. Life, she now understood, was a hazardous business. In fact, it was not *one* business at all, but several distinct ones, each of which called for a different approach. If she were to be successful in her chosen career, for example – if she were to climb the ladder of success in the male-dominated police force – then she must be bold, grabbing her opportunities before someone else snatched them away from her. But in her private life, caution was called for. Though she felt she would not be complete until she had a man of her own, it was vital to make certain he was the *right* man. She was determined she would not make the mistake of throwing herself at the first one who presented himself – as her mother had done.

She turned her back on the sea, walked over to her bed, and began to apply her mind to the murder of Punch Davies. Was the task her new boss had assigned of any real value – or was Woodend merely using it as a way to keep her out of his hair? And even if it were the latter, couldn't a smart woman like her find some way to turn it to her own advantage?

She lit a cigarette, and looked down at the notes she had made earlier.

'Would anyone being investigated by Davies be desperate enough to have committed murder to cover his trail?' she had written in her tight, neat handwriting. 'Would a cat burglar risk being hanged rather than face a few years in jail?'

The burglars she knew in Whitebridge regarded jail as nothing more than an occupational hazard – something to be tolerated in much the same way as non-criminals tolerated paying income tax and national insurance. Was there any reason to assume that the burglars in Blackpool would be any different?

What about the car-theft ring? she asked herself. A decade earlier, there would have been no call for one, but the number of car drivers had doubled since the early fifties, and it was now something of a growth industry. But not a *cottage* industry! Villains didn't nick cars off one street and try to sell them on again in the next. When they finally disposed of the stolen vehicle, it would be in another town – which meant the centre of the ring's operation usually had to be one of the big cities like Liverpool or Manchester.

Monika took a drag of her cigarette. She was back to the question of a strong enough motive for murder again, she realised. Say Davies *had* got a lead on the local branch of the car ring. Would the men running it decide he was a big enough threat to risk the rope for? No! Why should they, when all they had to do was close down the Blackpool end of things and concentrate on stealing cars from Burnley or Clitheroe instead?

Which left the hit-and-run case – and the more Monika thought about it, the faster her pulse began to race! The average perpetrator in a hit-and-run was not a felon like the ordinary criminal. He didn't regard a prison sentence as something which merely had to be endured. For him, it was the end of life as he had known it. And if the life he was about to lose was a good one, might he not risk the possibility of being hanged if that was the only way to protect it? So if Davies had had a good lead on the case, wasn't it possible that—?

She was on to something! She was sure of it!

Monika stubbed her cigarette out in the souvenir-of-Blackpool ashtray, which the landlady had provided. She had done a very productive hour's work, she told herself, and she was entitled to a reward. She wondered if any of the nearby pubs sold vodka.

The auditorium of the Gay Paree Theatre was dimly lit, which Woodend suspected was as much to mask the run-down nature of the place as to create an atmosphere. Most of the people who'd paid their admissions had chosen seats near the back of the room, but Woodend selected one close to the blue mock-velvet curtain currently drawn across the stage.

The seat was cramped, and creaked when he moved. It had probably been bought cheap from one of the cinemas forced to close down when television had become so popular, he thought.

He lit up a Capstan Full Strength and wondered if Inspector Davies had ever sat where he was sitting now. Could that be the explanation for Davies' apparent obsession with the Golden Mile? Could he have been no more than a lonely man – denied access to his wife's bed – who drew what vague comfort he could from watching semi-naked women?

The lights went down even lower – though not low enough to prevent Woodend from seeing the weedy middle-aged man who was sitting three seats up from him and was coughing nervously.

'Welcome to the show,' boomed the voice of the barker/magician who had enticed the audience in. 'Our first tableau this evening depicts the meeting between Cleopatra, Queen of the Nile, and Mark Antony, the mighty Roman general.'

So there was to be no drug-crazed Helga committing depraved acts, Woodend thought with a grin, as he sensed some of the other customers' disappointment.

The curtains rolled back noisily to reveal the scene. Mark Antony, 'the mighty Roman general', was dressed in a plastic helmet and cardboard breastplate which his ample stomach threatened to burst out of any second. His sandals, though not

Roman, at least looked leather, but Woodend couldn't help but think he'd have seemed a little more authentic if he'd bothered to take off his socks.

The general was standing next to a couch, on which lounged Cleopatra – the brassy blonde from outside – dressed only in her knickers, a plastic girdle and a blue, see-through top which was probably bri-nylon. Behind her stood two female attendants, both holding large feather fans and both naked to the waist. Any movement the assembled company made was purely involuntary – they knew the law. Except it was not *quite* true that there was no movement at all. Though the Queen of the Nile kept her body perfectly still, she let her eyes rove over the first two rows of the audience until they finally settled on Woodend. Then, just before the curtain was drawn again, her fixed expression melted into a broad smile which – there could be do doubt about it – had been intended solely for him.

There were six more tableaux – Queen Boadicea meeting the Romans; Christopher Columbus discovering native girls (who already seemed to have discovered Marks & Spencer's ready-wear for themselves); Dick Turpin (cardboard hat and cardboard mask) with his half-naked doxies. And during each of the scenes the star seemed to smile ever more broadly – and knowingly – at Woodend.

Then it was all over. The curtain was closed for the last time, the lights were raised and the punters climbed to their feet, feeling vaguely discontented.

Woodend squeezed his own large frame out of his flimsy seat, but made no move towards the exit. The barker, who was shooing the other customers through the door, noticed he seemed to have no intention of leaving, and walked over to where he was standing.

'I'm afraid you'll have to go now, sir,' he said.

'Are you the manager?' Woodend asked.

'No, but that's got nothing to do with—'

Woodend produced his warrant card. 'Central Lancashire CID,' he said. 'I'd like to see the manager.'

'The show was within the bounds of what's permitted by law,' the barker protested. 'Well within the bounds.'

'Maybe it was,' Woodend agreed. 'But I'd still like to see the manager.'

For a moment it looked as if the barker were about to argue further, then he shrugged his shoulders and said, 'You'd better follow me.'

He led Woodend to a door at the edge of the stage, knocked and then turned the handle without waiting for a reply.

'There's a bobby here to see you, Mr Gutteridge,' he said.

Over his shoulder, Woodend got a clear view of the office and the man the barker had been addressing. Gutteridge was in his early fifties, and had a mane of grey hair swept dramatically back, almost touching his shoulders. His office – in contrast to his own distinguished appearance – was little more than a cubbyhole. Most of the space was taken up by an old metal desk and two chairs. The rest was occupied by props from the various tableaux which, under the harsh light of a single naked bulb, looked even tattier than they had on stage.

'A bobby?' the manager repeated. 'A guardian of the law? But I was under the impression that all our little difficulties in that direction had been satisfactorily resolved.'

'He's not from the *local* force,' the barker said hastily. 'He's come from Central Lancs Headquarters.'

The manager ran the fingers of his left hand through his mane. 'I see,' he said thoughtfully. 'And he would be – ?'

'I would be Chief Inspector Woodend,' Woodend said, answering for himself. 'Would you mind if I asked you a few questions, Mr Gutteridge?'

'Not at all, my dear man,' the manager assured him. He turned his attention to the barker. 'Your public awaits you, Clive. Fly to them! Tread the boards like a colossus. Do all that is in your power to make them part with their five bobs.'

The barker shook his head as if he'd just been addressed in a foreign language – but had somehow managed to understand anyway – and departed. Woodend stepped into the office, closed the door behind him and manoeuvred his way around the props to the vacant chair.

'So how can I be of assistance you, Chief Inspector?' the manager asked.

'When your lad Clive told you I was from the police, you said you thought that – what were your exact words? – that the *matter* had been "satisfactorily resolved". What exactly did you mean by that?'

'That the difficulties we strolling players all so often have to face had been dealt with.'

'Would you care to be specific?'

Gutteridge laughed. 'I have toured the length and breadth of this great country of ours with my troop,' he said. 'I have given my audiences *Hamlet* and *Antigone*, *Doctor Faustus* and *Lady Windermere*. My company has brought tears to eyes of the many, but there are always the few – the groundling element – who have attempted to cause disruption. And if that is true of presentations of the classics, think how much more common it must be in a show which has less merit than the crudest Elizabethan burlesque.'

'You're sayin' you've had a bit of trouble with your punters,' Woodend translated.

'Precisely!' Gutteridge agreed enthusiastically. 'They come not to hear the immortal words of the Bard, but to gaze at naked flesh. Many of them arrive already fired up with alcoholic beverages –'

'Drunk,' Woodend supplied. 'Pissed. Legless.'

'As you say,' Gutteridge confirmed. 'And sometimes this human offal which poses as an audience wants more from a performance than my actors are allowed by the constabulary to provide.'

'Do you always take this long to get to the point?' Woodend asked.

Gutteridge smiled ruefully. 'Forgive me, my dear man. It is sometimes difficult to break the habits of a lifetime on the stage. These particular groundlings I was about to refer to infested us with their presence about two weeks ago. There were half a dozen of them, and they were – as you would say – pissed out of their tiny minds. Not happy with the spectacular we had presented, they refused to leave the auditorium until the girls had divested themselves of their few remaining garments. That was not possible, and so we called in the police.'

'An' what happened then?'

'Faced with the majesty of the law, the groundlings withdrew from the theatre without further resistance.'

An obvious question came to the forefront of Woodend's mind, but instead of asking it then – when it might be expected – he decided to file it for later.

'I'm surprised to find a man with a legitimate theatre background like your own in a place like this,' he said instead.

Gutteridge sighed. 'What can I tell you, my dear man?' he asked rhetorically. 'For years I dedicated myself to my art, with very little to show for it in material terms. Here, I may not earn golden opinions, but at least I can now look forward to the twilight of my years with a little less financial trepidation.'

'Aye, an' you're probably makin' more money an' all,' Woodend said, and before the manager had time to explain that was what he had meant, the chief inspector was on his feet and holding out his hand. 'It's been a pleasure to meet you, Mr Gutteridge,' he continued.

'The pleasure has all been mine, Chief Inspector.'

Woodend manoeuvred around the desk to the door, and was halfway out of the office when he turned and said, 'Oh, there is one more thing, sir.'

'Yes?'

'When you called in the police, was the officer who answered the call Mr Davies, by any chance?'

The manager only blinked once – but Woodend did not miss it.

'Who?' Gutteridge asked.

'Detective Inspector Davies,' Woodend repeated.

'The name sounds familiar. He wasn't the man who met an unfortunate end under the Central Pier, was he?'

'That's the feller.'

'Then no, it certainly wasn't him. The two officers in question were both in uniform – a sergeant and a constable, I believe. Now if that's all –'

'It isn't, actually,' Woodend told him. 'If I can quote you a second time, you said, "our little difficulties in that direction had been satisfactorily resolved".'

'I still fail to see—'

'I don't have your way with words, but that sounds to me as if you were talkin' about a long-term problem rather than an isolated incident involvin' a few yobs.'

For a moment, a confused expression filled Gutteridge's face. Then it cleared to be replaced by the look of a man who has realised that there might have been an honest misunderstanding.

'I see what you mean,' he said. 'The problem was not the incident itself, but whether it would have longer-term consequences. I was concerned that as a result of it, the constabulary might decide to take a less-than-favourable view of my establishment.'

'But they haven't?'

'No, the sergeant rang me a few days later to say that from his standpoint there was no more to be said on that matter. I expect he realised that we operate as a safety valve, and that if the Gay Paree was closed, something much more sordid would spring up to take its place.'

'Aye, that probably *is* what he thought,' Woodend said. 'Well, goodbye again, Mr Gutteridge.'

As he stepped through the office door, Woodend noticed the brassy blonde again. She was standing a few feet away from him and wearing the same towelling robe she had worn when she'd been on the platform. Now, however, it was so loosely belted that there was no longer a question of whether or not she was wearing a bra.

With a smile playing on her lips, she ran her eyes appraisingly up and down Woodend's body. 'Well, fancy running into you again so soon, Handsome,' she said.

Before there was a chance for the policeman to respond to her, Gutteridge emerged from the office and quickly inserted himself into the space between them.

'Where are my manners, allowing you to leave unescorted?' the theatre manager said. 'Let me show you the exit, *Chief Inspector*.'

Woodend allowed himself to be led away, but not before he had noted the look of shock which had appeared on the girl's face.

Gutteridge steered Woodend to the door. 'Come again, Mr Woodend,' he said. 'And next time do not feel obliged to part with any of your coins of the realm. For we humble players, the honour of your presence is payment enough.'

'That sounds a bit like bribery and corruption to me,' Woodend said.

The manager laughed – rather too loudly, the chief inspector thought.

'What a wit you are,' he said. 'What a loss to the stage was your decision to follow the path of law enforcement.' But even as he spoke, his hand – resting in the small of Woodend's back – was easing the chief inspector through the exit.

Woodend stepped out into the side street and saw that directly opposite was not only a row of boarding houses as he had expected, but also a brightly lit fish and chip shop.

'Now if that's not fate pointin' my way, what is?' he asked himself.

He crossed the road and entered the chip shop. There were no other customers at that moment, and the cook, a jolly-looking fat man, was standing behind the counter reading the evening paper. When he heard the bell over the door ring, he laid the paper on the counter and smiled at his new customer.

'What can I do for you, mate?' he asked.

'A fried cod an' a double ration of chips,' Woodend told him.

'Good choice. The cod's so fresh it hasn't stopped swimmin' yet.'

Woodend watched the fryer scoop the chips out of the bubbling fat in the range and place them, with the fish, into a neat newspaper parcel.

'Does the name Inspector Davies mean anythin' to you?' the chief inspector asked, as he handed over the money.

'I should say it does. He got himself topped last night – under yon Central Pier.'

'Did you know him personally?'

'Can't say that I did.'

'But you had no difficulty in recognising the name?'

'Well, of course not. We don't get many murders in Blackpool, an' as far as I can remember, we've *never* had a bobby killed before. So when one does get done in, it's bound to stick in your mind, isn't it?'

Exactly, Woodend thought as he picked up his parcel of fish and chips. *It's bound to stick in your mind.* But it hadn't stuck in Gutteridge's mind. When the name of the dead policeman had first come up, he hadn't recognised it at all. Or perhaps he'd only *pretended* not to recognise it.

The last end-of-the-pier show of the day was long over, the amusements had been closed for the night, and the Central Pier was in darkness. But it was not quite deserted. The glowing red end of a cigarette, moving through the night like a demented firefly, would have told any observer that at least one person had stayed behind.

Tommy 'Now Where Was I?' Bolton tramped relentlessly from one end of the pier to other, his mind wrestling with his problems.

Should he go to the police and tell them all he knew?

Could he dare to hope that because he would be helping them with a murder inquiry, they might, in turn, overlook what he would be forced to reveal about himself?

He shook his head angrily, cursing his own stupidity. How could they ignore what he'd done? It wasn't like a parking ticket or a littering offence. It was altogether more . . . more . . . significant.

So what was he to do? What choice did he have? None at all! He would have to keep quiet, and hope that the whole dreadful situation resolved itself of its own accord.

He had reached the very end of the pier, and slowly descended the steps to the fishermen's jetty. The waves below him – whooshing back and forth – could be so soothing on occasions. But they were not soothing now. Instead, they seemed to be roaring angry, urgent orders: *Jump in! Jump in!*

He was tempted to obey. One small step was all it would take – and his troubles would be over. But though his legs were shaking, they were unwilling to move an inch further forward. Acknowledging his failure to find the courage even to take the coward's way out, he turned and climbed the steps again.

He came to a stop near the entrance to the pier, and gazed loathingly across the promenade at the dim shape which he knew to be Gypsy Rose Elizabeth's fortune-telling booth. In the past he had often held strong grudges, and had been delighted to see those he resented eventually forced to face a painful humiliation. Sometimes, indeed, he had even engineered those humiliations himself. But he had never really *hated* before – never felt the vehemence he did towards the gypsy, a vehemence which was poisoning his whole life.

She did not deserve to live! The world would be better off without her. And in killing her, he would not just be settling his own scores – he was sure of that. He would be acting for others – dozens of people whose names he would never even know. And looked at that way, the murder would be almost an act of altruism.

But how to go about it – that was the question he must ask himself. How to eliminate this vile piece of human trash and not get caught.

It took an intelligent man to play the buffoon well, and he was a *very* good buffoon – as his income clearly demonstrated. Surely if he put his mind to it, he could come up with a plan which would not only guarantee her death but also ensure that he got away scot-free.

Twelve

The first thing Monika Paniatowski noticed when the shrill alarm clock forced her into consciousness was the vodka bottle sitting on her bedside table. The clear liquid had almost reached the screw cap when she'd bought the bottle the night before, but now the level had dropped to well below the top of the label – and she was fairly sure that was not due to evaporation!

She swung her legs out of bed, and inspected her room. It was a little cramped for her usual exercise programme, but she'd manage, she supposed. She began with a series of warming-up exercises, then got down on the floor between the bed and the wardrobe, and started doing her press-ups.

One . . . two . . . three . . .

She was drinking too much, she told herself. Worse, she was drinking *alone*. But what was the alternative? To go out on the piss with the lads? To have to endure their sexual innuendoes, which would only get more and more explicit as the evening wore on? To listen to their taunts that she was a bad sport when she repulsed their drunken embraces at the end of the session? To hear then sniggering together in the morning – because even if she didn't give them what they wanted, there would always be one or two of them who would claim that she had.

Four . . . five . . . six . . .

She must reduce her alcoholic intake. But it wouldn't be easy, because booze made the night easier to get through. She half-wished that her body would come to the assistance of her will power – that she could wake up in the mornings with a dreadful hangover. But she never did.

Seven . . . eight . . . nine . . .

The instructor had told her during her training that women could never match men press-up for press-up. And maybe he was right – maybe most of them couldn't. But she was determined to try – determined to show all those complacent bastards back at headquarters that having male genitalia didn't automatically grant them the keys to the universe.

By the time her nose had brushed against the floor thirty times, she'd had enough, but still pushed herself on to complete another ten. She'd be up to fifty press-ups soon, she promised herself, and once that barrier was broken, it shouldn't be impossible to reach a hundred.

She had washed, dressed and smoked her first two cigarettes of the day by the time she heard the gong in the hallway imperiously summoning her down to breakfast. As she walked down the stairs, she could smell the odours of a fry-up drifting from the kitchen, and remembered the times when her mother had carefully measured out what little food they'd managed to scrounge and advised her to eat it slowly. Well, those days were gone forever, thank God.

Her stomach was rumbling by the time she reached the bottom of the stairs, but then, through the open dining-room door, she caught sight of Woodend – already sitting at what would probably be *their* table for the whole of the investigation – and felt her appetite vanish.

The chief inspector's attention was focussed on the bowl of cornflakes in front of him, but once he had finished scooping the milk and cereal on to his spoon, he would undoubtedly look up and see her. Before he had the chance to do that, Monika strode quickly past the open door and on to the street.

Once outside, she took a deep breath of the salty sea air, and wondered why her instincts had ordered her to flee. Was it that she couldn't bear the thought of Woodend making a pass at her over the breakfast table? It didn't seem likely that he would. Experience had taught her that men trying to get into her knickers didn't make the offer and then give her all day to think about it. When they struck they were like snakes – one second pretending to be as harmless as dead wood and the next sticking their fangs into her.

So just what *was* it that made her so uneasy about being in the presence of her new boss? Could it be that she was worried that when he spoke of being a team and sharing the credit, he was actually being *sincere* – which made her own plans to always squeeze out of any situation only what was best for Monika Paniatowski seem almost treacherous? No! Woodend was as full of shit as the rest of them. He just had to be!

The bacon was crisp, the egg thick yolked, and the fried bread steeped enticingly in lard. As Woodend polished off the last few morsels of his fry-up, he told himself that whatever other headaches he would have to endure at the hands of Chief Superintendent Ainsworth, it was worth being back up North just for the food.

He was just finished his last piece of buttered toast when Mrs Bowyer strode meaningfully over to his table.

'There's a phone call for you,' she said accusingly.

'Who is it?'

'Didn't say. Just asked to speak to you.' The landlady gave a martyred sigh. 'This is most irregular, you know. The phone in the hallway is supposed to be for outgoing calls only – and then only in a real emergency.'

She was a real dragon, Woodend thought admiringly. If Saint George had had to face a creature like Mrs Bowyer in his quest to free the maiden, he would have abandoned the girl to her fate and gone off in search of the nearest pub.

He bit back an incipient grin and tried to look duly rebuked. 'It'll be somebody from Blackpool Central,' he explained. 'I'll tell them not use the phone in future. If they want to contact me, they can always send a constable round.'

'They can do no such thing!' the landlady said. 'This is a respectable house. No uniformed policeman has ever crossed my threshold on official business, and I'm not about to have them starting now.'

Woodend could constrain the grin no longer, and in order

to save the landlady the need to become righteously indignant, he climbed to his feet and turned slightly away from her.

'Better go an' answer the phone, then,' he said, half over his shoulder. 'You know how bad-tempered bobbies can be when they're kept waitin'.'

He walked into the hall and picked up the receiver. 'Woodend.'

'It's me, sir,' said a familiar voice.

So it wasn't someone from the local station at all! Instead, it was his faithful assistant – the Tonto to his Lone Ranger – Bob Rutter.

'Where are you, Bob?' Woodend asked, delighted.

'I'm in Whitebridge. I arrived yesterday – just after you'd left, as a matter of fact.'

'An' what do you think of it so far?'

'Seems a reasonable sort of place,' Rutter said cautiously.

'A reasonable sort of place!' Woodend repeated incredulously. 'You probably don't know this, lad, but when God created the earth, he started with Lancashire an' worked his way out.' He lit up a cigarette. 'Anyway, enough of the idle chatter. How soon can you get down here?'

There was an embarrassed pause on the other end of the line. 'I'm not sure I can get down there *at all*,' Rutter said finally.

'What are you talkin' about?'

'I had an interview with Chief Superintendent Ainsworth as soon as I reported for duty this morning. He's assigned me to another case.'

'*Another* case? What *kind* of case?'

'Car theft. There's apparently been a lot of it going on in the first place God created.'

Woodend felt his fingers crushing the cigarette he held between them. 'But that's outrageous!' he protested. 'Car theft's a job for the local flatfeet!'

'We *are* the local flatfeet now,' Rutter reminded him.

So they were, Woodend supposed. But that didn't alter the fact that he needed his right-hand man working with him on this case.

'You did point out to Mr Ainsworth that I'm investigatin' the murder of a policeman here, didn't you?' he asked.

'Not quite as subtly as you might have done, sir,' Rutter replied – and Woodend could picture the grin on his face. 'But I did remind him that I'm one of your team.'

One of his team? Bob Rutter *was* the team. 'An' what did he say to that?' Woodend asked.

'He told me that you already had a team in place. Then he went on to add that if I want to have any future in the Lancashire Constabulary, I'd do well to remember where my loyalties are supposed to lie.'

'Bastard!' Woodend said.

'Yes, you don't have to be here long before you start hearing rumours about Mr Ainsworth's parentage,' Rutter agreed.

Woodend deposited his crumpled – but still burning – cigarette in the souvenir ashtray next to the phone. If he'd been in Whitebridge at that moment, he'd have marched straight into Ainsworth's office and pointed out forcibly how vital Bob Rutter had become to his work. But he wasn't in Whitebridge when the blow fell – which had probably all been part of the Detective Chief Superintendent's machiavellian calculation.

'We'll get it clear just who you report to as soon as I've got this case wrapped up,' he promised. 'In the meantime, stay in touch.'

'I'll do that,' Rutter promised.

Not that it seemed likely to him that there would be much to stay in touch about.

When Monika Paniatowski arrived at the Incident Room, Sergeant Hanson and the three detective constables were already seated around the central Formica table. And they looked as if they had been there for a while – as if they had deliberately arrived early for the express purpose of having a private discussion before the outsiders from Whitebridge arrived.

The three constables merely nodded in her general direction, but Sergeant Hanson stood up and walked over to her.

'Did you sleep well?' he asked.

81

Monika felt her defensive shield slide into place, as it always did when she was with male officers. He'd asked her if she'd slept well, but had he really meant, had she slept *alone*? It wouldn't be the first time a man had used that gambit on her – not by a long bloody chalk.

'Sorry, I didn't mean to stump you with that question,' Hanson said, smiling. 'Should I have started with something easier?'

Monika felt herself returning his smile. 'I slept very well,' she said.

'And now I'll bet you're just bursting to get down to work. I've taken the liberty of assigning desks already, but if you're not completely happy with the arrangement—'

'I'm sure whatever you've decided will be fine.'

Hanson almost looked relieved. 'In that case, that'll be your desk over there – right next to Mr Woodend's. You'll find all the usual forms and requisition orders in the drawer. If there's anything else you want, you've only to ask me for it.'

'Thank you.'

'Do you fancy a cup of tea before you get started?' Hanson asked.

He was being very nice, Monika thought – but male officers had been nice to her before, and there was usually a price they expected to be paid.

We've filled in all the forms for you, Monika. The least you can do is show us a bit of leg.

I'll swap shifts with you, Monika, as long as you give me a quick kiss and cuddle in return.

'Oh dear, have I asked another difficult question?' Hanson asked, his smile back in place.

'I'd love a cup,' Monika said, looking round for the tea urn.

'Haven't got the catering side of things organised down here yet,' Hanson said, following her glance, 'so I'll have to pop up to the canteen for a cup.'

'If it's too much trouble –'

'No trouble at all. I'll be back in two shakes of a lamb's tail.'

Hanson disappeared up the stairs, and Monika wondered what she should do next. She could stay standing where she was until he returned, but that would make her look like a useless pillock. She could go and sit at the table with the three men who had barely acknowledged her presence. Or she could go over to her desk. She chose the desk.

The typewriter which rested on the desk was an Underwood – old, but serviceable enough. The pencils had all been sharpened to a fine point and there was a new sheet of blotting paper. She'd had no chance to form an opinion of Hanson as a detective yet, but he certainly knew how to organise an office – and that skill was rarer than most people seemed to appreciate.

As she leant over the typewriter and experimentally tapped one of the keys, she got a sudden sensation of being watched – studied, almost – by at least one of the men sitting at the table. It was not a new experience, yet somehow this time it was different. The inspection she was undergoing was not lascivious. If anything it was almost clinical – as if she were a laboratory rat being observed as she made her way through the maze.

She brushed the feeling aside, and reached for her desk drawer, intending to find out which kinds of forms Sergeant Hanson considered necessary for officers conducting a murder inquiry. As the drawer slid open – and she saw what was inside – she had to force herself to hold back a gasp.

All the forms were there, just as Hanson had promised her they would be, but in addition, resting on top of them, there was a rubber condom – a *used* rubber condom.

Behind her, she heard a loud snigger. She turned, slowly, towards the table. All three of the detective constables had their heads bent and seemed intent on their paperwork.

Paniatowski picked up the condom carefully between her thumb and forefinger and walked over to the table. Once there, she dropped it on a spot equidistant between the DCs. It fell on the table with a dull squelch. The three men first looked up – and then down.

'I don't know which of you has been having it off with my

drawer,' Paniatowski said, 'but whoever it is, somebody should explain to him that he's been wasting his money on condoms, because it's almost impossible for him to get a desk pregnant – especially if his tackle is so small that he can't fill a rubber johnny out better than this.'

The young Constable Eliot blushed, the ginger-haired Constable Stone giggled. Only Constable Brock, it seemed, did not find her remark either embarrassing or funny – and that told her all she wanted to know.

'Get rid of it, Brock,' she said.

'Me?' Brock demanded, outraged.

'You!' Paniatowski repeated. 'That is, unless, you'd rather it was still there when Mr Woodend arrives.'

Without waiting for a response, she turned and marched out of the room. As she mounted the stairs, she noted that her heart was galloping.

You're being stupid! she told herself. This isn't the worst thing you've ever had to put up with.

No, it wasn't. It was nothing more than the latest in a long string of indignities which had begun the moment she'd joined the Whitebridge force as a uniformed constable. But every time something like this happened, it got a little bit harder to cope with – every time, the light at the end of the tunnel seemed just that bit further away.

Rank hadn't insulated her from it – things were as bad now as when she'd been a rookie constable – and she had a nightmare vision of herself as a fifty-five-year-old Chief Superintendent, still having to put up with the crap. Of course, there was an obvious solution to the problem. She could resign from the force and take a job in something safe and mundane – like local government. But she didn't want to, dammit! She had earned her position as detective sergeant by guts and hard graft – and she was not about to relinquish it now without a fight.

By the time Monika Paniatowski had thoroughly scrubbed her hands in the ladies' toilet and returned to the Incident Room, Hanson was back with her tea, and Woodend was firmly ensconced in a chair at the head of the Formica table.

'Let's get down to business, shall we?' the man in the hairy sports coat suggested. 'I sent you lads out cloggin' it along the Golden Mile last night. Was it worth it?'

The three constables immediately looked to Hanson for guidance.

The sergeant gave a slight cough. 'Yes, sir. Apparently you were right,' he admitted.

'Oh aye? Right about what?'

'Several of the people we talked to admitted seeing quite a lot of Inspector Davies over the last two or three weeks.'

'An' not before?'

'Not since he was made up to inspector, which must have been three or four years ago now.'

Which pretty much confirmed what the rock seller had told him, Woodend thought.

'An' where did Mr Davies stop durin' these walks up the Mile?' he asked.

Hanson shrugged. 'There you've got us, sir. We've found plenty of witnesses who saw him going past, but none who actually saw him stopping anywhere.'

'Not even at the Gay Paree Theatre?'

'I beg your pardon, sir?'

'The manager of the Gay Paree – a self-important ham who goes by the name of Gutteridge – knows your Mr Davies.'

'Are you sure of that, sir?'

'I can't prove it, but I'm sure enough. Anyway, the interestin' question is – where did their paths first cross? It's highly unlikely they met on the golf links or at their local rotary club – I know some of these places can be quite liberal, but even they must draw the line at admittin' filth merchants. An' Mr Gutteridge doesn't strike me as the kind of feller who'd be interested in model aeroplanes, like Mr Davies was.'

'Perhaps Punch . . . Mr Davies was a . . .' – Hanson was searching for the right word – '. . . a patron of the theatre, sir.'

'If he'd been a "patron", as you so delicately put it, he'd just have sunk into the darkness like everybody else, and Gutteridge wouldn't have known him from Adam,' Woodend said. 'There has to be more to it than that.' He paused for a second. 'I was readin' somewhere about a town in America called Las Vegas,' he continued. 'Apparently it's in the arse-end of nowhere – slap-bang in the middle of the desert, to be precise.'

'Really, sir?' Hanson asked politely, though it was obvious he had no idea where this particular line of thought was leading.

'Aye,' Woodend said. 'It seems that the reason it exists at all is that these gangsters in California had a lot of money they didn't know what to do with – so they decided to invest it in creatin' a town dedicated to gamblin'.'

'You're wondering if the same thing could have happened here and there's British gangsters' money behind the Golden Mile?' Hanson asked.

'Well, it's a thought, isn't it?'

Hanson shook his head doubtfully. 'I'll look into it, sir, but don't expect me to come up with too much. As far as I know, there's two kinds of businesses on the Mile – the big ones, which are owned by legitimate entertainment companies like Rank and Mecca, and the small ones, which sell hot dogs, postcards and rock, and are pretty much one-man operations. I can't see scope for organised crime in either of them.'

'I think I agree with you there,' Woodend said. 'But the fact remains that *somethin'* was drawin' Mr Davies – who was an experienced an' dedicated police officer – to the Golden Mile – an' so far we've bugger all idea what it was.' He lit up a Capstan Full Strength and inhaled deeply. 'Get out on the streets again, lads. An' really put your backs into the job, because by the end of the day I want to know what that mysterious *somethin'* is.'

The four local men rose to their feet. Paniatowski was about to do the same when she noticed Woodend gesturing to stay where she was.

'So, tell me, Sergeant, what little expeditions have you got planned for today?' the chief inspector when the local men had gone.

'I've got a meeting with the sergeant in charge of the stolen car ring inquiry in an hour, sir,' Paniatowski said. 'And I've arranged to meet the team who were working with Mr Davies on the hit-and-run just before lunch. Once I've had a talk with both of them, I should have a clearer idea of where to go next.'

Half the sergeants he'd worked with in the past would have given a much longer outline of what they intended to do, Woodend thought – and have been watching him intently for signs of approval or disapproval as they spoke. He liked the fact that Paniatowski did not do that. On the other hand, after seeing the way she'd conned Mrs Davies the previous day, he was going to have to look out for her taking short cuts.

'I expected to see you at breakfast, Sergeant,' he said. 'You never turned up.'

'I don't eat much breakfast, sir,' Paniatowski lied.

'Maybe you don't,' Woodend replied. 'But I like to see the people I'm workin' closely with first thing in the mornin'. So as from tomorrow, I'll want to see you – bright-eyed an' bushy-tailed – sittin' across from me at breakfast table. Understood?'

'Understood, sir,' Paniatowski agreed.

Thirteen

'I used to get frustrated about only being a sergeant – but not any more,' George Collins said, after glancing briefly out of the café window to check that the sea was still there. 'Now I'm quite happy to serve out my last few years with three stripes on my arm.'

'What happened to make you change your attitude?' Monika Paniatowski asked.

'Oh, nothing dramatic,' the white-haired sergeant answered. 'I think I just grew out of being ambitious. I began to see that I'd get more satisfaction out of doing the job I had well than I would by constantly hankering after promotion. You'll probably get to feel that way yourself, in time.'

Like hell, I will! Monika thought. I'll never be happy as long as there's even *one* more step to climb.

'Tell me what Mr Davies was like as a boss,' she said.

'All in all, not bad. If you needed the overtime, he found some reason for you to stay on the job for a couple of hours more, and if you wanted to nick off early on the odd occasion, he'd generally turn a blind eye.'

He was probably very kind to stray dogs and little children, too, Paniatowski thought – but that's not really what I'm interested in.

'How would you rate him as a detective?' she asked.

'Pretty solid,' Collins said, after some thought. 'Very reliable. I'm not saying there aren't smarter detectives in the Blackpool CID, but none of them have his determination. He was like a terrier – once he'd got his jaw clamped around something, he wouldn't let go.'

'Tell me about this stolen car ring.'

'We used to get one or two vehicles a week reported stolen, and at least half of them would be found abandoned within a few days. Now we have four or five a week going missing, and if even a couple of them turn up again, we count ourselves lucky.'

'Is there any pattern to the thefts?'

'None. They disappear at all times of day, and from no particular area of town. I've tried planting a few decoy cars, and that's led to the arrest of a couple of local tearaways – but I'm sure they're not responsible for the majority of the thefts.'

'Any common thread running through the types of cars which were stolen?' Paniatowski asked.

Collins reached into his pocket and produced a piece of paper. 'I've brought you a list,' he said.

Paniatowski smoothed the paper out on the table, and ran her eyes quickly down the columns. It was all pretty much what she would have expected – Ford Anglias and Morris Minors at the bottom end of the scale, Austin Princesses and Vauxhall Victors at the top end. But there, right in the middle of the list, was a car which didn't belong at all.

'A Rolls Royce Silver Cloud!' she exclaimed. 'Who, in Blackpool, drives a *Rolls Royce Silver Cloud*?'

Collins grinned. 'Don't be taken in by appearances, lass,' he said. 'Blackpool may not look much when compared to London, but there's some real money in this town. Take Sam the Donkeyman, for example.'

'Who?'

'Scruffy little feller who's got a few donkeys down by the South Pier. See him on the street, and you think he hadn't got two ha'pennies to rub together. But as soon as the season's over, he's off to his luxury villa in Spain.'

'Is that who the Rolls belongs to?' Paniatowski asked. 'A donkey man?'

'No. He's got one of them big American cars. The Rolls belongs to Tommy Bolton.'

'Who?'

Collins looked incredulous. 'Tommy Bolton,' he repeated.

'The comedian!' He adopted the puzzled comical face which had become Bolton's trademark. ' "Now where was I?" ' he asked, in a fair imitation of Bolton's bemused tone.

'I think I've seen him on the telly,' Paniatowski said.

'Bound to have done,' Collins agreed. 'He's never off it. Anyway, first he bought himself a bungalow out in Lytham St Anne's – frightfully posh – and then splashed out on a brand new Roller. Didn't have it long, though. There can't have been more than a couple of hundred miles on the clock when it was nicked.'

'Where was it stolen from? The promenade?'

Collins chuckled. 'If you had a Rolls, would you leave it on the prom for all the riff-raff to mess with?'

'No, I suppose not.'

'And neither did Tommy Bolton. Somebody broke into his garage and took it.'

'And neither he nor his neighbours noticed anything?'

'The theft happened in the middle of the afternoon. Tommy was doing a matinee on the Central Pier, and most of his posh neighbours were out playing golf.'

Paniatowski frowned. She'd intended this interview to be nothing more than a smokescreen behind which she could hide from Woodend the fact that what she was really interested in was the Fleetwood hit-and-run. But now, much to her surprise, she found herself becoming intrigued by the case of the stolen Rolls Royce.

'Doesn't it bother you that this particular vehicle was so much more valuable than all the other cars on your list?' she asked.

'Not really.'

'Why not?'

'The way I look at it is like this. The gang mostly steals popular models because it knows they'll be easy to shift. But it knew it could get rid of the Rolls easily, too.'

'I don't see that,' Paniatowski confessed. 'If you were looking for one particular stolen Anglia, then you'd have quite a task on your hands because there are thousands about. But there aren't many Rollses.'

'That's the point,' Collins told her. 'Rollses are in short supply, and even if you have the money you can't just go out and buy one. Last time I checked there was a two-year waiting list – and people who are rich aren't used to waiting for anything.'

'So you're saying –?'

'In my opinion, Tommy's car isn't in this country any more. Even as we speak, it's probably being driven around the desert by some rich Arab with a tea towel on his head.' Collins paused to light up a Park Drive. 'I have to say that in this case I think it's partly Tommy Bolton's own fault.'

'Why?'

'Driving around in a flash car like that, he was asking for it to be nicked.'

Yes, Paniatowski thought – just like, by walking around in a reasonably attractive female body, I've been asking for all the stuff I have to put up with.

'Anyway, I'm sorry I've not been of much use, but that's really as far as I've got,' Collins continued.

Something had been bothering Monika Paniatowski all through the interview, and now she had finally managed to put her finger on it.

'One more question,' she said. 'You keep saying, "I did this," and, "I did that." What's the reason?'

'I beg your pardon?'

'In my experience, sergeants normally use "we" – meaning themselves and their bosses. I was wondering why you hadn't.'

Collins looked embarrassed. 'Just a slip of the tongue?' he suggested hopefully.

'Or was it that you didn't use "we" because there wasn't any "we" on this case – because it was just *you*? You said earlier that Mr Davies was dogged and determined. Were you just feeding me – a fellow sergeant – the kind of flannel you'd feed to the brass?'

'No, he was usually dogged and determined.'

'But not on this particular case?'

'On this case, no,' Collins admitted. 'I'd brief him and then ask him what to do next, and it was plain from his answer that he hadn't been listening to me at all.'

'Why do you think he was so distracted? Something to do with his home life?'

'It's possible,' Collins conceded, 'but I don't really think so. I think there was something about the job that was getting to him.'

'Like what?'

'I've no idea. But it was there all right – deep inside – eating at him like a worm.'

A wise chief inspector would be sitting in the Incident Room pretending to co-ordinate the reports which were coming in from the men on the street, Woodend thought as he ambled along the prom. A wise chief inspector would be available to answer the phone should Detective Superintendent Ainsworth deign to ring him. Aye, well, he had never claimed to be a wise chief inspector – and it was far too nice a day to be stuck in a stuffy basement.

He looked down on to the beach – at the row upon row of occupied deckchairs; at the small children scraping out moats around their castles for the incoming tide to run through; at the donkeys cantering along the sand – and at the screaming kids on their backs, holding on tight and only occasionally daring to free one hand to wave to their parents.

A tall, thin tent made of striped red and white material had been erected just near the steps leading up to the prom, and a crowd of youngsters was sitting in front of it, gazing up in fascination.

The Punch and Judy Show! The late Inspector William Davies' nickname had been Punch, Woodend reminded himself, as he walked down the steps to get a better view of the spectacle.

The performance was already well under way and there were two glove puppets on the parapet, behind which the puppeteer crouched hidden. One of the puppets wore a floppy cap and had a grotesque hooked nose. Mr Punch himself. The other puppet was his wife, Judy – which was what half the Blackpool police seemed to call Edna Davies.

'Give-us-a-kiss, Judy,' Mr Punch said in a wheedling, squeaky voice.

'Yes, I'll give you a kiss,' Judy replied.

The puppeteer bent his hand, and Judy disappeared below the parapet. When she emerged again, she was carrying a stick.

'Here's a nice kiss,' she screamed, beating Punch. 'And another . . . and another.' She chased her husband around the stage, raining blow after blow on him. 'I hope you like my kisses, Mr Punch.'

Punch stopped trying to escape, and instead wrested the stick from his wife. 'Thank you, Judy, for your kisses,' he shrieked. He hit her. 'Thank, you, thank you, thank you.'

Judy cowered under the blows. 'Enough, Mr Punch,' she pleaded. 'No more kisses.'

'Just one more,' Punch told her, hitting her so hard this time that she fell motionless.

Punch poked her experimentally with his stick, then, when she showed no sign of movement, he rolled her to one edge of the stage.

'That's the way to do it,' he told the children. 'What-a-pity, what-a-pity.'

Punch was like so many of the killers he had encountered over the years, Woodend thought – full of bravado when first admitting the crime, then slowly becoming anguished as the full horror of what they'd done started to hit home.

The chief inspector turned to face the sea. Punch Davies hadn't beaten his wife, by all accounts, but there were other ways to make a woman suffer besides inflicting physical pain. And was Judy's violent response to Punch's request for kisses so different from Mrs Davies' action in exiling her husband to the spare bedroom?

Woodend swung round to face the tent again.

A policeman had come to arrest Mr Punch for Judy's murder, and the two were engaged in a ferocious struggle, cudgelling each other with all their might. The kids, sitting on the sand, were watching the scene wide-eyed.

Punch caught the other puppet a heavy blow, and the policeman fell down dead.

It was a strange form of entertainment, Woodend thought. Mr Punch killed without compunction, and yet somehow managed to remain the hero, and later – when he cheated the hangman by tricking him into putting his own head in the noose – the audience would cheer him just as much as it had done at the beginning, when he had appeared before it without a stain on his character.

Perhaps there was something primeval about it, the chief inspector thought. Maybe by confronting evil and laughing at it, that evil somehow became less frightening.

He shook his head in self-mockery. He was a simple bobby, and abstract thoughts like that were far too deep for him. Perhaps Bob Rutter – with a grammar school education – could explain it all simply, but he was buggered if he could.

The bright green crocodile – another stock character in the Punch story – had appeared on stage – and grabbed Punch's large nose in his jaws. But there were no crocodiles in Blackpool, and however Punch Davies had earned his nickname, it certainly hadn't been by coming to grips with a slimy reptile.

Woodend decided that he had seen enough, and – reaching in his pocket for his Capstan Full Strength – he headed back to the promenade.

Fourteen

B ob Rutter drove along the ring road which skirted Whitebridge, trying to convince himself – unsuccessfully – that he liked what he was seeing. So, according to Charlie Woodend, God had created Lancashire first and then worked his way out, had he? Well, He might be omnipotent, but He didn't seem to have been any more immune to the Monday morning blues than anybody else starting their week's work.

The town Rutter was observing had been founded at the bottom of a valley, then slowly spread up the hills which surrounded it like a creeping plant. It had been, for a time, one of the main centres of the British textile industry, churning out woven cotton to meet the needs of a hungry Empire. But those days were long since past. Though some of the mills were still working, many had closed down as the manufacturers had shifted production to India, where labour was cheaper and more compliant. Now the abandoned factories stood starkly against the skyline – skeletal evidence of the place's dead glory.

It was the Lancashire climate which had brought the town and the cotton industry together, Rutter had been told. In order to prevent the cotton thread from snapping, it needed to be woven in a moist atmosphere – and Whitebridge had moisture enough and to spare. There were even local jokes about the weather!

'See that tower up on top of the hill?' one of the inspectors had said earlier. 'It was erected to celebrate Queen Victoria's Diamond Jubilee, but *we* use it as a weather vane.'

'Is that right?' Rutter had asked.

'Aye. If you can see the tower, it's about to rain. An' if you can't, then it already *is* rainin'!'

95

The new boy had laughed politely – as had been expected of him – but he couldn't help thinking that after a while the joke would start to wear a bit thin.

Rutter checked the street map which was resting on his knee. Another quarter of a mile, he calculated, and he should be looking out for a turning to the left. He wondered how Maria, his blind Spanish wife, who was already fairly heavy with their first child, would take to Whitebridge – and whether he should ever have put her in a position where there was little choice.

'Well, there's no point in worrying about that now,' he said to the road ahead of him.

Nor was there. For better or worse, he was stuck in his posting in Whitebridge for at least three years – and he would just have to come to terms with living in a foreign land.

He reached the junction he'd been looking for, and signalled to the left. The road he turned on to was wide, but desolate. On one side lay the rubble of what must once have been countless rows of terraced houses. On the other stood the towering – long since deserted – Calcutta Mill.

Rutter ran his eyes quickly over the building. It had high windows, designed to admit the maximum light possible into the weaving sheds. Its tall chimneys were sturdily constructed in Accrington Iron Brick. The mill must once have belched out enough smoke to cover the whole valley in a sooty pall – but it was years now since the chimneys had been fired.

He tried to picture the scene as it had been when Charlie Woodend was growing up. The mill's hooter sounding before first light had even broken. The sound of clogs on cobbles, as the workers made their way to the gate. The huge cacophony of noise within the mill itself – a noise so loud that, according to Woodend, the weavers had learned to lip read, which was a handy talent to have acquired when they went deaf (as, inevitably, they did) in early middle age.

Just beyond the mill was the place he had come to visit – a single-storied, somewhat ramshackle garage which, in addition to selling petrol, offered speedy repairs at economical prices.

As Rutter pulled up in the forecourt, his front wheels ran over a rubberised wire which rang a bell in the office. The man who answered the summons was wearing a blue boiler suit which encased his plump little body like a second skin. White stubble covered his chin, and a greasy cloth cap was perched on his head. He was at least sixty, Rutter thought – possibly older – but though the harsh Lancashire weather had taken a toll on his skin, his eyes were bright and sharp enough to have belonged to a much younger man.

By the time Rutter had got out of his car, the old man had drawn level with him.

'I'm looking for the owner of this garage,' Rutter said.

'That's me,' the old man replied. 'Albert Grimsdyke. What can I do for thee?'

'Police. Detective Inspector Rutter.'

Rutter reached inside his jacket pocket for his warrant card, but Grimsdyke shook his head.

'Dunna bother theesen about no papers,' he said. 'Tha'll be that new bobby – up from London – willt'a?'

'How did you know that?' Rutter asked.

'It's not easy keppin' things like that quiet in a town like Whitebridge,' the old man said. 'What can I do for thee, lad?'

'I'm making some inquiries – of a routine nature – at all the garages in the area.'

'An' what tha' wants to know is if any bugger's offered me a second-hand car wi' no logbook at a knockdown price,' the garage owner said.

'Why should you assume that?'

'In the old days tha' could leave anythin' tha' owned out on the street, an' be sure it'd be there when tha' got back,' the old man said. 'But times have changed. There's bin a lot o' cars pinched from round here recently, an' now here tha' ist – sniffin' around like a hound that's got a whiff o' the fox. Well, it dun't tek a genius to put them two things together, dust it?'

'And *has* anyone offered you a second-hand car with no log-book?' Rutter asked.

The garage owner shook his head. 'They'd ha' more sense. They'd know I'd be on the phone to the nearest cop shop afore they'd even had time to scratch their arses.'

Rutter grinned. 'Have you always been in the garage business, Mr Grimsdyke?'

The old man took off his cloth cap and rubbed his bald head. 'How old dust tha' think I am, lad?'

'Fifty-eight,' Rutter said, veering on the side of the complimentary.

'I'm seventy-two,' Grimsdyke told him, 'an' when I were growin' up, there wasn't enough motor cars in Whitebridge to kepp one garage goin', let alone the fifteen or twenty there must be now. I started out in th' mills, like me father an' gran'father before me. What I've learned about engines, I've picked up as I've gone along.'

A new figure appeared from behind the garage – a young woman. Like Grimsdyke, she was dressed in a blue boiler suit, but in her case the curves it hugged were much more appealing.

She saw the two men talking, and made a beeline for them, but once she'd drawn level she ignored Rutter, and spoke directly to the old man.

'Does the customer have a problem, Grandad?' she asked.

'He's not a customer,' the old man told her. 'He's a bobby. From London.'

The girl raised a quizzical eyebrow. 'From London?' she repeated.

'I used to work in London,' Rutter explained. 'Now I'm in the Central Lancs Police.'

Not quite true, he reminded himself. He *would* be a member of the local force, but not until the next day. Any investigation he was doing now was strictly unofficial – an attempt to get one jump ahead of the game.

He took a closer look at the girl's face. She was around twenty, he guessed. She had dark brown hair, a button nose and Cupid's bow mouth. There was a smear of grease on one of her cheekbones which, despite himself, he found erotic. And she was frowning as if she had found herself in a situation she would much rather have avoided.

'Can you just check when Mr Metcalfe's booked in for his oil change, Grandad?' she asked the old man.

'I know exactly when it is,' the old man replied. 'Half-past two this afternoon.'

'You might have got the time wrong,' the girl told him gently. 'You do that, sometimes, you know.'

'I'm sure—'

'Please just check it for me,' the girl said insistently. 'The book's in the office.'

'A' reet. If it'll kepp thee happy,' Grimsdyke agreed.

The girl watched the old man walk to the office, waiting until he was inside before she turned to Rutter, allowing her brown eyes to flash with anger.

'Have you got any identification?!' she asked brusquely.

Rutter produced his warrant card. The girl examined it carefully.

'What do you think you're doing bothering an old man like that?' she demanded fiercely, when she was satisfied that he really was who he said he was.

'Could I know who I'm talking to?' Rutter countered.

'Jenny Grimsdyke. The old man's my grandfather.'

'I'd gathered that. Well, Miss Grimsdyke, I'm conducting an official inquiry and—'

'But why bother the old man?' Jenny Grimsdyke repeated.

'He is the owner of the garage, isn't he?'

'On paper,' Jenny Grimsdyke admitted, 'but half the time he's no idea what's going on.'

'He seemed sharp enough to me.'

'So you caught him on a good day.' Jenny Grimsdyke's aggressive expression melted away, and was replaced by one which could almost be called pleading. 'Listen, would you like to know how things really are round here?'

'Certainly.'

'The business is struggling to keep its head above water. I'm putting in fifteen-hour days just to meet the bills. It would be better all round if Grandad retired and gave me a chance to get on with my own life.'

'But I take it he doesn't want to do that?'

Jenny Grimsdyke snorted. 'He built the business up from nothing. He had a few good years in the fifties – but now it's nothing again. Only he won't accept that. He loves the place. So I keep it running for him for him as best I can.' A trace of her earlier anger returned to her eyes. 'And I don't want him bothered. Do you understand that? If you need any help in your "official inquiries", then come to me – because I'm the only one around here who really knows what's going on.'

'All right,' Rutter agreed. 'In that case, I'll ask you same question I asked your grandfather. Have you been offered any second-hand cars at under their market value?'

Jenny Grimsdyke threw back her head and laughed out loud. 'Look at this place!' she said. 'Do you think we've got the spare cash to buy *any* car, even a beaten-up old crock?'

'So I take it the answer's no.'

'If I was trying to sell a stolen car, this is the last place I'd bring it,' Jenny Grimsdyke replied.

She had a point, Rutter thought.

'Thank you for your help, Miss Grimsdyke,' he said. 'I don't think I'll be bothering you again.'

He turned and walked back to his car. He was just climbing behind the wheel when the old man emerged from the office.

'I was reet a' along,' Grimsdyke called to his granddaughter. 'Mr Metcalfe's service is booked in for two-thirty.' He turned his attention to Rutter. 'Ist thee off, lad?'

'Yes, I am.'

The old man favoured him with a smile. 'Well, come again,' he said. 'Only next time tha' might be wise to bring an interpreter wi' thee.'

Fifteen

Fleetwood, where the hit-and-run accident had so recently occurred, was in many ways a poor relation to Blackpool – a resort which had both sands and sea, yet had never quite caught on. Some people did spend their holidays there, it was true. And there were always day-trippers who came to see what lay at the very end of the tramline. But any dreams the town might once have had of being a mecca of entertainment had long since dimmed, and now its main claim to fame lay in being the home of Fisherman's Friend throat lozenges.

Bounded as it was by the Irish Sea to the west and north, and the River Wyre to the east, Fleetwood stuck out like a raised thumb on the fist of the Fylde Peninsula, and the corner of Blakiston Street and Walmsley Street – which was where Monika Paniatowski was standing at that moment – could probably best be described as in the right-hand tip of that thumb's jagged nail.

'The old lady was actually on the zebra crossing when she was knocked down, was she?' Monika asked.

'Right slap-bang in the middle of it,' the man next to her confirmed.

Monika looked first to her left and then to her right. The road was as straight as an arrow in both directions.

'Can you give me some more details?' she asked.

Detective Sergeant Colin Howarth nodded. He was a young-ish man, perhaps no more than a year or two older than Paniatowski herself, but unlike the white-haired Sergeant Collins, who still took his job seriously, Howarth had an air about him which suggested he was already mentally coasting towards retirement.

'The vehicle involved in the accident was travelling south,' the local sergeant said.

'How can you be sure of that?'

'The victim took the impact of the crash on her right side. We know what point she started out from and where she was going to, so unless she'd turned back on her own tracks – which she had no reason to do at that time of night – she was crossing from this side of the road to the other when the vehicle hit her, which must mean that the car was coming from over there,' he pointed up the road, 'and heading out of Fleetwood.'

'What else have you got?'

'From the extent of her injuries, we know that the vehicle hit the poor old biddy at considerable speed – possibly as high as sixty miles an hour. She was thrown right up into the air, as you'd imagine.'

'Must have done her a lot of damage.'

'It killed her!'

Paniatowski sighed. 'What I mean is, the injuries which led to her death must have been quite horrific.'

'Broke at least a couple of dozen bones, I think.'

You think? Paniatowski repeated to herself. You *think*. You should bloody *know*!

'And then there was the cut on her back,' Howarth added.

'What cut on her back?'

'It was about two inches long and a quarter of an inch wide.'

'And what caused it?'

'The pathologist is still working on that.'

Getting information out of Howarth was like pulling teeth, Paniatowski thought.

'Any forensic evidence?' she asked.

Howarth shrugged. 'A few paint scrapings. A bit of glass.'

'And have you learned anything from them?'

'The boffins in Whitebridge are working on it, but they haven't been able to identify them yet. And even if when they can, I don't see what good it will do. Say the paint comes from a Vauxhall Victor. Do you have any idea how many Victors there are in Lancashire alone?'

'What about witnesses?' Paniatowski said – almost snapped.

'There were none that we could find. It was gone midnight, you see. The pubs had all been closed for well over an hour, and everybody who'd been out drinking had gone home to bed.'

'Except for the victim and the driver,' Paniatowski pointed out.

'Yes, except for them.'

'What was *she* doing out so late at night?'

'Her daughter and son-in-law had been attending some sort of company dinner in Preston. She was babysitting her grandchildren. The son-in-law offered to drive her back home, but she said it wasn't far, and she'd be perfectly all right walking. And so she would have been, if some nutter hadn't ploughed into her.'

'You think he'd been drinking?'

'Seems likely, doesn't it? It's hard to see how he could have missed seeing her on the crossing if he'd been sober.'

Paniatowski opened her handbag and took out her cigarettes. 'Do you have *any* real leads?'

'None,' Sergeant Howarth admitted. 'We've conducted a door-to-door inquiry that's taken in half the population of Fleetwood, and I've had my lads ring up every garage within a twenty-mile radius to check if anybody's tried to book in a car that had some unexplained damage. And it all got us absolutely nowhere.'

'But you *are* still investigating it?'

'Of course we are,' Howarth replied, without much conviction. 'But like I said, unless a surprise witness suddenly comes forward – or the driver suffers a bout of remorse and gives himself up – I can't see us getting a result on this one.'

'Was that Inspector Davies' opinion, too?' Paniatowski asked.

'Sort of.'

'What does that mean?'

'To tell you the truth, I don't think Mr Davies cared much about the case one way or the other.'

'And why was that, do you suppose?'

'I think he had other things on his mind.'

'Such as?'

'I've absolutely no idea,' Howarth said – and Paniatowski was sure that he was lying.

Monika flicked her lighter open and lit a cigarette. 'Thank you for your help, Sergeant,' she said.

'That's it?'

'You've told me all you know, haven't you?'

'Well . . . yes.'

'Then there doesn't seem much point in taking up any more of your valuable time.'

'I'll drive you back to the station,' Howarth said, gesturing towards his car.

'If it's all the same to you, I think I'd like to spend a bit more time in Fleetwood,' Paniatowski told him.

'Any . . . er . . . particular reason for that?'

'No. No *particular* reason,' Paniatowski lied.

'I'll see. Well, if you'd like to tell me what time you'd like picking up again –'

'I'll take the tram back,' Paniatowski said firmly.

'There's no need—'

'I know there isn't,' Paniatowski agreed, 'but I still fancy a tram ride.'

The café just behind the Winter Gardens was a favourite haunt of tram drivers and policemen. When Sergeant Hanson arrived, his team had already assembled and were sipping strong tea out of white enamel mugs.

'What happened with Sergeant Paniatowski this morning?' Hanson said, as he spooned a heaped teaspoon of sugar into his mug.

'What do you mean, Sarge? What happened to her?' DC Stone asked.

Hanson took a sip of the tea. God, it was so strong you could build bricks out of it. 'When I went to get her a cuppa, she seemed fine, but she when she passed me as I was coming back from the canteen, she looked as if she'd just heard her mother had died,' Hanson said. 'Now why was that?'

'Told you we'd got to her,' Brock said to Stone in an undertone.

'What was that?' Hanson demanded.

Brock shrugged. 'Some women just don't have a sense of humour.'

'Much as I love riddles, there are times when I'd prefer a straight answer,' Hanson said, with an impatient edge creeping into his voice. 'So I'll ask you again – what happened?'

'She . . . we . . .' DC Eliot mumbled.

'Spit it out, lad,' Hanson ordered.

'I put somethin' in her desk drawer,' Brock admitted, slightly sheepishly.

'Did you, indeed? And what was it, exactly?'

Brock shrugged again. 'A nodder.'

'A nodder! You put a contraceptive in her desk?'

'It was only a bit of fun.'

Hanson laid his mug down on the table. 'Outside, Brock,' he said.

'You what, Sarge?'

'You heard me.'

The sergeant stood up and walked to the door. Brock hesitated for a second, followed him.

'There's three ways I can handle this,' Hanson said, once they were out on the street. 'Can you guess what they are?'

'No,' Brock said sulkily.

'The first is that I can go along with the rest of you, and treat what you did to Sergeant Paniatowski as nothing more than a joke. But I have a problem with that, because I'm a sergeant too.' He paused. 'The second alternative is to report the incident to Chief Inspector Turner.'

'You wouldn't do that, would you, Sarge?' Brock asked, slightly panicked.

'No, I wouldn't,' Hanson admitted, 'but only because I don't believe in shopping any of my lads, even if he is a toe-rag like you. So I'm left with the third alternative, aren't I?'

'And what's that?' Brock asked, some of his cockiness returning.

'We forget rank for a few minutes, find a nice quiet spot somewhere, and settle this man-to-man.'

'You'd fight for her?' Brock asked.

'No,' Hanson told him. 'I'd fight for her right to get the respect her stripes have earned her.'

'I could take you, you know,' Brock said menacingly.

'Maybe you could,' Hanson agreed. 'I don't think so myself, but maybe you could. Anyway, it shouldn't take us long to find out, should it?'

Brock shook his head. 'I don't want any trouble with you, Sarge.'

'Then you'd better make sure that you don't make any more trouble for Sergeant Paniatowski,' Hanson told him. 'Am I making myself clear?'

'Yes.'

Hanson slapped Brock on the shoulder. 'Good lad,' he said. 'Now let's get back inside and I'll buy you another cuppa.'

As a detective, Sergeant Howarth would have made a good hat-stand, Monika Paniatowski thought as she walked down Victoria Street, Fleetwood, towards the waterfront. He had instigated door-to-door inquiries and rung all the repair garages because that was what the police manual said he should do in cases like this. What he *hadn't* done, while following the generalised theory, was to pay any attention of the specifics of this particular case – especially the ones involving geography.

She ran these geographical factors quickly through her mind. A driver who knocked down his victim in London might live a hundred miles away from the city and merely have been travelling through it on the way to somewhere else. But that couldn't have happened in Fleetwood, because there was *nothing* beyond the north edge of town but the sea. All of which led her to conclude that the driver hadn't been in the relatively small area bounded by the sea and the river as a result of chance, but had had some definite purpose. And what purpose *could* he have had, so late at night?

She had reached the river, and gazed across the slightly choppy water at the Knott End Golf Course. Most of the senior officers back in Whitebridge seemed to spend half their time playing golf – either that or rolling up their trouser legs at meetings of their Masonic Lodge. Those were the ways to get on in the police force, but she couldn't see herself doing the former, and was barred by her sex from the latter. So it looked as if any significant promotions she won would have to be through talent and sheer bloody-mindedness – and she was blessed with an abundance of both.

Monika turned left on to Queen's Terrace. Ahead of her stood the lighthouse – a solid, slightly ornate Victorian structure which could as easily have been a part of the town hall complex as a beacon to guide shipping. Beyond that she could see Fleetwood Pier, which was nothing more than a stunted relative of the three much longer piers which could be found, just a short tram ride away, in Blackpool.

It was the building between lighthouse and pier which took her by surprise. For a start, it was four stories high, which made it much taller than any of the other structures in the vicinity. Then there was its shape – it was built in a crescent, rather then being square or oblong. It seemed to the sergeant to be altogether far too grand to be in a place like Fleetwood and judging from the name spelt out in individual letters along its frontage – The Palace Hotel – that was an opinion its owners shared with her.

Monika stopped to light a cigarette. The hotel was nothing more than a monument to unfulfilled hopes, she thought. Yet despite the fact that Fleetwood had never become the swish resort the builders had anticipated, the Palace was still there – still doing business. How had it managed to survive after it had become clear that there would never be enough holidaymakers – and certainly not the right *kind* of holidaymakers – to fill up all its rooms?

A triumphant smile found its way to her lips. It was obvious, she told herself – there was only one way it *could* have survived.

Sixteen

It simply wasn't in the nature of Northern males to have a fuss made over them, even when they were no longer around to see it for themselves, Woodend thought – which was why he hated men's funerals in general and the idea of his own in particular. And a funeral of a police officer was even worse than most.

All those uniforms!

All that pomp and ceremony!

It was enough to make a corpse cringe, and he hoped that when his time came, Joan would have him popped into the ground with as little bother as possible.

Still, full-blown funerals like this one did serve a function, he admitted as he stood in a corner of Blackpool's Layton Cemetery – even if that function was only to help those left behind to come to terms with death. And perhaps, especially in a case like that of Detective Sergeant William Davies – a man cut down in his prime – the family needed to be assured that his contribution had been appreciated and his presence would be missed.

You're thinkin' too much, Charlie, he told himself.

That was another thing about funerals – they made you think too bloody much.

The funeral cortège was approaching – a coffin carried shoulder-high by officers in full dress uniform, and followed by a sea of navy-blue serge interspersed with islands of grey and black, which denoted the civilian mourners. The Blackpool police must have galloped through the forensics and all the other formalities in order to make this happen so quickly, Woodend thought. Maybe they'd done *that* out of respect for the family, too. But there was at least a part of him which couldn't help seeing the whole thing as an unseemly rush – which couldn't help wondering whether the hurried funeral was any more than one part of a process aimed at getting Davies buried and forgotten as quickly as possible.

Wishing he could light up a cigarette, he moved a little closer to the hole in the ground which was to be Punch Davies' last resting-place. The widow took up her position next to the grave. She was wearing a black dress with a veil. Standing beside her were her two children. The boy, who looked around eleven years old, was unnaturally pale, and was gripping his mother's right hand tightly. The girl, by contrast, had a vacuous look on her face, as if – as far as she were concerned – it didn't matter whether she was here or in some other place entirely. Her hand was in her mother's, too, but in this case it was Edna Davies who was maintaining a tight grip.

Though he was too far away to hear the actual words distinctly, Woodend could see the vicar's lips moving, and knew that the service had begun. He turned his attention back to the widow and her children. The girl – Susan – was gazing uncomprehendingly at what was happening in front of her. On the other hand, the boy – Peter, was it? – seemed to be becoming increasingly agitated.

Woodend watched in fascination as the pale child tugged at this mother's arm, seeking – no, more like, demanding – attention. The widow finally gave way, bending her head so that the boy could whisper something in her ear. She nodded. The boy spoke again, and this time she shook her head. Peter's agitation was, if anything, increasing. He was pulling so hard now that his mother was in danger of overbalancing.

The boy broke free. His mother stood there uncertainly. She had a husband to bury, a retarded daughter to look after, and a wayward son to control. She couldn't do all three, and when the boy took a couple of steps backwards, cannoning into those people standing behind him, she could do nothing more than shrug helplessly.

Peter disappeared into the forest of adult legs. Poor little bugger, Woodend thought, it had obviously been too much for him. He could only hope that one of the adults attending the funeral had the presence of mind to try to calm the child down.

Peter appeared again at the very edge of the half-circle of mourners. He was crying, but there was a determined expression on his face, as if he knew exactly what he was doing. He began to move quickly, cutting a wide arc around the funeral party and heading in Woodend's direction. It was perhaps thirty seconds before the chief inspector realised that the child was not *just* heading in his direction – he was making directly for *him*.

Another fifteen seconds and they stood facing each other – the big policeman and frail, pallid boy.

'My mummy says you're the man who's going to catch the man who killed my daddy,' Peter said, without preamble.

Going to catch! By God, what it was to be young, Woodend thought – to believe that right would always prevail.

He crouched down, so that his eyes were at the same level as the boy's. 'I'm certainly lookin' for him,' he said softly.

'He's a very *bad* man,' Peter replied, as if he expected that would make Woodend's task easier.

'Yes, he is,' Woodend agreed.

The boy cocked his head to one side, as though he was looking at Woodend as a person for the first time.

'Do you have any children?' he asked.

'One,' Woodend told him. 'A girl. But she's a bit older than you.'

'A girl,' Peter repeated in disgusts. 'Girls are soppy. Why couldn't you have a boy?'

'She's what the stork brought me,' Woodend said. 'And I love her very much.'

'My daddy loved me,' the boy said defiantly.

'Of course he did,' Woodend agreed. 'He still loves you, even though he's in Heaven. And you still love him too, don't you?'

'Yes,' the boy said seriously. 'I still love him. My daddy did a very bad thing once, but . . .'

'But what?'

'But he was still a very *good* daddy!'

Woodend became aware of another person – a woman who looked like a younger version of Peter's mother – standing a few feet away from them.

'Who are you?' she asked, not quite sure yet whether she ought to be suspicious or grateful.

'Chief Inspector Woodend. And you'd be Peter's auntie?'

'That's right,' the woman agreed.

'Peter and I have been havin' a nice little talk,' Woodend told her, 'but I think it's time he went back to his mummy and sister.' He reached into his pocket and extracted two half-crowns. 'Here you are,' he said, holding them out to the boy. 'Buy yourself some sweets when you get home.'

Peter looked up questioningly at his aunt, and, when she nodded, he extended his arm, like a well-mannered little boy, so that Woodend could drop the coins into the palm of his hand.

'Say thank you,' the aunt ordered.

'Thank you,' Peter said dutifully.

'And I'd like to thank you, too,' the aunt said.

Woodend shrugged awkwardly. 'I didn't do anythin',' he told her. 'Like I said, me an' Peter were just havin' a nice little chat.'

The aunt put her hand on Peter's shoulder, and shepherded him, unprotesting, back towards the open grave.

Woodend straightened up. '*My daddy did a very bad thing once . . . but he was still a very good daddy,*' he said softly to himself.

'Sir,' called a voice to his left.

Woodend turned to see Sergeant Hanson standing there.

'I thought I'd find you here, sir,' the sergeant said.

'Oh aye? An' *why* should you have thought that?'

'Because if I'd been in charge of the investigation, it's where I would have been.'

Hanson was a good bobby, Woodend thought – his kind of bobby.

'Why didn't you attend the funeral?' he asked the sergeant. 'Didn't you want to pay your last respects to Inspector
Davies?'

'I did consider coming,' Hanson admitted, 'but it seemed
me that the best way to show my respect to Billy was to do
all I could to catch the man who killed him.'

'An' are you getting' anywhere?' Woodend asked.

'It's too early to say for sure, sir,' Hanson told him. 'But I
think I might finally have come up with a good lead.'

Seventeen

T he lobby of the Palace Hotel, Fleetwood, was in a different
world to the entrance hall of the Sea View boarding house
in Blackpool. There was no danger in the Palace of new arrivals
barking their shins against their suitcases as they bent over to
sign the guest book. The lobby was a celebration of space. Its
front desk would have more than filled Monika Paniatowski's
living-room. It had polished wooden floors and a jungle of
palms sitting complacently in brass pots on top of delicate
inlaid tables. Yet for all its pretensions, the sergeant noted,
its grandeur had a faded edge to it – the leather sofas showing
distinct signs of cracking, the wood panelling crying out for a
little maintenance.

Paniatowski walked over to the desk. Behind it stood no
harridan who looked as if she would measure the soap to see
if the guests were washing too much, but a pleasant young
man in a grey suit and grey and silver checked tie.

The young man looked up from the ledger which he'd
been studying, and gave Paniatowski a smile which was
more practised than welcoming.

'How can I help you, madam?' he asked.

'Police,' Paniatowski replied, producing her warrant card.
'I wonder if I could ask you a few questions?'

As if a switch had been clicked in the back of his head,
the young man's smile evaporated, and he was suddenly very
guarded. 'What kind of questions, exactly?' he asked.

'Routine questions,' Paniatowski replied, deadpan.

'Is this about the night of the hit-and-run accident in
town?'

'It might be. And what if it is?'

'Well, then you're wasting your time. We've already had a policeman here asking questions about that.'

'Inspector Davies?'

'Inspector Davies? The officer who was murdered?'

'That's right.'

'No, it wasn't him. It was a detective sergeant. I think his name was Howarth.'

Ah, Sergeant Howarth – Blackpool's answer to the wet sponge! Paniatowski thought.

'What exactly did the good sergeant want to know?' she asked.

'If we'd catered a function on the night of the accident.'

'And had you?'

The clerk smirked. 'We cater functions most nights of the week. We have quite a reputation. People come from all over the North West to attend them.'

Paniatowski slipped a cigarette into her mouth, and looked expectantly at the counter clerk. He gaped at her for a second, then produced a lighter from his pocket and flicked it open.

'Thank you,' Monika said, inhaling deeply. 'Now what's the answer to my question?'

'What question?'

'Whose "do" were you catering on the night of the accident?'

'I'll have to check,' the receptionist told her.

He reached under the counter and produced an old, leather-bound ledger. Laying it out grandly in front of him, he opened it at the bookmark and ran his index finger down a column which had been filled in with tight handwriting.

'This shouldn't take a minute,' he said, looking up at her.

It shouldn't take any time at all, Paniatowski thought. The man had already given this information to Sergeant Howarth, and that was not something he'd be likely to forget.

'Ah, here it is,' the clerk said unconvincingly. 'Last Thursday we catered a function for the Golden Mile Association.'

'And who might they be?' Paniatowski asked. 'People who've got businesses on the Golden Mile?'

The receptionist laughed, deprecatingly. 'Oh dear me, no.

The Golden Milers – as we call them – are all very prominent figures in the community. The Mayor of Blackpool himself is their honorary president.'

'And what exactly do they do?'

'Exchange ideas about how Blackpool can be improved. Raise money for various charities. That kind of thing.'

'I see,' Paniatowski said thoughtfully. 'Were you on duty that particular night?'

'I was, as a matter of fact.'

'So you'll know what time this "do" of theirs broke up?'

'The bar was open until eleven.'

'But they didn't *leave* at eleven, did they?'

'Some did,' the receptionist said evasively. 'Most of them, in fact.'

'But not all?'

'I've already told all this to Sergeant Howarth.'

'So there's no harm in telling it again – to me. You were saying that not all the guests left when the bar closed at eleven.'

The receptionist shrugged. 'You know what it's like when you get a group of good friends together. It seems a pity to break up the party, and they take their time to get moving.'

'So some of them could have left much closer to mid-night?'

The receptionist stuck his jaw out. 'No, they'd all gone well before that,' he said stubbornly.

'I'd like to see a guest list for the Golden Milers' function,' Paniatowski told him.

'I'm afraid I can't give you one.'

'Because it doesn't exist?'

'Because I'd need the manager's permission to do that.'

Paniatowski picked up the receiver off the telephone cradle and handed it to the receptionist. 'Then *get* his permission,' she suggested.

With a great show of reluctance, the receptionist took the receiver from her with his left hand, and dialled a single number with his right.

'We have a detective sergeant in the lobby,' he said. 'No,

not from here. From Whitebridge. She wants to see a list of people who attended the Golden Mile Association function . . . Yes, that's right . . . She seems adamant . . . Yes, I'll do that.' He placed the phone back on its cradle, and stepped from behind the counter. 'Wait here a moment, please,' he told Paniatowski.

Then he scuttled off through the lounge like a man with a great deal on his mind.

The manager of the Grand Hotel had grey hair, a large nose and horsy teeth. He could have passed – in poor light – for a diplomat or the chairman of a large company, Paniatowski thought. He had been sitting at a large mahogany table when she entered the room, an ideal position from which to spring gallantly to his feet and shake her hand.

There were two straight-backed chairs facing the manager's table, but instead of inviting her to sit in one of them, he waved her to the other side of the room, where two armchairs stood, one each side of a coffee table.

Paniatowski took one of the armchairs, and the manager the other. The manager crossed his legs, and placed his clasped hands over the upper knee. Paniatowski found herself disliking the gesture almost as much as she instinctively disliked the man.

'Would you care for something to drink, Sergeant?' the manager asked. 'A pot of tea?' He winked. 'Or perhaps something a little stronger?'

Paniatowski shook her head. 'No, thank you.'

The manager guffawed. 'You're the first detective I've ever met who turned down a drop of the hard stuff,' he said. 'Maybe that's because you're the first *lady* detective I've ever met.'

Paniatowski looked down at the oriental rug in front of her chair, and wondered how difficult it would be to clean if she vomited all over it.

'Your receptionist tells me he needs your permission to hand over guest lists,' she said.

'Quite right,' the manager agreed. 'He was doing no more than his job.'

'But I take it you have no objection to giving that permission.'

The manager favoured her with what he probably considered an endearingly perplexed frown.

'I gave Sergeant Howarth a list, and he has already used it to eliminate everyone who was here that night,' he said, avoiding answering the question directly.

'And how do you imagine he was able to do that?' Paniatowski asked.

'Oh, it shouldn't have been too difficult,' the manager replied. 'Given the time of the accident, anyone who left before eleven-thirty should be in the clear, shouldn't they?'

'Probably,' Paniatowski agreed reluctantly.

'And of the minority who were still here after that, most had chauffeurs to take them home.'

'But some didn't?'

'There were a few who drove themselves.'

'Or got their wives to do it?'

'Ah . . . no. You see, this was a gentlemen-only evening – a short break from the pleasures of domestic bliss.'

'So we're still left with a few of them who could have been travelling down Blakiston Road at the time of the accident,' Paniatowski persisted.

'No. As I think Robert at the desk may already have told you, all the guests left well before midnight. Besides, they're all respected members of the community, and if they'd seen anything, I'm sure they would have reported it.'

Paniatowski looked the manager squarely in the eyes. 'If Sergeant Howarth has a list, why won't you give me one?' she asked.

'Sergeant Howarth is a local policeman, and therefore sensitive to . . . err . . . the local situation. I was sure he'd handle the information I gave him in the proper manner.'

'Whereas a bobby from Central Lancs HQ might be less than impressed with the local bigwigs, and could stir up all kinds of dirt?'

The manager's eyes hardened. 'I'll be frank with you, Sergeant Paniatowski,' he said. 'Before I agreed to see you,

I took the opportunity to call up Sergeant Howarth. According to him, you are here to investigate the murder of Inspector Davies – and only that. The accident has nothing to do with you.'

'Unless it's connected with the murder.'

The manager laughed. 'How could the murder possibly be connected with a case of drunk-driv—' He came to a sudden halt.

'Drunk-driving?' Paniatowski said. 'I don't remember anyone mentioning drunk-driving.'

'Given the nature of the accident, I think it is a fair assumption that the driver was drunk,' the manager said. He glanced down at his wristwatch. 'I'm running late for another appointment, so if there's nothing else, perhaps we could end our meeting now.'

'You won't give me the list?'

'Sergeant Howarth has one. Perhaps he will be willing to show you his. Failing that, I'm afraid you'll have to get a court order.'

And how easy would that be? Paniatowski asked herself. Considering that all the magistrates in Blackpool were probably members of the Golden Mile Association, it should be bloody near impossible.

She stood up, and ignored the hand which was being offered to her. 'I can find my own way out,' she said.

She turned the door handle and stepped into the corridor. The manager had said he had another appointment, but Paniatowski was hardly surprised to see that there was no one waiting outside.

The sergeant made her way back to the lobby. Robert the receptionist was back behind the counter, and reading the expression on her face, he smirked again.

Paniatowski glanced over the counter at Robert's little kingdom – a switchboard, a desk, a safe and *two filing cabinets*. She wondered how far he would go to protect that kingdom of his – how many lies he would be willing to tell to pervert the course of justice.

She stepped through the main door and out on to the

promenade. A breeze had blown up, and she greedily gulped in the fresh sea air.

The meeting with the manager had been a waste of time, as she'd known it would be. But it had been a *necessary* waste of time, if she were to avoid arousing his suspicions. Opening her handbag, she took out her notebook, flipped it open to the last page she had used, and scanned what she'd written.

> Councillor Conway
> Dr Pearce
> Sir Henry Rathbone
> Alderman Sutcliffe . . .

Receptionists who wanted to keep their secrets truly secret should be more careful, she thought. More specifically, they should make sure that when they left their posts to consult the boss, they locked their filing cabinets first.

Eighteen

Chief Inspector Turner and Detective Sergeant Hanson sat in one of the shelters close to the Central Pier, apparently doing nothing more than watch the green and cream trams rattle by.

Though it had been Hanson who had requested the meeting, he seemed reluctant to speak, and finally it was Turner who said, 'Don't you think you'd better tell me what's on your mind?'

'I don't know how much longer I can protect Mr Davies,' Hanson blurted out.

'Protect Mr Davies?' Turner repeated, questioningly.

'Protect his reputation, then.' Hanson fumbled with his packet of cigarettes. 'I'm a good bobby, sir.'

'I know you are.'

'And I've always done my job to the best of my ability.'

'Unquestionably.'

'But I'm finding myself in a situation in which I can't do my job properly any more.'

'What's brought this on?'

'I've found a witness who may be able to assist the investigation.'

'Isn't that good?'

'Yes! If she can help us find out who killed Punch. No, if she puts the idea into Mr Woodend's head that he should take a closer look at what Punch was doing just before he died.'

Turner nodded gravely. 'I see.'

'Isn't it time we stopped trying to walk the tightrope?' Hanson pleaded. 'In some ways what Punch did is our fault

– all our faults – because we had our suspicions and we did nothing about them. Don't you think we should accept the consequences of that?'

Turner put an avuncular hand on Hanson's shoulder. 'You're a sergeant, and you're seeing things from a sergeant's viewpoint, which is only natural,' he said. 'But I'm a chief inspector, and I have to take a much wider look at things.'

'I know that, but . . .'

'When you talk about coming clean, you're thinking in terms of a reprimand on your record – which is something you could easily bury with a couple of years of good police work. I, on the other hand, have to consider the overall consequences. Do you imagine, even for a second, that if we tell them all we suspect, those bastards in Whitebridge will just sit on their hands and wait while we put our own house in order?'

'Probably not,' Hanson admitted gloomily.

'Definitely not,' Turner countered. 'They'll have a couple of their hatchet men down here before you can say "Board of Inquiry". And what will they do? They'll turn us upside down. For all our faults, we're an effective police force. But we won't be when they've finished with us. I know. I've seen it all before.'

'So what do we do?' Hanson asked.

'Just what we have been doing up to now – trying to solve Punch's murder without going too deeply into his background. All right?'

'All right.'

'You don't sound convinced.'

'When I uncovered the witness this afternoon, I felt elated,' Hanson told him. 'Then I thought – what if all I'm doing is stirring up some muck on Mr Davies? And for maybe ten minutes, I was considering not telling Mr Woodend about the witness at all. Do you know how that made me feel, sir?'

'No, I don't.'

'It made me feel like something the cat had dragged in.'

*   *   *

121

Woodend stood in front of the garishly painted gypsy's booth. Most of it was covered with signed pictures of celebrities posing with Elizabeth Rose, but squarely in the centre of the display was an elaborate scroll in a glass frame:

> Are you looking for a real friend? One to whom you can tell all your worries and problems. If so, this lady is the answer to your prayers. She has helped hundreds of people in all walks of life with her sound advice and powers of concentration. Your visit is treated in the strictest confidence and you may unburden your mind to her and leave here lighter in heart then ever before.

It was all a bit different from the fortune-tellers he remembered as a kid, Woodend thought. No mention here of 'good luck' or 'tall, dark, handsome strangers', but then he supposed that gypsies, like everybody else, had had to move with the times.

He slid open the dark-blue velvet curtain, and stepped inside. The booth was gloomy, apart from a single light placed strategically behind the gypsy to give the outline of her body a golden glow.

'Sit,' Elizabeth Rose commanded.

Woodend lowered himself into a chair which, despite his size, put him at a level well below that of the gypsy.

'You are troubled,' Elizabeth Rose said.

Her voice was deep and husky. Part of that was put on for effect, Woodend thought – though another part of it he recognised was the result of the gypsy being a chain-smoker like himself.

'You are troubled,' she repeated.

'Tell me, is there anyone who visits you who isn't troubled?' he asked. 'Come to that, is there anybody in the whole of Blackpool – the whole of England – who isn't troubled in some way?'

'You have only one child,' the gypsy said, ignoring his question. 'It's a daughter, isn't it?'

Woodend felt the hairs on the back of his neck stand on end. How could the gypsy have known that?

'Answer me,' Rose Elizabeth commanded. 'Is the child a girl?'

'Yes,' Woodend admitted.

'You worry about her. You are troubled that you may have taken a decision which will ruin her life.'

The gypsy was exaggerating things out of all proportion, Woodend told himself. It was true that Annie hadn't exactly been enthusiastic about the idea of moving away from London and leaving her friends behind. True, too, that because her accent was more Southern than Northern she might feel slightly self-conscious in Whitebridge – at least for a while. And it could be argued that there were better times for her to change school than one year before School Certificate. But none of those things was really a big problem. She would soon make new friends – and she was bright enough for the move not to damage her academic progress.

Sweat was forming around Woodend's collar. He'd been more worried about his daughter than he'd been prepared to admit, he now realised. Though he'd managed to hide it from himself until that very moment, the thought must have been nagging at the back of his mind that perhaps all the changes would hurt Annie's chances of going to university – of having the opportunities he'd never had.

His throat felt suddenly very dry. 'Am I right to be troubled?' he found himself croaking.

'Do you really want to know?' the gypsy asked him.

He was not sure that he did – not sure that knowing would make it any easier. What he really wanted to do, if he were honest with himself, was to leave the gypsy's booth and never return, because though he had seen action in North Africa and forced himself to keep his nerve while cataloguing the heaps of dead in Dachau, he did not think that he had ever been so frightened before.

He was not there to be intimidated by husky voices, tricky light effects and wild guesses, he argued as he gripped the sides of his chair. He had a job to do, and he had better get on with it. He took a deep breath, but instead of clearing his mind it only served to fill his lungs with the sickly-sweet smell of the booth.

'What about me?' he asked, fighting back. 'You've told me about my daughter, now tell me about me.'

'You are a traveller who has returned to his home,' the gypsy said, 'only to find that that home is no longer there. You are a ship which has lost its anchor and is now drifting helplessly on a sea of doubt.'

If she was guessing, she was making a bloody good job of it, Woodend thought. Too bloody good. This was *his* interview. He was supposed to be in charge – and he clearly wasn't.

'I'm not here to ask you about the future,' he said, running his finger around his shirt collar. 'I've come to ask you about somebody else's past.'

'This, too, I know.'

'So if you'll just tell me how much I owe you for the consultation –'

'There will be no charge.'

'I insist.'

'You cannot force me to take your money – even if you are a policeman.'

'How did you know that?' Woodend demanded. 'How did you know I was a bobby?'

'I didn't,' the gypsy told him, and though the arrangement of the lights made it impossible to see her face, he was almost sure that she was smiling. 'Yet I knew that you were a man of authority, a man used to asking questions – and not only of himself.'

'I want to know about Detective Inspector Davies,' Woodend said.

'Ah yes, he came to me.'

'An' accordin' to the witnesses we've talked to, it was more than once.'

'It was three times,' the gypsy agreed.

'An' what did he want?'

'What does anyone who comes here want? Peace. Tranquillity. An answer to all life's problems.'

'Let's be a little more specific,' Woodend said. 'What particular problems did Davies have?'

'I am not a lawyer or a doctor,' the gypsy said, 'but I take my responsibilities equally as seriously as they do, and what is said in this booth is never allowed to leave it.'

'I'm conductin' a murder inquiry,' Woodend told her.

'Then you have heavy responsibilities, too,' the gypsy replied. 'But what Mr Davies told me can be of no help to you.'

'You can't know that,' Woodend countered. 'You're not in a position to judge.'

'Perhaps not, in any sense you would recognise. But I am in a position to *see*.'

'I could take you in for questionin',' Woodend warned her.

'You would learn nothing.'

'Or I could get the local police to make your life uncomfortable. Post a couple of uniformed bobbies outside your booth, and you'd be surprised how quickly your business drops away.'

'It is a brave man – or a foolish one – who threatens a gypsy,' Elizabeth Rose said.

And despite himself, Woodend felt his heart miss a beat.

'Perhaps we could reach a compromise,' he suggested.

'Perhaps,' the gypsy agreed.

'Would it be possible to talk – in general terms – about what Inspector Davies said to you?'

'You have much in common with him. He, too, was troubled over his daughter – worried that he had failed her, as you worry you have failed yours.'

'But his daughter's retarded,' Woodend protested, aware, as he spoke, that the policeman in him was receding and the father was reasserting himself. 'She couldn't have gone to university. There was nothin' he could really do for her.'

'How little you know,' the gypsy rebuked him. 'How little you understand.'

'Do you know who killed Inspector Davies?' Woodend asked, forcing himself to put the interview back on track.

'Did you know beforehand that he was *goin'* to be killed? Do you have a picture of the murderer in your mind?'

Elizabeth Rose laughed softly. 'It is not so simple,' she said. 'To reach the future, we must all walk down a long, dark passage. For those like me – who have better eyes than most – it is possible to pick out vague shapes at the end of that passage, and to draw intelligent conclusions from them. But those conclusions are sometimes wrong.'

'Can't you tell me anythin'?' Woodend persisted. 'The man's age? Why he felt Davies had to die?'

'Mr Davies had to die because he was in the way,' the gypsy said. 'But I am telling you nothing that you don't know already. In every murder case, the victim has to die because he is in the way.'

It was a relief to be out on the prom again – to see Blackpool Tower standing just where it had when he was a child, to hear the reassuring rattle of the trams and the cries of the bingo callers. Woodend lit up a Capstan Full Strength and let the smoke snake around his lungs.

He found himself thinking about Annie, who was probably at that very moment packing up her room – the room which had been hers for fifteen years – ready for the move to Whitebridge. Any difficulties she experienced as a result of his decision, he would deal with, he promised. If she was lonely, he would find out which were the best youth clubs in town and drive her there himself. If she were falling behind in her studies, he would hire her a private tutor. And if things were still not working out, he would sacrifice his own career, move back to London, and take a job in private security.

Those options – or any even vaguely resembling them – had not been open to Punch Davies. When he had gazed into his daughter's blank eyes and known that – however much he tried – he could never really reach her, it must have broken his heart.

The sight of a uniformed constable reminded Woodend of why he was in Blackpool, and for the third time in less than half an hour, he forced himself to cast aside his own worries and anxieties, and think like a policeman. There would have been no point in taking the gypsy in for questioning, he argued. However much pressure he had put on her, she'd have said no more at the station than she'd told him freely in her booth. Yet even as these thoughts raced around his head, he found himself wondering how much he was being guided by bobby's logic – and how much by a fear of the unknown!

Nineteen

M onika Paniatowski had been expecting it to be something of an effort to return to the basement after the
incident with the contraceptive, but even so she was surprised
by just how difficult it was turning out to be. As she walked
down the steps she was straining her ears for sounds of the local
DCs – for sounds of the enemy – but the only noise they seemed
capable of picking up was the unreasonably loud clatter of her
own reluctant heels.

Bang, bang, bang! Bang, bang, bang!

She stopped halfway down the stairs, telling herself she'd
done it so that she could hear more clearly – but knowing that
what she was really doing was putting off the moment when
she'd have to face whoever was down there.

What if it was Brock? No one should have to deal with a
slimy creep like him after a hard day's work. But perhaps she
wouldn't have to! Perhaps he'd learned his lesson.

She shook her head, angry at her own attempt at self-
deception. Men like Brock *never* learned. They were like
jack-in-the-boxes – however often you slapped them down,
they came bouncing back up again.

Monika took a deep breath and forced herself to press on.
Three more steps and she reached the basement level. Two
more steps and she was inside the incident room. And Brock
was not there! The only member of the team sitting at his desk
was Sergeant Hanson.

Monika nodded to him – and he nodded back.

She walked over to her own desk. She needed paper, and
without even thinking about it, her hand reached for the drawer.
Then she *did* think about it – and felt her body freeze.

'It's all right – you won't find anything unpleasant in there,' said Hanson's voice behind her.

She felt the use return to her limbs at the same moment as a fresh wave of anger surged through her. She swung round, furious at herself for her moment of weakness – and even more furious that she had let it show.

'I don't know what you're talking about!' she said.

Hanson smiled. 'I think you do,' he said. 'There was an unpleasant incident this morning. Well, I've taken steps to see that nothing like it occurs again.'

'I don't need you to fight my battles for me,' Paniatowski said.

If Hanson noticed the lack of graciousness in her tone, he did not take offence. 'It was my battle as well,' he said mildly.

'Oh yes?'

'Certainly. My main function – as I see it – is to make sure that things round here run smoothly, so that the whole team can concentrate on the job in hand. Badger wasn't just being bloody rude to you this morning – he was undermining my authority as well. And I can't have that.'

He was behaving decently towards her and he deserved to be treated decently in return, Paniatowski thought, starting to feel slightly ashamed.

'Thanks,' she said.

'I was only doing my job,' Hanson assured her. He paused for a second. 'Got any plans for tonight, Sergeant?'

'Not particularly,' Paniatowski admitted. 'Why do you ask?'

'Blackpool's not all fish and chip shops, you know. There are a couple of nice restaurants tucked away in quiet corners.'

'Are you asking me out?' Paniatowski asked suspiciously.

'I'm suggesting that two sergeants might have a meal together so they can discuss the case – and anything else of interest which might crop up during the course of the evening.'

'And will you tell your wife about it?'

'I'm not married.'

'I can easily check up on that, you know,' Paniatowski warned.

Hanson laughed. 'Ask anyone you like. I'm not married. I've never even been engaged. I broke up with my last steady girlfriend more than two years ago. Not that that should have anything to do with it, one way or the other. Like I told you, it'd just be two very professional police officers havin' a bite together. So what do you say?'

Paniatowski smiled. 'I say yes,' she replied.

Bob Rutter looked around the hotel room the Central Lancashire Police had booked him into. It didn't take long. The room contained a single bed, a dressing table, a wardrobe and a sink. There had to be better ways to spend his first evening in Lancashire – the first evening of his new life – than sitting alone in this box, he thought.

He'd noticed a television set in the residents' lounge downstairs, and for a moment he was tempted to go and watch it. Then he remembered that it was 'Bonanza' night, and the lounge was sure to be crowded. The flicks, then? According to the local paper, they were showing *The Guns of Navarone* at the Plaza, but somehow he wasn't in the mood for a gung-ho war film, either.

He sat down on the bed and tried to analyse his vague feelings of discontent. Perhaps they came from the fact that he was spending the night away from home. But he'd done that often enough before, so why should it be any different this time? And then he had it – he was used to being away, but he was *not* used to spending time in alien territory without Cloggin'-it Charlie by his side.

He grinned ruefully. He was a big boy now. He was going to learn to do without Woodend's reassuring presence and caustic comments.

Why not go for a walk? he asked himself. A good long walk – punctuated by a pause for a couple of pints – would help him to sleep.

For the next hour or so, Rutter wandered aimlessly, but quite happily, through the streets of Whitebridge. In some ways, the town was still old-fashioned enough to remind him of the London he had known as a child. Everything had seemed fresh and exciting in those days, he thought, enveloping himself effortlessly in a cosy blanket of nostalgia. Even shopping had been an adventure back then.

He remembered going down to the corner store, where butter and biscuits had been sold from large barrels, and bacon sliced off the bone before your very eyes. A smile came to his lips as he recalled the complex network of spring-loaded overhead wireways the assistants used to send the customers' money to the cashier's desk. Now, only a decade or so later, the corner shops were all being replaced by large, impersonal self-service stores in which the assistants didn't know your name, and the smell of cheese was smothered by plastic packaging. And where London had led, Whitebridge would soon follow. It was progress of a sort, he supposed but –

But he was starting to sound more like Charlie Woodend with each day that passed, he thought with some chagrin.

It was time to stop and have that drink he'd promised himself, he decided, coming to a halt in front of a pub called The Grapes. He had a choice of two doors just inside the main entrance, one leading to the saloon bar and the other to the public. In the days before he'd started working with Charlie Woodend, he would automatically have selected the saloon, but now he pushed the public bar door open.

There were only four customers, and he was surprised to find that although he'd been in the town for less than a day, he recognised one of them.

He walked across to the man with a scrubbed red skin and a few cotton balls of white fluffy hair on his head, and said, 'Hello, Mr Grimsdyke. Do you remember me?'

The old car mechanic looked up. 'Aye,' he said. 'Tha's that bugger from the South what can't speak the Queen's English proper.'

Rutter grinned. 'I'm just going to order myself a pint. Can I get you one in at the same time?'

The old man held his glass up to the light. There was perhaps an inch of beer left in the bottom of it.

'Aye, tha might as weel get me one,' he said.

It was strange what effect being away from home could have

on him, Rutter thought, as he waited for the pints to be pulled. If he'd been in London and come across someone he'd only met once, he'd simply have nodded politely. In the wilds of Lancashire, on the other hand, he found he was inordinately pleased to see even a vaguely familiar face.

He took the drinks over to the table. 'How much did that cost thee?' the old man asked, picking up the pint Rutter had bought him. 'One an' fivepence, were it?'

'Something like that,' Rutter agreed.

'When I were a lad, tha could buy a pint for a penny 'alfpenny. An' it tasted a damn sight better than the stuff we're suppin' now.'

The old man was drunk, Rutter realised – and while not exactly legless, he'd certainly had enough to make whatever anyone else had to say much less important than what he had to say himself.

'Aye, a penny 'alfpenny a pint,' the old man repeated. 'Tha could get a decent meal for a tanner in them days, an' all.'

'Things change,' Rutter said.

'They do that. An' usually not for the better. When I were a lad, tha could go out for the day an' leave tha back door unlocked. Can tha do that now? Can tha hell as like.'

Rutter was starting to regret sitting down, and wondering how soon he would be able to make his excuses and leave.

'Tha can walk for twenty mile these days an' still not come across an honest man,' Grimsdyke continued. 'It's enough t' mek thee weep.'

'I'm sure it's not as bad as that,' Rutter said soothingly.

'Tha'd be surprised what's goin' on, even in a little place like Whitebridge,' the old man countered. 'That granddaughter o' mine thinks it all goes over my head. But it dun't. I see what's happenin', right enough. An' let me tell thee somethin' for nothin' – a lot of what's goin' on just isn't right.'

'What do you mean by that?' Rutter asked, starting to get interested.

'I'm sayin' na more,' the old man replied, his expression suddenly guarded. 'If truth be told, I've probably said too much already.'

*   *   *

132

The prawn cocktail had been served on crispy lettuce, the steak had been cooked to perfection, and the waiter was just opening a second bottle of wine. Monika Paniatowski leant back in her chair and tried – though not *too* hard – to throw off the feeling of well-being which she felt was so inappropriate to a business meal with a colleague.

'What's your opinion of Sergeant Howarth?' she asked.

'Howie?' Frank Hanson repeated. 'He's all right, in his own way, I suppose.'

Paniatowski felt she wanted to giggle, but instead she said, 'That's a case of damning with faint praise if ever I heard one.'

'Your question wouldn't have anything to do with the fact that Howarth's investigating a hit-and-run in Fleetwood – and you were up in Fleetwood yourself this afternoon – would it?' Hanson asked.

'How do you know about that?'

Hanson grinned. 'If you had bobbies from a different area tramping all over your patch, wouldn't you make it *your* business to know where they'd been?'

Monika returned his grin. 'I suppose so.'

'And *does* the one thing have anything to do with the other?'

'It might,' Paniatowski replied.

She was feeling very light-headed, she thought – far more light-headed than she should have been after what she'd drunk. Perhaps it was the rich food. Or maybe the relief at finding she had at least one ally within the Blackpool police force. Or could it be – could it possibly be – that it was a long time since she'd been attracted to a man as much as she was finding herself attracted to Sergeant Hanson?

'I'm not one to talk out of school,' Hanson said, delivering his words slowly and carefully, 'but given a choice between working with you on an important case, and working with Howarth on it, I'd choose you any day of the week.'

'He's not likely to make waves, then?' Paniatowski asked.

'How do you mean?'

'Say he suspected that someone important in this town was involved in a serious crime. Would he go after them – or would he prefer to leave the case unsolved?'

'Are we still talking about the hit-and-run?' Hanson asked.

Paniatowski nodded. 'The night the old lady was knocked down, there was a meeting of the Golden Mile Association at the Palace Hotel.'

'Was there, by God?'

'You didn't know?'

'I had no idea.'

'The car which killed her was coming from the direction of the hotel, at a time when the pubs had been closed for over an hour. And the driver was drunk – even Howarth agrees on that point. So what does that tell you?'

'It tells me that if I'd been assigned to the case, I'd be concentrating my efforts on talking to the people who'd attended the function.'

'Exactly,' Paniatowski agreed. 'But Sergeant Howarth's been through them in record time, and decided that none of them had anything to do with it.'

Hanson scooped up his remaining vegetables on to his fork and popped them into his mouth.

'Where's all this taking us?' he asked.

'I'm here to investigate a murder – but if I discover that another serious crime has been committed and it's not being properly investigated, what am I supposed to do?'

'Are you sure that seeing justice done is your only motivation?'

'What's that supposed to mean?'

'If Mr Woodend solves this murder – as I'm sure he will – you'll get some of the credit for it. But not much. Whereas, if you were to wrap up a hit-and-run case entirely on your own, you wouldn't have to share the credit with anybody. Now don't tell me that hasn't crossed your mind.'

'It's crossed my mind,' Paniatowski admitted. 'It may even be what first persuaded me to push this thing further. But it's not my only motive.'

'No?'

'No! Look, that old lady was out minding her own business when she was hit by a car going at nearly sixty miles an hour. The impact crushed I don't know how many bones, and threw her into the air. The medical report says she died almost instantly. But what's *almost* instantly? Who's to say how much agony she suffered before everything went black? She was an innocent. She didn't deserve to die. And I want to nail the bastard who killed her.'

'And you want me to help you?'

'I didn't say that.'

'But it's what you meant.'

'Perhaps I won't need your help,' Paniatowski said. 'Perhaps I can do it all on my own.'

Hanson shook his head. 'You know that's not true. You can maybe make a start on it yourself, but there'll come a point when you need local support.'

'Will I get it?'

Hanson looked down at his wine glass. 'Throughout my entire career, I've tried to be a good bobby and always do the right thing,' he said heavily. 'I think you're trying to do the right thing here, but . . .'

'But what?'

'Sometimes you find yourself faced with a choice between doing what's right by the victim and doing what's right by your colleagues and the community you live in. It's not an easy choice, but it has to be made.'

'This conversation isn't about the hit-and-run any longer, is it?' Paniatowski asked. 'All this "rights of the victim" and "rights of the community" stuff has to do with the murder of Punch Davies.'

'Yes . . . no . . . well, maybe,' Hanson said, looking confused. 'I think I might have had a bit too much to drink. Look, let's forget the murder and stick to the point. You're going to go ahead with your own personal investigation into the hit-and-run whatever I say, aren't you?'

'Yes,' Paniatowski agreed. 'I don't want to, but it feels like I don't have any choice.'

'Then I *will* help you, because I *do* think you're doing the right thing.' Hanson told her. 'But only so far.'

'Meaning?'

'Meaning, when all this is over, I still have to live here. So if you decide to go to the ropes on this one, there's no point in looking over your shoulder to check if I'm still there – because I won't be. If you take a fall, you'll have to do it on your own.'

Twenty

Woodend stood in the tiny lobby of the Sea View Hotel, the telephone receiver clasped tightly in his big hand.

'Can you hear me, Joan?' he asked.

'Clear as a bell,' his wife replied. 'Is somethin' the matter, Charlie?'

'Why should somethin' be the matter?' Woodend asked defensively.

'I don't know. It's just somethin' in your voice. An' you never ring me when you're workin' on a case – except, of course, when you're comin' home an' you want me to stock up with pork sausages.'

Woodend forced himself to chuckle. 'Aye, I'm a bit of a bugger, aren't I?' he said. 'Is everythin' all right at home?'

'Very hectic. The removal men come tomorrow, so as you can imagine, there's been a lot to do.'

'An' how's Annie?' Woodend asked, dreading the answer.

'A bit moody – but then girls are at her age, aren't they?'

'Could I speak to her?'

'She's not in.'

'But it's after ten! What's she doin' out at this time of night?'

'One of her friends has been throwin' a goodbye party for her,' Joan said.

A goodbye party! Woodend thought. It sounded so final. But wasn't that just what it was? True, Annie might take the occasional weekend excursion to London and stay with one of her mates, but essentially that part of her life was over. And it had been his choice, not hers.

'What time is she expected home?' he asked.

137

'You're not suddenly goin' to start playin' the Victorian father, are you?' Joan countered.

'No, that's not the reason I want to know. I just thought I'd ring again when she got back.'

'I've told her to be in by eleven, but you know she's not exactly a dab hand at punctuality,' Joan said. 'So you'd better leave it until around eleven-thirty. If you'll still be up.'

'Oh, I'll still be up,' Woodend assured her.

Because of one thing he was certain – until he had spoken to his daughter, sleep would elude him.

They had been far from the last couple to enter to the restaurant, but they were the last to *leave* by a wide margin, and when they had finally stood up to go, the waiters were already relaying the tables for the next day's business, while the cashier, having already totted up everyone else's bill, was drumming her fingers impatiently.

Now they were driving along the promenade. They had already passed the North Pier and were entering the Golden Mile. The bingo halls were closed, the hamburger stands and fish and chip shops had shut for the night. Lights still burned in the pubs, but the last few customers were being shown the door. Another ten minutes and the scene would look very much like it had the night Detective Inspector Punch Davies had taken his final – fatal – walk under the Central Pier.

Hanson was at the wheel. He had had a little too much to drink, but unlike many drivers in his condition he recognised the fact, and was keeping his speed well below thirty miles an hour.

The local sergeant turned slightly towards his passenger. 'Are you tired?' he asked.

'More relaxed than tired,' Paniatowski replied. 'Was that an idle question, or was there some motive behind it?'

'I was just thinking it would be a pity to end the evening so soon,' Hanson replied.

'So what do you suggest? A late-night drinking club?'

'There aren't many of those in Blackpool. And the ones that do exist are pretty seedy places.'

A smile crept to Paniatowski's lips. 'But you have an alternative?' she said.

'My cleaning lady was round this morning, so this is the one night of the week when my flat doesn't look like a pig sty.'

'Is that so?'

'And there's a bottle of twelve-year-old malt whisky in my booze cabinet that I've been saving for a special occasion.'

'Which is how you'd classify this?' Paniatowski asked lightly.

'Yes, it's how I'd classify this,' Hanson replied seriously.

'Before we go to your flat – *if* we go to your flat – I'd like to make one thing clear,' Paniatowski said.

'And what's that?'

'There are enough complications in my life already, Frank, so I'm not looking for a steady boyfriend. If anything should happen tonight, it happens *tonight* – and then that's it. Understood?'

'Understood.'

'You don't sound too happy about it.'

Hanson signalled a left turn, and pulled off the Mile. 'If there's one thing I've learned in this life, it's that if you can't have what you want, you might as well settle for what you can get,' he said.

Annie had not returned when Woodend phoned at eleven-thirty, nor when he called again at eleven-thirty-five or eleven-forty. In fact, it was not until ten minutes to twelve that a tired-sounding Joan told him she'd finally arrived and was waiting to talk to him.

'You were late!' were Woodend's first words. 'Don't you know how your mother worries about you when you're late?'

Annie gave an audible sigh. 'I came home in a taxi,' she said. 'Mum knew I was going to do that. Why should she have been worried?'

He was being far too heavy-handed, Woodend thought.

'Was it a nice party?' he asked, softening his voice a little.

'It was all right,' Annie replied – giving away nothing.

'I think you're goin' to like it up North,' Woodend told her. 'I'd forgotten just how pleasant it can be.'

There was only silence from the other end of the line.

'Did you hear what I said?' he asked.

'Yes.' Sullen.

'I was always brought up to believe that when a grown-up asks you a question, you give them an answer,' Woodend said – aware that he was handling the conversation badly again, yet not knowing how to handle it well.

'Was there a question?' Annie asked. 'I didn't hear one.'

She was right, of course. He hadn't asked a question, he'd simply told her she'd like it up North. But what he had meant was: will you try to like the North, Annie? Will you *really* try – just for me?

'It's not so far off your sixteenth birthday,' he said. 'We'll have to be thinkin' about buyin' you a scooter.'

Again, silence.

'Annie . . .' he said tentatively.

'If you're waiting for me to thank you for taking me away from all my friends, Dad, then you'll be waiting a long time,' Annie said bitterly.

'If you feel like that, why have you never mentioned it before?' Woodend asked.

'Because you're never here to mention it *to*, Dad. You're just never here.'

'That's not quite fair,' Woodend protested weakly.

'Isn't it?' Annie countered. 'When was the last time you were here for my birthday?'

'I can't remember,' Woodend admitted.

'Exactly. You can't remember. Well, I can. I was ten – and halfway through my party you were called away on an important case. But then they're *all* important, aren't they, Dad?'

'Listen, we'll talk more about this when we meet up in Whitebridge,' Woodend said.

'There isn't anything to talk about,' his daughter told him. 'The decisions have already been made, haven't they? We're going to live in Lancashire whether I like it or not.'

The line went dead. The receiver in Woodend's hand felt as if it were made of lead. He replaced it on its cradle, and made his way slowly upstairs to his bedroom.

'*You had much in common with him,*' the gypsy had said, speaking of Inspector Punch Davies. '*He, too, was troubled over his daughter – worried that he had failed her, as you worry that you have failed yours.*'

They might have had things in common, just as the gypsy claimed, Woodend thought, but there was one big difference between them – there was so much less that Davies would have been *able* to do for his daughter.

It was almost one o'clock in the morning when the phone on Gypsy Elizabeth Rose's bedside table rang.

She reached groggily for the receiver. 'Who the hell is this?' she demanded.

'Who the hell do you *think* it could be?' asked a voice which chilled her to the bone. 'Is there anybody else who'd call you at this time of night?'

All traces of sleep drained instantly from her body. 'What do you want?' she asked.

'Did he come to see you?'

'Yes, he came.'

'And what did you tell him?'

'What we agreed I should tell him. That he was probably failing his own child as Davies had failed his.'

'And was he convinced?'

'About himself?'

'About the reasons you gave for Davies going to see you?'

'I think so.'

'But you're not sure.'

What had started as a tight ball of fear in Gypsy Rose Elizabeth's stomach had grown and grown until it now encompassed her whole body.

Why had she ever become involved with this man? she asked herself.

Surely even the limited psychic powers she had should have been enough to tell her that he was very, very dangerous.

'I said, you're not sure you convinced him, are you?' the man repeated.

'I'm sure,' Elizabeth Rose told him – praying that he believed her.

'Then you're probably right,' the man agreed. 'But it's better to be safe than sorry.'

'What do you mean by that?'

'I think you should go away – just until all this has all died down.'

'Go away?' Elizabeth Rose repeated.

'That's right. You've been under a lot of strain lately. You could use the rest. Why not go to Capri? You like it there, don't you?'

The gypsy's mouth felt as dry as a desert, and she did not need to look at her hand to know that it was trembling. 'I . . . I can't afford to go away at the height of the season,' she croaked.

The man laughed. 'What are you worried about?' he asked. 'Money? Money's no problem. I can give you more than enough to make up for what you would have earned in the next two months.'

'But if I disappear, the police will think—'

'The police will think that, like all gypsies, you get nervous when you know they're watching you and have decided to take off. It will be no more than that, I promise you.'

She wanted to tell him to go to hell – but she simply couldn't summon up the courage.

'When . . . when would I have to go?' she asked.

'I think that it should be as soon as possible. Don't you?'

'Yes,' she agreed, because she dared give no other answer.

'I've already got the money,' he said. 'A suitcase full of it. Why don't you meet me by the South Pier in half an hour?'

'Couldn't it wait until morning?' the gypsy asked, the panic gripping so tightly now that she thought it would strangle her.

'By morning, you could be in a police cell, waiting for Chief Inspector Woodend to find the time to interrogate you,' the man said. 'I've met him. I know what he's like. He's not

142

one of those bobbies who give up. Once he's got his teeth into something, he'll go on and on at you until you tell him everything. And you know what that means, don't you?'

'Yes,' Elizabeth Rose said, dully.

'Tell me. Put it into words.'

'I'll go to jail.'

'You'll go to jail for a long time. And prison is a lot harder on gypsies than it is on normal people, Elizabeth Rose. Even if you only did five years – and you'd be very lucky to get away with so little – you'd be like an old woman when you came out.'

It was true what he was telling her – so what choice did she have? 'What happens after you hand over the money?' she asked.

'I drive you to Preston, and you catch the early morning train to London. Once there, you buy yourself a first-class air ticket – there'll be plenty of money for that – and by tomorrow afternoon you could be dipping your toes in the Mediterranean Sea. So what do you say, Elizabeth Rose? Will you be at the South Pier in half an hour or not?'

No! a voice inside her screamed. *No, no, no!*

'I'll be there,' she said.

'Good!' the man answered – and hung up.

Twenty-One

It was the sunlight streaming in through the window – and shining mercilessly on her face – which woke Paniatowski up. She opened her eyes, then instantly closed them again. She felt awful. A steam hammer was pounding in her head, and she was willing to swear that something furry had crawled into her mouth and died there.

The bed she was lying in felt unfamiliar. It was not her own bed, she was sure of that. Nor was it the lumpy, iron-framed one which Mrs Bowyer provided at the Sea View Hotel. No, this bed was bigger and firmer. It was a bed in which it would be comfortable to make love.

It was all coming back to her! Entering Frank Hanson's flat. Their first kiss. Tumbling back on to the sofa. Tearing at each other's clothes. Coupling once – and then coupling again.

She heard the bedroom door click, and – bracing herself for the shock – she opened her eyes again. Frank was standing in the doorway, a white towel around his waist and a tray in his hands.

'I thought you might like a bit of breakfast,' he said. 'Tea, toast and freshly squeezed orange juice. If you fancy egg and bacon, I can do you that, too.'

Paniatowski groaned. 'How can you be so bloody cheerful?' she demanded.

'Why shouldn't I be? It's another beautiful day outside, and the memories of last night still haven't quite faded.' He frowned slightly. 'You do remember last night, don't you? I'd hate it if you didn't.'

'I remember,' Paniatowski said.

'God, you were wonderful,' Hanson said sincerely. 'I don't think I've ever been with a woman quite like you.'

'And exactly how many women *have* you been with?'

'A few. Enough to recognise someone special when I come across her.'

Paniatowski groaned again, as the steam hammer in her head shifted gear. 'Don't you have a hangover?' she asked, inviting him to share her misery.

'I had a bit of a headache when I woke up,' Hanson admitted. 'But it's gone away now.'

'God rot you!' Paniatowski said, through clenched teeth. 'Why did you let me drink so much?'

Hanson grinned. 'You don't seem to me to be the kind of woman who needs anyone's permission to do *anything*.'

True, Paniatowski thought. She had no one to blame but herself.

'I should never have had that last whisky just before we went to sleep,' she said, self-pityingly. 'I was all right without that last whisky.'

'You'll be fine once you've got a bit of food inside you,' Hanson assured her. He laid the tray on the bedside cabinet. 'Look, I've cut the toast into soldiers to make it easier to swallow. So why don't you eat your breakfast like a good little girl?'

Paniatowski sat bolt upright. It hurt.

'Breakfast!' she exclaimed. 'What time is it?'

'About a quarter to eight. Why?'

Paniatowski sprang out of bed. She was naked, but it seemed pointless to start coming over modest after all that had happened the night before.

She began a frantic search of the floor, looking for the clothes she had so carelessly abandoned in the heat of passion.

'What's the hurry?' Hanson asked. 'The morning briefing isn't until nine o'clock.'

'Yours might not be,' Paniatowski told him, picking up her stockings and bra, 'but mine's with Cloggin'-it Charlie over breakfast, and if I'm not there on time he'll have my guts for garters.'

*   *   *

145

Woodend was just eating the last bit of his kipper when Paniatowski entered the dining-room and sat down opposite it.

'You look like hell,' the chief inspector said.

'Mornings aren't my best time, sir,' Paniatowski told him.

'Bollocks!' Woodend snorted. 'You were out on the razzle last night, weren't you?'

'I may have had a couple of drinks,' Paniatowski admitted.

'I don't care if you had a couple of *dozen* drinks,' Woodend told her. 'I don't care if you were so pissed you couldn't find your bed. What you do on your own time is entirely your own business. But what I do insist on, Sergeant, is that when you're on *my* time, you're able to keep your eye on the ball. Have I made myself clear?'

'Yes, sir,' Paniatowski said meekly.

'Right, we'll see if we can order you up some breakfast,' Woodend said raising his arm in the air to signal the waitress. 'Though I'm far from convinced the dragon who runs this place will be willing to serve anybody who's had the temerity to turn up late.'

'It's all right, sir, I'm not hungry,' Paniatowski said. 'All I want's a cup of tea.'

Woodend bad mood suddenly evaporated, and he chuckled. 'Virtue might not always be its own reward,' he said, 'but vice is usually its own punishment. I'd go more carefully next time, if I were you.'

'Yes, sir,' Paniatowski said.

But she was thinking: Will there *be* a next time? Do I want to see Frank Hanson again? Can I afford to put myself in a position where I might start getting involved?

Only the skeleton of the kipper lay on Woodend's plate now. He pushed it to one side.

'So have you got anythin' to report, Sergeant?' he asked. 'Or were your investigations yesterday just a waste of time?'

'Why don't I tell you what I found out, and see what you think, sir?' Paniatowski suggested.

'Aye, go on then,' Woodend agreed.

Paniatowski merely sketched out her meeting with Sergeant Collins and what he'd told her about a possible stolen car ring, but when she came to Sergeant Howarth and the hit-and-run, she was much more thorough – though she omitted to mention her brief excursion behind the reception desk of the Palace Hotel.

Woodend listened in silence until she had finished, then nodded his head. 'It doesn't seem quite right,' he admitted, 'but I don't see what it's got to do with us.'

'If a crime's been committed, sir –'

'Then much as I deplore it – much as I hate hit-an'-run drivers – it's really none of our business.'

Paniatowski had been prepared for this, and even in her post-hangover haze she had her counter-argument prepared.

'What if it's *not* just a local matter?' she said. 'What if it's connected with Mr Davies' murder?'

'Go on,' Woodend said, noncommittally.

'We know that everyone who belongs to the Golden Mile Association is influential in the community, and so has a lot to lose if there's even a breath of scandal. But this is much more than a *breath*. One of them gets blind drunk and kills an old woman – and he knows that if he's caught he'll be exchanging his big detached house for a prison cell before he's even had time to say "involuntary manslaughter".'

'I'm still listenin',' Woodend told her.

'He manages to get home without being discovered, and his first thought is that he's in the clear. After all, there are thousands of cars in Lancashire, and the driver of any one of them could have been responsible. But then the doubts start to set in. What if the police pin down the hit-and-run driver to the Golden Milers, he asks himself, and then narrow it down further to the last ones to leave? He won't be one of thousands of suspects any more – he'll be one of only a handful. Now let's just say he knows both the men leading the investigation. He doesn't see any difficulties with Sergeant Howarth – all he has to say is that he had nothing to do with the accident, and Howarth will believe him. But Inspector Davies is another matter. He has a reputation for never letting go of a case until he's solved it.'

'At least, he had until recently,' Woodend mused.

'The driver decides that the only way to be sure he's safe is to get rid of Mr Davies. He lures him under the pier on some pretext or other, and kills him.' Paniatowski spread out her hands like a magician who'd just completed a successful trick. 'What do you think of that, sir?'

'I'm not convinced a man would risk life imprisonment to avoid three or four years in jail.'

'Life or three or four years, it makes no difference – it's all the same to him.'

'You'd better explain that.'

'He's at the top of the mountain, and he likes it there. If he once falls it doesn't matter whether he only rolls a few feet or ends up right at the bottom – because however small the fall, he knows he can never reach the top again.'

'You've got a way with words, I'll give you that,' Woodend said. 'So do you really think the hit-and-run and the murder are connected?'

'I do,' Paniatowski said.

Well, it wasn't completely beyond the bounds of possibility that they were, she told herself.

'If you were goin' to take this particular investigation any further, you'd need a list of the folk who actually attended this function,' Woodend said.

'I've got one.'

'Have you, now?' Woodend asked. 'From Sergeant Howarth?'

'No, sir.'

'From the manager of the Palace Hotel?'

'No, sir.'

'Then from where?'

'I'd rather not say, sir.'

Woodend rubbed his chin with the palm of his hand. 'I'm known for cuttin' corners, Sergeant,' he said, 'but I always make sure I stay within the bounds of the law.' Well, usually, anyway, he added as a mental qualification. 'Have you kept within the bounds of the law in obtainin' this list, Sergeant?'

'I believe so, sir,' Paniatowski said – or at least, if she hadn't, nobody would be able to prove it.

'An' who's on this list of yours?'

'As I said, it's exclusively local bigwigs. Doctors with private practices, a few successful solicitors, a builder, a couple of bank managers, three or four magistrates . . . According to Sergeant Hanson you don't get invited to join the Milers unless you're a true pillar of the community. You get the picture?'

'Aye, I get the picture,' Woodend said. 'So despite the fact it's called the Golden Milers Association, it's really nothin' to do with the Golden Mile. For example, there was nobody there from behind the scenes in what you might call the "entertainment industry".'

'No, sir.'

'Nor any of the stars from the shows?'

'No, sir.'

Woodend pondered for a second. 'It's a dicey business goin' up against local power an' influence – you could be puttin' both our careers on the line – but I'm goin' to let you do it, anyway,' he said.

'Thank you, sir,' Paniatowski said – and wondered if Woodend would have been quite so willing to back her if he'd known that as well as the solicitors, doctors and builders who had been at the function, it had also been attended by the chief superintendent in charge of the Blackpool police.

Twenty-Two

L ife went on, Edna Davies told herself, as she reached up into the cupboard over the sink for the breakfast bowls. There were times when you thought it couldn't possibly – but it always did. Bill had died in the most horrific way. His face had been so smashed up that it had been almost impossible to recognise him. So what? Did that mean the washing-up didn't need to be done any more? Or that it was no longer necessary to get Peter ready for school?

She filled the kettle and thought about her husband. He'd been a good man, she acknowledged. A decent man. In his whole life, he had made only one real mistake – and even that had been an accident. She should have been able to forgive him. She should have been able to accept the fact that their life was tough enough without there being any bad blood between them – that they needed to be able to draw strength from each other. But she hadn't be able to do that, and though she would never have wished Bill dead, she couldn't quite suppress the feeling that he had only got what he deserved.

Edna glanced up at the kitchen clock. Twenty past eight. If Peter wasn't down soon, he would be late.

She walked to the foot of the stairs. 'Your breakfast is on the table!' she called.

No answer.

'Can you hear me?' she shouted.

Still, Peter did not respond. Perhaps he'd fallen asleep again. Or maybe he'd merely drifted into one his daydreams, leaving – as he always did on such occasions – the real world far behind him.

She began to climb the stairs. 'Do you want me to lose my temper with you?' she called out.

She wondered if she'd said the right thing. The boy's father had only just died. Shouldn't she be giving him some slack? Or was that the wrong way to go about it? Now that she was both mother *and* father to Peter, should she be laying down firm ground rules even in the midst of the boy's mourning?

Bill would have known what to do, she thought. He had been a good father who had done everything he could for Peter. He'd done all he could for Susan, too – after it had been too late really to do anything at all.

Peter's bedroom was empty. Edna checked the bathroom, but he was not there either.

She opened her own bedroom door and looked across at the bed she and Bill had once shared – the bed that a much younger Peter had crawled into on the nights he'd been woken up by a bad dream. She could almost feel the three of them snuggled together, sharing their body heat and their love. But that had all been before Susan had been born.

There was no sign of Peter in his father's room – which meant there was only place where he could be. Her heart starting to beat a little faster, Edna made her way to the box room.

She knew what she would find inside – she had put it all there herself – yet still she hesitated on the threshold.

Her breathing was becoming irregular now.

I should never have done it, she thought. I should have used the room for storing bits of junk in, like everybody else does.

She grasped the knob, and opened the door. The room contained a single bed, neatly made up. Shelves ran around the walls – Bill had not wanted to put them up, but she'd insisted – and on those shelves stood the toys she'd bought over the years. The golliwog she'd given Susan for her second birthday. The doll's house she'd bought when her daughter had turned six. It was with these toys that she'd recorded the passing of the childhood Susan had never really had, and though she'd told herself that one day . . . one day . . . the girl would be able to take as much pleasure in these playthings as normal children did, she'd known, deep in her heart, that day would never come.

Peter was standing in the corner of the tiny room, a glazed look in his eyes.

'What are you doing here?' Edna asked softly.

'I don't know.'

'If you don't hurry up, you'll be late for school.'

'That doesn't matter.'

'It does matter,' Edna said urgently. 'If you don't get on at school, you'll never get on in life.'

'Who cares?'

The slap was so sudden and so violent that it surprised even Edna herself. One second her arm was resting by her side, the next her hand made contact with her son's right cheek, causing a resounding crack which echoed around the narrow room.

At first the boy was too shocked to cry, then the first tears appeared and soon he was sobbing uncontrollably, his thin body shaking as if he had just been pulled out of icy water.

Edna knelt down beside him, and hugged him tightly to her. 'I'm so sorry,' she said, starting to cry herself. 'I don't know why I did it. I don't know what came over me.'

But she did. Peter – her son – had opportunities in front of him that his sister would never know – and he was treating them as if they were nothing.

Oh God, please grant me this one wish, she prayed as she clasped her son ever tighter to her. Please, please, let at least one of my children lead a normal, happy life.

Woodend looked down the table at his team – his blonde-haired bagwoman, the solid Sergeant Hanson, the fresh-faced Constable Eliot, the brooding Constable Brock and the ginger-haired – almost feline – Constable Eric Stone.

'Listen, I'm not sayin' you're not workin' hard,' he told them, 'but I *am* sayin' that you're not gettin' the results. The Golden Mile's not that big a place when all's said an' done, an' we know Mr Davies was spendin' a lot of his free time there. Why did he do it? Because he needed to meet somebody connected with one of the businesses on the Mile! Probably more than one person, in fact. So you should be able to come up with witnesses who either talked to him themselves or saw somebody else talkin' to him. An' with the notable exception of Gypsy Rose Elizabeth, you've drawn a complete blank.'

'Has the gypsy been able to contribute anything to the investigation, sir?' Hanson asked hopefully.

'Not as yet,' Woodend replied, a vague feeling discomfort sweeping over him as he remembered what Rose Elizabeth had had to say about his own problems. 'But even if she does prove to be of some use later, we can't go buildin' the whole case around the word of one Romany.' He paused, and let his eyes sweep the table. 'You,' he continued, addressing DC Eliot, 'what have you come up with, lad?'

A blush broke out on Eliot's face, and he immediately turned towards Sergeant Hanson for guidance.

'Look at me, lad, not him!' Woodend ordered. 'Who've you talked to?'

'The . . . the sarge asked me to concentrate my efforts on the bingo callers, sir.'

Woodend nodded. 'Not a bad avenue of inquiry, that,' he told Hanson approvingly. 'Bingo callers are always on the look-out for extra customers, so they're not likely to miss much of what's goin' on around them.' He turned his attention back to Eliot. 'An' what have these bingo callers been able to tell you?'

'Not a lot,' the detective constable admitted. 'Some of them knew him, and some of those who didn't recognised him from his photograph. But the only thing any of them could tell me was that they'd seen him walking past their places of business on a fairly regular basis.'

'The Golden Mile's a village,' Woodend told his team. 'You understand what I mean when I say that, don't you?'

But from the blank expressions which greeted this remark, it was plain that they didn't. Even Monika Paniatowski, whose abilities he was coming to appreciate more all the time, looked at him as if he were talking gibberish. If Bob Rutter had been there, he would have understood, the chief inspector thought regretfully. Bob wouldn't have needed it spelling out for him.

'A village is anythin' which is tied together by a common interest or culture,' Woodend continued. 'In what most people think of as a village – a collection of houses, a church and maybe a pub – what ties the people together is that they need each other. If one of them takes sick or there's a fire, there's no point in waitin' for help to come from the nearest town, because that'd take too long. So they have to rely on each other. Now the Golden Mile's a village, too, but for a very different reason. The people who work there are tied together by a *shared experience*. They share the experience of workin' while everybody around them is havin' fun. They share the experience of havin' to put up with drunks while keepin' a smile on their faces. They all know what it's like to be looked down on by people who probably don't make half the money they do. Do you see where I'm goin' with this?'

His team all nodded, though he was not sure whether he was really getting through to them or not.

'They're like bobbies in some ways. There's only two groups of people as far as they're concerned – themselves and the civilians. An' like any bunch of villagers, they know a hell of a lot about each other.' Woodend laid his hands flat on the table. 'There are people out there who have all the answers we need. All you have to do is find them.'

There was a pause, which perhaps indicated that the team were digesting what he'd said – or might merely have meant they were hiding their incomprehension behind a wall of silence.

Then Hanson said, 'We'll do our best, sir. We want Mr Davies' killer caught as much as you do.'

But did they? Woodend wondered. Did they *really*? He had an uneasy feeling about this case. He felt, for much of the time, as if he were stumbling around in a thick fog, while the rest of them stood on the edges of it – making sure that he didn't find his way out.

'If anythin' comes up that I should deal with durin' the next few hours, I can be contacted at Whitebridge headquarters,' he said, and, noticing a couple of raised eyebrows, he added, 'Detective Chief Superintendent Ainsworth wants me to bring him up to speed on what progress we're makin' with this investigation – an' in order to avoid him havin' a heart attack, I'm goin' to have to lie through my teeth.'

He stood up, and walked to the door. Sergeant Hanson waited until the chief inspector's footsteps had receded up the stairs before addressing the rest of the team.

'Right, you heard Mr Woodend,' he said. 'Get out there and bring back some results.' He turned to Paniatowski. 'If you could spare me a few minutes, Sergeant, I'd like a quick word.'

'Of course,' Monika agreed.

The three detective constables trooped out of the room. Hanson got up from his chair, and took the one directly opposite Paniatowski's.

'I meant what I said just before you dashed off this morning,' he said. 'Last night was wonderful.'

Yes, it was pretty spectacular, Paniatowski thought. But aloud, she said, 'I usually try not to get my social life and my professional life mixed up even *after* working hours, Frank. I'm certainly not going to do it *during* them.'

Hanson looked a little chastened. 'Fair point,' he said.

'So if there's nothing else –' Paniatowski said, starting to get up from her chair.

'There is. I've been in touch with one of the waiters who works at the Palace Hotel. He didn't want to talk about the night of the Golden Milers' do – like everybody else, he'd rather not get on the wrong side of the people who matter – but he owes me a couple of favours, and when I reminded him of that he agreed to co-operate as long as I'd promise that what he told me couldn't be traced back to him.'

'What *did* he tell you?' Paniatowski asked, doing her best to hold back her excitement.

'According to him, the show finished at around eleven, and the entertainers buggered off soon after that.'

'What kind of show was it?' Paniatowski asked.

'Do you know, I didn't think to ask,' Hanson admitted. 'It was probably a band or something.'

Unlikely, Paniatowski thought. Bands were for dancing, and the Golden Milers' function had been an all-male affair. But now was the time to listen, not to raise questions.

'Go on,' she said encouragingly.

'The Milers started to drift off at around a quarter past eleven, but there was a hard-core who stayed on after that. It wasn't a free bar, and the hotel hadn't got an extension on its licence, so there should have been no more drinks served, but – though nobody's ever going to admit it – it wouldn't surprise me if a few glasses of the hard stuff still managed to find their way under the towels.'

'It wouldn't surprise me, either.'

'Now we come to the bit where you get lucky,' Hanson continued. 'As near as we can establish, the old lady was knocked down sometime between ten past and a quarter past twelve – and at midnight, when the manager of the Palace appeared and said he really was going to have to close, there were only five Milers left in the bar!'

And the last of them to leave – or at least the last to have driven down Blakiston Street – must have been the one who hit the old woman, Paniatowski thought. Unless . . .

Unless it had been one the *first*, and the others, arriving on the scene *after* the accident, were covering up for their highly influential mate! Now *there* was a convincing scenario!

'Do you have the names of these people?' she asked.

'Yes I do. But before I give them to you, I want you promise me you'll tread carefully. We don't want you charging round like a bull in a china shop, looking for conspiracies everywhere, now do we?'

'Of course not,' Monika agreed.

Twenty-Three

Detective Constable Eliot was walking along the promenade, eating chips from a newspaper, and wishing – not for the first time – that people wouldn't always get a false impression of him. The problem was, he told himself, that when they saw his baby-faced features and noticed how often he blushed, they immediately classified him as someone who would never amount to much.

Well, they were wrong! If only they'd give him the chance, he'd prove that he could be as tough as any of the hardboiled cops he'd seen in the American detective films. Maybe even tougher! And as for ambition – he'd had plenty of that. In his mind's eye he could clearly see himself as Lancashire's youngest-ever chief constable. Then he would show them! Under his leadership, the crime rate in the county would plummet, and villains from Warrington to Preston would shake at the mere mention of his name. All he needed was one lucky break to help him on to the first rung of the ladder.

He stopped to deposit his chip-paper in a waste bin, and noticed that he was standing next to Gypsy Elizabeth Rose's fortune-telling booth. The door of the booth was closed and securely padlocked – which was surprising. If he'd been a fortune-teller, he thought, he would have opened up hours ago in order to entice inside all the holidaymakers who were walking round with their money burning holes in their pockets. But maybe gypsies weren't like policemen – maybe they only worked when they felt inspired.

He paused for a moment to look at the pictures of the celebrities, frozen forever behind a sheet of plate glass on the side of the booth. There were comedians and singers, acrobats and magicians, all of them – apparently – great friends of Elizabeth Rose's. One day he himself would be important enough to merit a place next to them, Eliot thought – though perhaps not until the Queen had conferred his knighthood on him.

'Want to buy a toy that'll keep your kids amused for hours?' asked a voice to his left.

Flattered that someone considered he looked old enough to have children of his own, Eliot turned and saw a tiny brown-skinned man holding a bunch of toy monkeys on sticks in his right hand.

'Marvellous things, these monkeys,' the street vendor continued. 'First they climb up the sticks, an' then they climb down again. Don't ask me how they do it – it's one of the miracles of modern science.'

'Have you got a licence to sell those things?' Eliot asked.

'What's that got to do with you?' the man countered.

'A lot,' Eliot told him. 'I happen to be a detective.'

'A detective?' the tiny man repeated incredulously. 'You mean you're like Bailey an' Spencer on *Seventy-Seven Sunset Strip*?'

'No, I'm not a private eye,' Eliot said, with just a hint of regret in his voice. 'I'm a bobby.'

'Get away!' the vendor said, his disbelief still evident.

'I am,' Eliot insisted. 'I've got a warrant card in my pocket. You can see it, if you want.'

The vendor scoffed. 'You can buy a genuine-looking warrant card down at the House of Jokes for one an' a kick,' he said. 'Tell you what – if you're really a detective, why don't you show me a bit of detectin'?'

'How do you mean?'

'Have a look at them pictures on Elizabeth Rose's booth, an' tell me what's odd about them?'

Eliot did as he'd been told. 'I can't see anything wrong with them,' he confessed, after he'd studied them for perhaps a minute.

'You mean to tell me, Mr Detective, that you can't spot a fake when you see one?'

'A fake?'

'Take another look at the photo of Elizabeth Rose with Lonnie Donegan,' the vendor suggested.

Perhaps the vendor was suggesting the man wasn't really Lonnie Donegan at all, Eliot thought, but he certainly *looked* like the King of Skiffle. The constable cocked his head sideways to see if that would help. It didn't.

'I still don't get it,' he said.

'You notice that Lonnie's standin' close to Elizabeth Rose, but not actually touchin' her?'

'Yes.'

'An' can you see that while most of him is in sharp focus, the side of his body next to Elizabeth Rose is a bit blurred?'

'I suppose it is, now that you mention it.'

'That's because it's two different photos that have been fitted together.'

'Are you sure?' Eliot asked. 'Can they actually do that?'

The other man shook his head in mock despair. 'It's as easy as fallin' off a log if you know a little bit about photography,' he said.

'But why would she bother to fake the photographs?'

'Because it's good for business. Look, your average punter comes along an' he sees these pictures, an' what does he think? He thinks, well, if she's good enough to tell the fortune of a big star like Lonnie Donegan, then she's certainly good enough to tell mine.'

'Are all the photos fakes?' Eliot asked.

'No,' the vendor said. 'Not *all* of them. A few are the genuine article. Like that one there.' He pointed at the picture of a slightly rotund man who was grinning broadly and had his arm draped over Gypsy Elizabeth Rose's shoulder. 'She knows Tommy "Now Where Was I?" Bolton, all right. Matter of fact, I saw him comin' out of the booth only last week, though I have to say he wasn't lookin' half as cheerful then as he does in the picture.'

'Wasn't he?'

'He was not. Judgin' by the expression on his face, I'd have said he was all set to kill somebody. Of course, it could just have been indigestion.' The vendor glanced down at his watch. 'Well, if you'll excuse me, there's somewhere else I have to be. See you around.'

'See you around,' Eliot replied.

'An' keep practisin' with that detective work. You never know, one day you might get good at it.'

The vendor sauntered calmly down the prom, and it was not until he had completely disappeared from sight that Eliot realised that the little man had never produced the trading licence he'd been asked for.

Monika Paniatowski had spent some considerable time select-ing the clothes she would wear that morning. She had finally settled on a black-and-white check suit which was both smart and businesslike, and which – she hoped – would create the right impression with the important people she planned to meet. Initially, the suit had done the trick – at least for her – and when she'd set out from the police station, she'd been brimming with confidence. But now, as she sat in the main hall of Tideswell's Bank – watching the customers depositing and withdrawing money, and trying to look as if it didn't bother her that she'd been kept waiting for over forty-five minutes – she felt some of that confidence start to ebb away.

'Sergeant Paniatowski?' asked a voice.

She looked up. A young man in a grey suit was hovering over her.

'Yes, that's me,' she said.

'Mr Lumsden will see you now.'

She followed the clerk down a long corridor until they reached a door on which had been fixed an impressive brass plate inscribed with the words 'J. Lumsden, Manager'. The young man knocked on the door, opened it, ushered Paniatowski in, and discretely withdrew.

Paniatowski got her first look at the man who'd been one of the last of the Golden Milers to leave the Palace Hotel on the night of the hit-and-run. Lumsden was between forty-five and fifty, she guessed. He had greying hair which was parted to the left, and wore thick-framed horn-rimmed glasses. And he was very impressed with himself. Even from a distance, she could detect the aura of self-congratulation that shrouded him like a thick cloak.

Lumsden did not get up. Instead, he glanced at a piece of paper on the heavy oak desk which separated them.

'It's Miss Paniatowski, is it?' he asked, looking at her over the tops of his glasses.

'It's *Detective Sergeant* Paniatowski,' Monika corrected him.

'Quite so,' the bank manager agreed, only slightly awkwardly. 'Won't you take a seat, Sergeant.'

Paniatowski chose one of the two chairs in front of the desk, and sat down. She crossed her legs slowly – just to see what would happen – and was not at all surprised to note that Lumsden was following the action with his eyes.

'Now what exactly was it you wanted to see me about?' the bank manager asked, when he'd finally forced himself to stop admiring the detective's legs.

'I believe you attended a function organised by the Golden Mile Association last Thursday—' Paniatowski began.

'Is this about that blasted hit-and-run in Fleetwood?' Lumsden interrupted her curtly. 'Because if it is, that matter's already been dealt with.'

'What do you mean?' Paniatowski asked suspiciously. '*Dealt with*?'

'I mean that I've spoken to the local police about it.'

'Who did you talk to? Was it Sergeant Howarth?'

'Yes, I believe that was the officer's name. Not that I can see why it matters, one way or the other, who I actually—'

'Sergeant Howarth is investigating a hit-and-run accident, as you've already pointed out,' Paniatowski said. 'I, on the other hand, am investigating the murder of Detective Inspector Davies.'

'You're surely not suggesting the two are connected, are you?'

Not really, Paniatowski thought. In fact, the more I think about it, the less likely it seems.

'There may *very well* be a connection,' she said.

'What kind of connection are we talking about?'

'I'm afraid I'm not able to reveal the nature of my inquiries.'

'*Your* inquiries?' the bank manager repeated. 'If you don't mind me saying so, you seem to have taken rather a lot of responsibilities on yourself for a mere detective sergeant.'

The bastard was doing his best to intimidate her, Paniatowski told herself. Well, she wasn't going to let that happen.

'I have the full confidence and support of my chief inspector, Mr Woodend,' she said. 'And Mr Woodend, in his turn, has the full confidence of the chief superintendent,' she continued, stretching the truth well beyond breaking point, 'If you have any doubts about that, sir, perhaps you'd like to give Mr Woodend a ring.'

'That won't be necessary – at least for the present,' the bank manager said. 'What would you like to know about that particular night, Sergeant?'

'You were one of the five guests who stayed behind when all the others had departed—' Paniatowski began.

'I'm not sure you've got your numbers quite right,' Lumsden said.

'I am,' Paniatowski assured him, reeling off the names that Sergeant Hanson had given her. 'You do *remember* them all being there, don't you?'

'Yes, I suppose so,' Lumsden said reluctantly.

'What I'm really interested in is the sequence of departure,' Paniatowski told him.

'I beg your pardon?'

'When you did all finally drive back to Blackpool, I assume that you stayed together in a sort of unorganised convoy until you had left Fleetwood, and then went your separate ways,' Paniatowski said, giving Lumsden the opportunity to place himself neatly in the centre of her conspiracy theory.

'Then you'd be wrong,' the bank manager replied. 'As a matter of fact, I can't really tell you what the others did, because I was the first to leave.'

As befits the chief rat on a sinking ship, Paniatowski thought caustically.

162

'Do you happen to remember which way you drove home?' she asked.

'Why should you want to know that?' the bank manager countered sharply.

Paniatowski shrugged. 'You may have seen something which meant nothing to you at the time, but could have relevance to our inquiries.'

'Your inquiries into how Detective Inspector Davies came to be found dead under the Central Pier – several miles away from Fleetwood – a few nights later?' Lumsden asked sceptically.

'That's right,' Paniatowski replied, deadpan.

Lumsden sighed. 'As I recall, I took Blakiston Road down as far as Poulton Road, and from there I went on to the Broadway.'

'In other words, you travelled down the road on which the hit-and-run incident occurred.'

'Yes, I did. But I can assure you there was no old woman lying in the street when I passed by. If there had have been, I would certainly have stopped.'

It was perfectly possible that he was totally innocent, Paniatowski thought. On the other hand, if he *had* killed the old woman – and was sure that there were no wit- nesses to the act – the smartest thing he could do would be to stick fairly closely to the truth, thus minimising the possibilities of being caught out over any inconsistencies later.

'Would you say that any of the friends you left behind was particularly drunk?' she asked.

The moment the words were out of her mouth, she realised that she had gone a step too far.

The bank manager gave her an angry glare. 'None of my friends were in *the least* drunk,' he said. 'We are all far too responsible to indulge in that kind of behaviour.' He glanced down pointedly at his wristwatch, although there was an expensive carriage clock sitting on the desk right in front of him. 'And now, if you will excuse me, Miss Paniatowski, I have a rather important appointment.'

He had said all he was prepared to say, Paniatowski decided, and to try and push him any further would simply be a waste of effort.

'Thank you for your time,' she said.

She rose from her seat carefully – so as to avoid giving Lumsden the undeserved reward of a second show of leg – and walked over to the door.

'Oh, there is one more thing,' she said, as her hand reached for the brass door handle.

'Yes, yes! What is it?'

Lumsden sounded impatient, but also off his guard, Paniatowski thought.

'It's nothing really very important, just something I was curious about,' she said.

'Get on with it.'

'The cabaret – which is what I suppose you'd call it in your social circle – left right after the show was over, didn't it? At around eleven o'clock?'

'Something like that.'

'The point that's been puzzling me is the *kind* of cabaret you could put on for a group of gentlemen having a night out. I thought of a band at first, you see, but then I couldn't imagine the gentlemen dancing with each other.'

For a few seconds Lumsden merely gaped at her, then he took a spotless white handkerchief out of his pocket, and quickly wiped it across his brow.

'No, a band wouldn't have been appropriate,' he agreed, somewhat shakily.

'So what sort of cabaret was it?'

'It was . . . it was a magician,' Lumsden said. 'That's right. A magician. He's appearing at one of the shows in town, though I couldn't tell you which. He was rather good,' he added weakly.

'Thank you again for your help,' Paniatowski said, biting back a small smile of triumph.

Then she closed the door behind her, and was gone.

Lumsden mopped his face again with what had been a pristine handkerchief a few moments earlier, and was now stained with sweat.

He should have anticipated that last question, he thought angrily. He should have been ready with a quick answer. But the bitch had deliberately blind-sided him by seeming to be only interested in the hit-and-run, so he'd fallen right into her trap – and now the damage was done.

He picked up the phone and dialled the operator.

'Blackpool Central Police Headquarters,' said a voice on the other end of the line when he was connected. 'Can we help you?'

'I want to speak to Chief Superintendent Richardson,' Lumsden said.

'If you'll tell me what the problem is, I'll connect you to the right department,' the switchboard girl told him.

'I don't want *any* bloody department,' Lumsden said, aware that he was shouting, but not being able to do anything about it. 'I want to speak to Mr Richardson personally.'

'I'm afraid that won't be poss—'

'My name's Lumsden. I'm the manager of Tideswell's Bank. I happen to be a close friend of Mr Richardson's, calling about a matter of some importance, and if you don't put through in the next few seconds, I wouldn't like to be in your shoes when he finds out about it.'

'Connecting you to his office now, sir,' the girl said, her polite words larded with dislike.

Richardson would make things all right, Lumsden told himself, mopping his brow again. Or if he couldn't, he would know someone higher up the chain of command who could.

Twenty-Four

G ilbert Sidebotham, a tackler from one of the biggest mills in Rochdale, leant back in his deckchair and sighed with pure pleasure. This was the life, he thought – sitting on the beach with your bare feet exposed to the fresh sea air. This was what you worked for all year round – one week of the magic of Blackpool.

Sidebotham took in the scene spread out in front of him with a lazy contentment. The donkeys were racing along the seashore, carrying screaming, excited kids on their backs. A few people were wading into the sea, retreating with a shriek when an unexpected high wave came in. The deckchair attendants were manoeuvring their way between tight knots of people, the change in the pockets of their white coats clinking as they went. There really was nothing like the seaside.

He turned his attention to his two sons, who were busy digging away in the sand with their buckets and spades. They were only five and seven, but they were big lads for their age, and Sidebotham couldn't help noticing – with some pride – that the hole they were digging seemed to be much wider and deeper than any of the holes the other kids had managed.

His eldest boy suddenly stopped digging, and called his brother over. Together, they examined the bottom of the hole with puzzled – possibly troubled – expressions on their faces. For a moment Sidebotham considered getting up and seeing what the matter was, but he quickly dismissed the idea. It was comfortable in the deckchair, and whatever was bothering the lads couldn't really be of much importance, he told himself.

His younger son jumped into the hole and began to clear away the sand with his hands. The mystery, whatever it was, would soon be revealed, Sidebotham thought, as he reached into his jacket pocket for his cigarettes.

The two boys suddenly froze, as if they had seen a ghost.

The tackler from Rochdale was starting to become con-cerned. 'I'll just go an' see what's up wi' yon lads,' he told his wife, levering himself out of his canvas seat.

'They're fine as they are,' Mrs Sidebotham replied. 'Give 'em a bit of peace, for goodness sake.'

'I'm not sure they *are* fine,' Sidebotham replied.

And events were, almost immediately, to prove him right. He had not covered even half the distance between the deckchair and the hole when his eldest son snapped out of his trance and released a blood-curdling scream.

Sergeant Paniatowski stood on the promenade at Fleetwood, watching the back entrance of the Palace Hotel. A telephone inquiry an hour earlier had elicited the information that Harry Granger – the waiter who had unwillingly provided Frank Hanson with the names of the lingering Golden Milers – was due to report for duty at half-past twelve. Since it was already twenty-five past twelve, the chances were that he should be along any minute.

It was at twelve-twenty-eight that the man finally appeared. He was walking quickly, probably to avoid clocking on late. Which was excellent – because men in a hurry were usually more than eager to get straight to the point.

Paniatowski stood perfectly still while Granger passed her, then fell in behind him. She deliberately matched her steps to his, and though she couldn't see anything other than his back, she could tell from his posture that he was starting to get worried.

He speeded up, and so did she. He slowed down, and she decreased her pace too.

He wanted to turn round, she thought, but as yet he was far from convinced that was a good idea.

Paniatowski waited until they almost reached the gate which led to the staff entrance before reaching out and tapping Granger on the shoulder. The effect was most gratifying. The waiter did not actually leap into the air – but he came fairly close to it.

He whirled round. 'Are you followin' me?' he demanded.

Paniatowski smiled. 'Of course I am.'

'Why?'

Monika produced her warrant card. 'Police. I'd like to ask you a few questions.'

'What about?'

'About the same thing you were discussing with Sergeant Hanson earlier this morning.'

'But he promised me that if I answered his questions, he'd leave me alone from now on,' Granger protested.

'He meant it,' Paniatowski replied. 'And I promised him that if he told me what you'd told him, I'd leave you alone too. Unfortunately for you, I lied.'

Granger glanced nervously at the staff entrance. 'If anybody sees me talkin' to you, I could be in big trouble,' he said.

'Then we'd better move away from the hotel, hadn't we?'

'But I'm on duty in a minute.'

'Won't do you any harm to be late for once,' Paniatowski said indifferently. 'Tell them your tram broke down.'

She took him by the elbow, and led him in the direction of the pier. 'I talked to one of the men on your list this morning,' she continued. 'Mr Lumsden – the manager at Tideswell's Bank. I tried to talk to the others, too, but they've been very difficult to contact. Now why do you think that should be?'

'I've no idea.'

'It couldn't be because Lumsden warned them off, could it?'

'It might be,' Granger admitted.

'But warned them off for what reason?' Paniatowski asked.

They had reached the sea front. She came to a halt, and released the waiter's elbow.

'Did you see them drive off?' she asked.

'Who?'

'The last five of the Golden Milers to leave,' Paniatowski snapped impatiently.

'I saw Mr Lumsden go. He was the first. But by the time

the others went, I was already back in the kitchen, stackin' the dishes.'

Paniatowski sighed. It would all have been so much simpler if Granger could have narrowed it down to one or two suspects, she thought.

'Let me ask you something else,' she said. 'Lumsden claimed that the entertainers left straight after the show. Was that true?'

Granger's eyes widened. 'Mr Lumsden told you about the *entertainers*?' he gasped.

Paniatowski nodded. 'But why don't you tell me about them, too?'

'It was a very tame show, really,' Granger said. 'I mean, you'd never have got away with puttin' on anythin' like it on the Golden Mile, but this was a *private* function.'

It was all starting the make sense. The men out alone for the night. Lumsden reaching for his handkerchief when she'd asked him exactly what kind of entertainment it was.

'How many girls were involved?' Monika asked.

'There were three of them,' Granger said. 'An' the feller. They put on a bit of an exhibition, if you know what I mean.'

'And when the "exhibition" was over, did any of the guests take one of the girls for a tour of the hotel – a tour including the bedrooms upstairs?' Paniatowski asked speculatively.

Granger looked shocked. 'No!' he said. 'The management would never have allowed things to go that far.'

So that was what Lumsden had got into such a sweat about, Paniatowski thought – something which, when all was said and done, amounted to nothing more than a giggling schoolboys' outing.

'*He* left at the same time as the girls,' Granger volunteered.

'Who did? The man who'd been doing mucky things on stage with them?'

'No!' Granger said dismissively. 'The comedian.'

'What comedian?'

'The one who told jokes between the acts.' A look of realisation suddenly came to Granger's face. 'You didn't know about him, did you?'

'No,' Paniatowski agreed. 'But now that I do, you'd better give me all the details.'

Granger was looking more and more worried. 'Listen, if it got out he was appearin' on the same stage as strippers, he wouldn't be very pleased. Wouldn't do his reputation any good, you see. I mean, he wasn't here for the money. He told me that himself.'

'So why was he here?'

'More as a favour than anything else. See, now that he's bought himself a bungalow in Lytham, he wants to start hobnobbin' with the people round here who matter, an' I expect he thought that puttin' on a show for the Golden Milers was a way of gettin' his foot in the door.'

'You still haven't told me who you're talking about,' Paniatowski said.

'Can't you guess?'

'I'm not in a guessing business. Why don't you just tell me who he is?'

'He's Tommy "Now Where Was I?" Bolton,' the waiter said.

Barton Lane was located right in the centre of the oldest part of Whitebridge, and had been in existence long before the first mill had appeared to scar the landscape. It was the kind of lane which twists and turns when you least expect it to. The kind of lane in which the pedestrian was always coming across strange and exotic businesses which appeared to have no place in the modern world of Whitebridge – taxidermists and chandlers, specialist tea vendors and old-fashioned bespoke tailors who filled their windows with pin-striped material which seemed to do little else but gather dust.

Lorries could not navigate their way up Barton Lane, and even the brewer's dray which delivered the barrels of beer – and was pulled by two magnificent shire horses – sometimes ran into difficulties. But however difficult it was, the dray's journey still had to be made, because halfway up the lane stood a pub which was officially known as the White Swan, but which all the locals called the Dirty Duck.

170

Woodend was at one of the tables in the upstairs bar, the remains of a steak and kidney pie in front of him. The man who had been until recently his trusted right hand – and was showing considerably less enthusiasm for Northern cuisine than his old boss – sat opposite him.

'How are things progressing in Blackpool, sir?' Bob Rutter asked.

'I wouldn't like to say,' Woodend admitted. 'I haven't really got a handle on this case, yet.'

'And your new sergeant?' Rutter asked – just a little too casually.

'She's got a lot of confidence,' Woodend replied. 'More than you had when you started workin' with me.'

The remark had not been intended to sting – but it did. 'I had plenty of confidence!' Rutter protested.

'You had confidence that you could handle any job I gave you,' Woodend told him. 'Paniatowski's confidence is of a different kind entirely. She's out to make a name for herself – an' not by bein' part of my success, but through what she does on her own.'

'Detection's a matter of team work,' Rutter said.

'Aye, it is,' Woodend agreed. 'But it's also a bit like football, in a way. If the team doesn't work together, they're lost. But there always comes a moment durin' the game when the individual player has to decide to take control of the ball an' run with it on his own. That's what you call star quality.'

'You sound as if you approve of her,' Rutter said.

An' you sound as if you don't, Woodend thought.

'She'll have to learn to bend a little to the way I work,' the chief inspector said, 'but I'm willin' to bend a little in her direction, as well. Call it a bit of a crusade, if you want to – I'd like to see more women doin' well in the police force. An' after all, she's reached the rank of detective sergeant, so she must have somethin' about her.'

'And I think I know what it is,' Rutter said, still sounding slightly aggrieved. 'At least, as far as you're concerned.'

'Do you now? An' what might that be?'

'She reminds you of yourself when you were a young bobby.'

'Do you know, you might be right,' Woodend said. 'I'd never thought of it quite like that.'

'The difference is that you were a young bobby in the forties, not the sixties,' Rutter pointed out. 'Policing's moved on a long way in the last twenty years, and Sergeant Paniatowski should realise that.'

What had caused this sudden outburst? Woodend wondered. Jealousy? Insecurity? In a way, he supposed both those things were understandable. Bob was like a young bird who had been kicked out of the nest before he was *quite* sure he could fly under his own power. Maybe later it would be necessary to chirp a few words of encouragement, but given Rutter's present mood the best course of action was probably to change the subject.

'Why don't you ask me what Detective Superintendent Ainsworth had to say for himself this mornin'?' Woodend asked.

'What did Chief Superintendent Ainsworth have to say for himself this morning?' Rutter repeated dutifully.

'That he'd expected a result by now.'

'But you've been on the case for less than two days,' Rutter protested, falling back naturally into the familiar role of confidant and soother.

'True,' Woodend agreed. 'But accordin' to Mr Ainsworth, two days should have been plenty of time. He doesn't have any of the details of the murder, mind – not a blind one – but he's got enough experience to know that even a rookie detective constable could have got to the bottom of it all by now.' He took a swig of his pint. 'What about you, lad? How are you gettin' on?'

'I've been handed an investigation that's already in its sixth week,' Rutter said. 'All the ground has already been covered several times, and the officers who've been working the case have come up with Sweet Fanny Adams. But that's not really their problem any more, is it? I'm in charge now, and if anybody has to bear the stigma of failure, it's going to be me.'

Woodend nodded gravely. 'They've got it in for both of us, haven't they?' he said.

'Ainsworth certainly does, for one,' Rutter admitted. 'So

what can we do about it? It's not going to be easy for Maria to pull her roots and move to Lancashire, you know. It's hard enough for a person who can see, but when you're blind . . . when you depend on knowing where things are, because you can't actually *see* them . . .'

And she wouldn't have had to go through any of that if it hadn't been for me, Woodend thought guiltily – because I'm the one who got Bob the promotion and the transfer.

'Then there's the fact that the baby's on the way,' Rutter continued. 'She'll have to learn to deal with that, too. And she's more than willing to do it. But I don't want to have to tell her she'll have to go through all the trauma of moving again in another six months.'

An' I don't want to have to tell Annie that I've made her leave all her friends behind for a new life that simply isn't goin' to happen, Woodend told himself.

'As I see it, we've got two choices,' he said. 'The first is that we can throw in the towel – like you've just hinted. If that's the course we take, then we either leave the force, or try to get another transfer to somewhere else. I don't fancy workin' for a private security firm, an' even a feller like me – a feller who's sabotaged his own career more times than he cares to remember – can see that it wouldn't be a good plan, prospect-wise, to move forces again so soon.'

'So what's the second choice?' Rutter asked.

'There've been several occasions in the past when I've asked you to do somethin' for me as part of an investigation, an' – because you're an idle young bugger by nature – you've suggested I give the job to the local police,' Woodend said. 'Do you remember any of those cases?'

Rutter grinned. Did he remember? Of course he did! He recalled tramping the street of Leeds in search of a bootmaker who might give them the vital clue which would help them crack the Swann's Lake case; visiting half the coffee bars of Liverpool – and drinking so much cappuccino in the process that he thought it would come out of his ears – in the hope that he'd find a lead on who killed young Eddie Barnes. Yes, he remembered – and so did his feet!

'The reason I mentioned it now – apart from bein' unable to resist a dig at you whenever the opportunity arises – is that every time you tried to skive off a job, I told you to stick with it because I didn't trust the local flatfeet to do it properly,' Woodend continued. 'I've been sayin' for years that one Scotland Yard man is worth five or six bumpkins from out in the sticks. Well, if we're goin' to survive in Whitebridge, we're goin' to have to prove that boast's true. So there's our second choice, lad. We'll do our job so well that we'll make ourselves bloody indispensable.'

A waiter appeared at the end of the table. 'Chief Inspector Woodend?' he asked.

'Aye, that's me.'

'There's a telephone call for you, sir.'

Woodend rose from his seat. 'I won't be a minute.'

Left alone, Rutter picked up his fork and listlessly moved the remains of his pie around his dish. He'd been delighted when he'd got his promotion, but now he wasn't sure it was such a good thing. They had to prove they were indispensable, Woodend had said. But were they? Or – more specifically – was he? Had he learned enough approaches and intuitive leaps from the master of bluff to make it on his own – or could he have benefited from a couple more years working as Woodend's bagman?

When the chief inspector returned to the table, he was looking as grim as Rutter had ever seen him.

'Has something happened, sir?' the newly promoted inspector asked.

'Aye, you might say that,' Woodend replied. 'Another body's turned up in Blackpool.'

'Does it have anything to do with your case?'

'It'd be a bloody miracle if didn't. The body in question belongs to a fortune-teller who worked on the Golden Mile. I was questionin' her about the murder only yesterday.'

Twenty-Five

The first dead body little Charlie Woodend had ever seen had been his grandmother's. He'd been eight at the time, and his parents – having decided that he was old enough to look death squarely in the face – had ushered him into the cold front parlour where her coffin lay. The old lady had looked so peaceful that he'd found it hard to believe that she wasn't just sleeping. Then his mother had told him he could touch his granny if he wanted to, and as his fingertips brushed softly against her cold, dry skin, he had accepted that she was lost to him for ever.

The body which lay before him in the Blackpool morgue had none of his grandmother's tranquillity. Gypsy Elizabeth Rose's mouth was wide open, and her eyes bulged so much that they looked as if they were about to burst.

Here was a woman who had known she was on the point of death, Woodend thought – and he wondered whether her killer had taken any pleasure from having so much power over another human being.

'Fill me in on all the details you've got so far,' he said to Chief Inspector Turner.

'The body was discovered just before noon, on the sands close to the South Pier. It had been buried in a shallow grave, no deeper than two and a half feet at any point. The kids who found her uncovered her left hand first. Initially they thought it was one of those you can buy at joke shops, but then they dug further, discovered there was an arm attached to it, and realised how serious the whole situation really was.'

'Why a *shallow* grave?' Woodend murmured, almost to himself.

'I beg your pardon?'

'If he was goin' to bury her, why not make a proper job of it? Why not take her out into the woods somewhere, an' put her under six feet of earth?'

'Beats me,' Turner said.

'He must have known that leavin' her there, she'd either be found by some kids – as she was – or uncovered by the tide. So we have to assume that he *wanted* her to be found.'

'A fair point,' Turner agreed.

'But if he wanted her to be found, why go to the trouble of buryin' her at all? Why not simply dump her in a quiet back street?'

'He might have been worried he'd be seen doing that.'

'Whereas he wasn't at all worried that somebody might see him diggin' a big hole in the sand, an' then carryin' a body to it?' Woodend asked. 'Buryin' her must have taken at least half an hour. Throwin' her from his car would have taken seconds. So I say again, why go to the trouble of buryin' her?'

'I don't know,' Turner said.

And he didn't seem very interested in finding out, either! Woodend thought. Turner was going through the motions as if he were one serious police officer presenting the facts of a murder case to another serious police officer, yet he somehow managed to give the impression that he was merely acting – that beneath his grave exterior there lurked a strong emotion he was doing his best to restrain.

'You've established that the cause of death was definitely strangulation, have you?' Woodend asked.

'Oh yes. And the pathologist thinks that whoever killed her must have been quite strong – which would seem to rule out a woman as the perpetrator.'

Woodend lit a Capstan Full Strength in the vain hope that it might deaden the smell of formaldehyde which permeated the whole building.

'I remember this woman who lived on our street when I was kid,' he said. 'Tiny little thing, she was – looked as if the slightest puff of wind would blow her away. But every Friday night, she'd be down at the pub door at eleven o'clock sharp, and when her sixteen-stone husband staggered out, she'd half-carry the drunken bugger home.'

'Meaning some women are stronger than they look?' Turner asked.

'Meanin' just that.'

'You're probably right.'

Woodend studied Turner again. The local bobby seemed quite open to accepting the idea that the killer might be a woman. In fact he seemed open to accepting *any* idea that his colleague from headquarters might care put forward about Gypsy Elizabeth Rose's murder.

'How about suicide?' Woodend suggested. 'Do you think there's any chance she killed herself?'

For a second, Turner was uncertain how to react, then he forced a reluctant grin to his face. 'You're making a joke, aren't you?'

'Aye,' Woodend agreed. 'I'm makin' a joke.'

But he was almost sure that if he'd put forward a theory that was even *slightly* less ludicrous, Turner would have gone along with it.

'Does the quack have any idea about the time of death?' he asked.

'Dr Philips is a little cagey about being too definite. If the body been left out on the beach, he could have made the standard calculation based on the drop in her body temperature, but the fact that she was buried under warm sand means the rate of cooling would have been slower. The only problem is, nobody's sure yet *how much* slower.'

'Well, that might answer one of my earlier questions,' Woodend said thoughtfully.

'What question would that be?'

'The one about why she was—'

Woodend bit back the rest of the comment, because he was not certain that he entirely trusted Chief Inspector Turner. Come to that, he was not certain he trusted *anybody* in the Blackpool police.

'What were you about to say?' Turner asked.

'Doesn't matter for the moment,' Woodend told him. 'Let's

get back to the matter in hand. Is the good doctor prepared to give any estimate *at all* as to the time of death?'

'He's willing to say it probably didn't occur earlier than ten o'clock last night or later than seven o'clock this morning.'

'That's somethin', anyway,' Woodend said. 'Now I suppose the next question is: "Does this murder belong to me, or is it bein' given to somebody else?" '

'Our chief super spoke to DCS Ainsworth about half an hour ago,' Turner said. 'They both think it's unlikely that two killings – so close together in both time and geography – could be unconnected. There was some talk of putting a second DCI on the Elizabeth Rose case, but in the end Mr Ainsworth decided that – for the time being at least – the two crimes should be treated as parts of one investigation.'

Aye, that will just suit Ainsworth, Woodend thought. Why should he nail me for failin' to solve one murder when he's got the chance of nailin' me for failin' to solve two?

'Will you be needing more of my men now the scope of the investigation's widened?' Turner said.

Would I like to invite more possible spies into my camp? Woodend asked himself. No, I bloody well wouldn't.

'I don't want any more men reportin' directly to me,' he said aloud. 'But I would appreciate it if your lads could save my team a bit of leg-work.'

'What do you want them to do?'

'I want to know as much about Elizabeth Rose's movements last night as you can come up with. What time did she leave her booth? Where did she go after that? Who was the last person to see her alive? You know the routine.'

Turner nodded. 'If you don't need me for anything else, I'll get on to it right away.'

'Aye, you do that,' Woodend agreed.

He turned his attention back to the body. Had there been any indication, when he'd been talking to the dead woman the previous day, that she'd soon end up like this? No, he didn't think there had been. So he had no reason to feel guilty, then. But he did – because however much he tried to persuade himself he couldn't have known, there was something inside him which said that he *should* have.

He walked over to the window and looked out on to the car park. DCI Turner had already left the building, and was heading towards his vehicle.

Woodend closed his eyes, and tried to visualise the other occasions on which he'd seen Turner walking away from him. Was there any difference in his demeanour this time? he wondered.

Yes! Yes, there bloody well was!

Turner had a definite spring in his step now – almost as if some heavy burden of responsibility had suddenly been lifted from his shoulders.

The chief inspector took a deep drag on his Capstan Full Strength. It wouldn't be strictly accurate to say that Turner was glad Gypsy Elizabeth Rose had been murdered, he thought – but the man was certainly relieved about *something*. Now why the hell should that be?

The team had been gathered together around the basement table, and they all looked suitably grave and responsible. But could they just be play-acting, as Turner had been earlier?

'We know for a fact that Mr Davies went to see the murdered woman,' Woodend said, 'but when I talked to her, she claimed he'd only dropped in for a consultation. Did he seem like the kind of man who'd believe in fortune-telling, Sergeant Hanson?'

'No sir,' Hanson said, without hesitation. 'Mr Davies was one of the most down-to-earth officers I've ever worked with.'

'So assumin' that the two murders are connected, then what Davies an' Elizabeth Rose said to each other could be of vital importance to the case. The only problem is, we can't ask them what it was – because they're both dead. We've found nothin' to connect Mr Davies with the gypsy, so what I want to do is turn the thing on its head, an' see if we can find anythin' to connect *the gypsy* with *Mr Davies*. Chief Inspector Turner's men are investigatin' what she did in the last few hours of her life – what I want you to come up with is what she did with the rest of it. Am I makin' myself clear?' The four local men nodded. 'Right,'

Woodend continued. 'Sergeant Hanson will co-ordinate. Get on with it.'

Woodend watched Hanson and three constables leave the room, then turned his attention to Sergeant Paniatowski, who had gone back to her desk.

'How's it lookin' from your end of things, Monika?' Woodend asked. 'Are you still convinced there could be a link between Mr Davies' murder an' the hit-an'-run?'

'More than ever,' Paniatowski lied.

'In that case, you'd better stick with it.' The phone rang on Woodend's desk. He walked over and picked it up. 'Yes? This is Woodend, sir. Yes, she has been considerin' the possibility that . . . No, I haven't . . .'

After making sure that his back was turned to her, Paniatowski quietly picked up the receiver on her own desk. 'I've been getting nothing but complaints about her all day,' she heard Ainsworth bark.

'That can sometimes be the sign that an officer's doin' his job – her job,' Woodend countered.

'You've got two murders on your hands. Isn't that enough for you, without upsetting everybody who matters in Blackpool?'

'My sergeant thinks there may be a connection.'

'And what do you think?'

'I won't know until she's completed her investigation and reported back to me.'

'Let me get this straight!' Ainsworth said. 'You've let Paniatowski loose on some of the most important people in Lancashire without a shred of evidence that she'll come up with anything worthwhile?'

'You have to have confidence in your team,' Woodend replied evenly. 'Besides, if there's one thing I've learned over the years, it's that in order to come up with a few right answers, you have to ask a lot of what will probably turn out to be pointless questions.'

'Do you want to be taken off this investigation, Chief Inspector?' Ainsworth asked threateningly.

'No sir. But if I can't conduct it the way I see fit, then I might as well be.'

'You're relying on the chief constable to protect you, aren't you?' Ainsworth demanded. 'You think you can pull the old-pals act on him. Well, let me tell you, Woodend, he's got his own position to protect, and he's not about to sink himself just to keep you afloat.'

'I quite appreciate that, sir.'

'So you'll call Paniatowski off?'

'I'll have to think about it,' Woodend said.

'Will you, indeed? Well, if I was you, I wouldn't think about it too long, Chief Inspector.'

There was the sound of the receiver being violently slammed into its cradle, and then the line went dead.

Paniatowski replaced her own receiver just as Woodend was turning to face her. The chief inspector's eyes looked troubled, and there were lines on his brow she'd never even noticed before. It came as a shock to her to see how much he could change during the course of one brief phone call.

'Was that Mr Ainsworth?' she asked.

'What makes you ask that?'

Paniatowski forced herself to grin. 'I caught you saying the occasional "sir" and, being a trained detective, I worked out that you must be speaking to someone of a higher rank than you. So it was a good bet you were talking to the DCS.'

Woodend returned her grin with a weary smile of his own. 'Aye, it was him,' he admitted.

'Did he want anything important, sir?'

'Not really. He was just askin' me to keep him up to speed on the investigation.'

Paniatowski turned back to the notes which lay on the desk in front of her. She almost had it cracked, she told herself. Five names – five possible hit-and-run drivers. They'd kept up a united front so far, but when she finally used the implied threat of revealing what she knew about the 'entertainment' – when they realised that their wives might learn what they'd been up to their boys' night out – one of them would break ranks and give her the name of the guilty party. All she needed was a little more time – and Woodend had completely surprised her by buying that time for her. But at what cost, both to his investigation and to his position in the Central Lancs police?

You have to have confidence in your team, he'd said.

And he'd been talking about her!

'I've been reviewing my notes, sir,' she said, across the empty room.

'Have you now? An' have you come up with any conclusions?'

'Yes, I have. I now think that I was quite wrong in what I said earlier. There *is* no connection between the hit-and-run case and Mr Davies' murder. I'd be much more valuable to the team following another line of investigation.'

Woodend gave have a long stare which seemed to be reaching down right into the depths of her soul.

'I wish you'd told me that about five minutes ago,' he said. 'You're sure you've got it right this time?'

'Yes, sir. I'm sure.'

Woodend picked up the phone. 'Could you get me Chief Superintendent Ainsworth in Whitebridge Headquarters, please?' he asked the switchboard operator.

And suddenly Monika Paniatowski knew that she was not brave enough at that moment to hear a second conversation between the man who had trusted her and the other man who seemed hell-bent on destroying him. Feeling both ashamed and confused, she rose from her desk and tiptoed to the door.

It was almost nine o'clock when Monika entered Dutton's OBJ Tavern and saw Frank Hanson – a welcoming smile on his face – waiting for her at a corner table.

As Paniatowski flopped into the seat opposite him, Hanson, noticing her anxious look, and his smile transformed itself into concern. 'Want to talk about it?' he asked sympathetically.

'You did a good piece of work for me this morning,' Monika said tiredly. 'I'm almost convinced that one of the last five men to leave the Palace Hotel is guilty of manslaughter.'

'But –?'

'But Mr Woodend's in charge of investigating *two* murders now, and they have to take precedence over anything else.'

'You've changed your tune,' Hanson said.

'I know I have,' Paniatowski admitted. 'Or maybe I've just finally heard somebody else's tune, and decided it's my job to dance to it.'

'I've never been very good at riddles,' Hanson said. 'Would you mind explaining that particular one to me?'

'Not tonight. I'm a bit too confused to even explain it to myself.'

The waiter came over and deposited the vodka Paniatowski had ordered on the table.

Hanson paid for it. 'You need something to take you out of yourself,' he said. 'How about a spot of dancing at the Tower Ballroom?'

'I don't think so.'

'Come on,' Hanson said encouragingly. 'I know you don't want to take me on because you've noticed I've got feet the size of coal barges – but appearances can be deceptive. I have it from a number of sources that dancing with me is like walking on air.'

Paniatowski reached across the table and touched his hand. 'It's not you,' she said. 'It's me. The mood I'm in tonight, I wouldn't be any fun.'

'So there's no chance you'll be coming back to my flat for a nightcap?'

'I'm afraid not. I need some time on my own – time to think things through.'

'Is this a brush-off?' Hanson asked. 'Because I'm a big boy now, and if that's what it is, there's no need to sugar the pill.'

'It's *nothing* like that,' Paniatowski assured him. 'Look, Frank, I don't know how things are going to turn out with us, but maybe once the case is closed we'll be able to get a clearer picture.'

'So there's a chance that what we had could turn out to be more than a one-night stand?'

'A good chance. But I'm afraid you're going to have to be patient.' Monika paused. 'I'm asking a lot, aren't I?'

'Yes, you are,' Hanson agreed. 'But if a thing's worth having, it's worth waiting for. And you, Detective Sergeant Paniatowski, are worth a long, long wait.'

Twenty-Six

From his table in the breakfast room of the Sea View Hotel, Woodend looked across the road at the uniformed constable who was leaning against the cast-iron railings which ran along the promenade.

'Is something wrong, sir?' asked Monika Paniatowski, as she finished off her fry-up with a gusto Bob Rutter could never have hoped to emulate.

'Wrong?' Woodend repeated abstractly.

'Yes. You seem to have something on your mind this morning.'

Woodend took an automatic sip of his tea. 'Have you ever seen a bobby on duty over there on the sea front before?' he asked.

'Can't say I have,' Paniatowski admitted.

'Me neither,' Woodend said thoughtfully. 'So I wonder what the bugger's doin' there now.'

There was a second uniformed constable positioned on the promenade at the corner of Barton Avenue, and a third a little further down. It was when he saw the fourth, posted near St Chad's Road, that Woodend decided he had had enough.

The constable noticed him crossing the road and turned to look towards the Pleasure Beach. He was still looking at it – gazing at the Big Wheel with a fixed intensity – when the man in the hairy sports jacket drew level with him.

'What's this all about, son?' Woodend asked.

'I beg your pardon, sir?' the constable said, trying to act as if Woodend's approach had taken him by surprise – and failing miserably.

'When you called me "sir" just now, were you bein' polite to a member of the general public – or were you givin' rank its due?' Woodend asked.

The constable looked confused – as well he might.

'I . . . I . . .' he spluttered.

'You know who I am, don't you?' Woodend demanded.

'Y-yes, sir. I . . .'

'But I don't know who you are. Have we been introduced?'

'No, sir. You . . . you must have been pointed out to me in the canteen.'

'Bollocks!' Woodend told him, and before the hapless constable had time to reply, he turned and walked away.

They were watching him, Woodend thought as he walked along the sands. They were bloody well watching him. And not only that, but they were making no secret about it. They wanted him to know he was being observed – wanted him to be intimidated by the fact. Well, sod them! He'd solved more murders than the local flatfeet had had hot dinners, and he wasn't about to let them stop him solving this one.

He took the steps down to the beach. Let the buggers follow him along the sands if they wanted to. Let them find out for themselves what effect the sight of three or four uniformed bobbies would have on the packed ranks of holidaymakers who associated bobbies with summonses for having no lights on their bikes or passing illegal betting slips – and who had come to Blackpool to get away from that kind of thing.

Just ahead of him, he saw the Punch and Judy booth he'd noticed a couple of days earlier. Two or three dozen kids were sitting cross-legged in front of it, waiting for the show to start, and Woodend saw no reason why he shouldn't join them – if only to see a nosy uniformed policeman puppet get a pasting!

The grotesque Mr Punch appeared above the parapet and bobbed around. 'Hello, hello, hello,' he screeched at the top of his thin voice.

'Hello, hello, hello,' his young audience screamed back.

Punch's wife, Judy, entered from the left. 'What's all this noise, Mr Punch?' she demanded.

A sound of crying came from off-stage. Judy looked towards it, and then back at Mr Punch. 'I do believe you've woken the baby,' she complained.

'Oh no, I haven't!' Punch protested.

'Oh yes, you have!' shouted Judy, and her young audience joined in with cries that, yes, he had.

'Oh no, I haven't!'

'Oh yes, you have!'

His earlier irritation vanishing, Woodend felt a broad grin come to his face. It was like being in the time machine again, he thought. Little Charlie Woodend, sitting on the sand and ignoring the fact that the sun was burning his legs – though he knew he would pay for it later. The Punch and Judy show had seemed nothing short of a miracle back then. But that was before the days of television. He wondered how much longer shows like this would survive now that there was a box in the corner of the living-room that seemed able to deliver so much more.

Judy disappeared for a second, and returned holding a swaddled bundle in her arms.

'The baby *is* crying,' she told Punch, 'and now I'm going to make *you* take care of it.' She handed the bundle over to him, then turned to the audience. 'Now boys and girls, I want you to make sure that Mr Punch looks after the baby properly. If he doesn't, you will call me, won't you?'

'Yes,' shouted the children – and one middle-aged adult in a hairy sports jacket.

The baby continued to cry after Judy had left the stage. Punch looked down at it. 'What a cross baby you are,' he said.

Some of the children were already calling for Judy to come to the rescue, but Woodend did not join them. Instead, he had fallen into a thoughtful silence.

'Naughty baby!' Punch screamed. 'Naughty, naughty baby. Do shut up! Do shut up!'

Woodend stood frozen to the spot, cursing his own stupidity. The indications had all been there, he told himself, and he had seen the Punch and Judy show often enough to know it backwards. He should have made the right connection long ago!

The puppet baby was still crying loudly. In exasperation, Punch banged its head on the playboard and threw it out of the booth. The children were calling for Judy even louder now, but when she appeared Woodend was not there to see her, because the chief inspector was already striding at a furious pace towards the promenade.

Edna Davies opened her front door to find the chief inspector from Whitebridge standing awkwardly on the step.

'What is it this time?' she asked.

'I've got a few more questions I need to ask you,' Woodend told her. 'I'm afraid they're goin' to be rather painful ones.'

'It wasn't exactly easy talking to you the last time,' the widow countered.

'Last time all we were talkin' about was the few days before your husband's death,' Woodend said. 'This time, we're goin' to have to go back a lot further.'

Mrs Davies' shoulders slumped. 'You know,' she said.

'I've guessed,' Woodend replied. 'But I still need you to fill in some of the details.'

Edna Davies nodded, resignedly. 'What, exactly, do you want to know?'

'Your daughter, Susan, wasn't born backward, was she?'

'No,' Edna Davies admitted. 'She wasn't.'

'But she was a difficult baby. Always cryin' – never letting up even for a second.'

Mrs Davies put her hands on her hips as, in a split second, resignation turned to fury.

'Is that what you think?' she demanded angrily. 'Do you really think that Bill abused his own baby – just because she wouldn't keep quiet?'

'That isn't what happened?'

'No, it isn't what bloody happened. He dropped her, all right?! He lost his grip on her and she landed on her head. There was brain damage.'

Woodend believed her. Inspector Davies had never beaten

his daughter, as he'd initially suspected, but the fact that he had dropped her had been enough for police humour – made harsh by its daily contact with the worst kinds of reality – to christen him Mr Punch.

'You don't blame him?' Woodend asked.

'Of course I blame him!' Mrs Davies replied, almost screaming. 'How could I not blame him! He'd been drinking.'

'Was he drunk?'

'No,' the woman replied. 'He'd just had enough to make sure that he couldn't take proper care of my sweet little angel.' Tears were welling up in her eyes. 'He tried his best to make up for it. He was a perfect father after that. He'd show Susan more patience than I could ever have managed. But it was all a bit too bloody late then, wasn't it?'

'I'm sorry,' Woodend said. 'If there's anything I can do –'

'You've got what you wanted,' the widow told him. 'You've heard what a mess Bill made of all our lives. Now will you please just go.'

She was right, Woodend thought. There was nothing more he could say – no consolation he could offer her. He turned and made his way quickly down the garden path and out on to the street.

The Alderman Salter School for Children with Special Needs was set back from the sea at a point roughly midway between Blackpool and Cleveleys. It was a large, ugly nineteenth-century edifice, and had probably once been the seaside retreat of a cotton magnate who had made his fortune from the dark, satanic mills further inland. The building was surrounded by pleasant, landscaped grounds, but they did nothing to disguise the fact that it was also surrounded by a high wall, and had a heavy iron gate which was permanently manned.

As Woodend made his way up the drive which led from the gate to the main building, he looked around him. There were a number of children out in the grounds. Some of them were playing games with each other, and could have been mistaken for normal kids. But there were others – solitary figures – who sat on benches under the watchful eye of nurses and gazed blankly into space.

The principal's office was on the ground floor at the front of the house. The principal herself was an attractive, energetic woman in her late forties. She gestured Woodend to sit down, then stretched across her desk to offer him a thin black cigar from a silver box.

'We don't get many visits from the police here,' the principal said, when Woodend had politely turned down her offer and lit up a Capstan Full Strength instead. 'In fact, I don't think we've ever had any at all. The children we look after can be naughty, and even antisocial, but we take great care to ensure that they are given very little opportunity to do anything criminal.'

She was probably making a joke, Woodend decided – an institutional joke – but he kept his smile halfway between friendly and amused, just in case he was wrong about that.

'I'm here in Blackpool to investigate the death of Detective Inspector Davies,' he said.

The principal lit up one of her thin cigars, and blew the smoke down her nostrils. 'I thought that might be the case. Which made me wonder why you decided to visit us. We are a combination of school and hospital, and on both counts we are bound by a code of confidentiality not to reveal any details of our pupils' records.'

'I understand that,' Woodend replied. 'It's Mr Davies himself, not his daughter, that I'm here to ask you about. Do you think you can talk about him without breaching your code?'

'Possibly,' the principal said cautiously. 'What would you like to know?'

'I've just been talkin' to his wife, an' I came away with the impression that he's been a carin' an' lovin' father to his daughter.'

'You came away with the right impression. Mr Davies visited his daughter at every possible opportunity. His patience with her was a marvel to behold. There was nothing he wouldn't have done for her, although – to be brutally honest – there was not much he *could* do.'

'The brain damage is irreversible, then?'

The principal shot him a warning glance. 'We rarely use words like irreversible in this school. This is an institution built on hope – however slender that hope may be. And perhaps when Susan moves to the new school – if that is, Mrs Davies decides that she *should* still move—'

'Hang on,' Woodend said. 'What new school are we talking about here?'

'It's in Switzerland. Mr Davies read about it somewhere, and asked me what I thought. I had to tell him that it appeared to have produced some remarkable results.'

'But Switzerland! Wouldn't that have been expensive?'

'Very expensive indeed. I'm told that Eton College charges four hundred and sixty pounds a year to educate the future leaders of this country. The school in Switzerland costs more than twice that amount, even without the extras.'

DCS Ainsworth, the most highly paid detective in Lancashire, couldn't be earning more fifteen hundred quid a year, Woodend thought. Yet Punch Davies, a humble inspector, was considering sending his daughter to a school which would cost close to a thousand pounds.

'Do you have any idea where he was hopin' to get the money from?' Woodend asked.

'Yes, I do, as a matter of fact. He told me that he was due to come into an inheritance. A rich relative had died, and Mr Davies was, apparently, the sole heir to his estate.'

An' if you could swallow a story like that, Woodend thought, then swallowin' a double-decker bus should be a doddle.

Twenty-Seven

If Chief Inspector Turner's lackeys had followed his taxi out to Edna Davies' house and then on to the special school, Woodend had certainly not spotted them. But from the way the constable posted on the promenade opposite the corner of New Bonny Street was so studiously ignoring him, there could be no doubt that he was back under surveillance again now.

Woodend walked up to the constable and waved his hand in front of the man's face.

'Yes, sir?' the constable asked.

Woodend shook his head. 'Wrong reaction, lad,' he said. 'You should have seemed surprised when a complete stranger came up to you and did that.'

'I'm afraid I don't know what—?'

'Of course you don't,' Woodend agreed. 'But do you know where the nearest police phone box is?'

'Yes.'

'Good,' Woodend said. 'Now listen carefully, lad. I'm goin' in there –' he pointed to the Gay Paree Theatre – 'an' I expect to be about half an hour. Then I'll be payin' a visit to your chief inspector. I think he might appreciate some advance warnin' of that – especially when he finds out where I've been – so if I was you, I'd give him a call the moment I've gone. Understood?'

'But sir, I—'

'Just do it!' Woodend advised him.

He turned on his heel and crossed the road. The platform outside the Gay Paree was deserted and the coloured lights which spelled out its name were switched off, but that didn't necessarily mean there was no one inside. Woodend strode up

191

to the side door opposite the fish and chip shop, and began hammering furiously.

It was Clive, the barker and very amateur magician, who opened the door. He did not seem very pleased to find Woodend standing there.

'We're closed,' he said sullenly.

'Aye, so you are,' the chief inspector agreed. 'An' if you don't do exactly what I say, that could pretty soon become a *permanent* state of affairs.'

'What are you talkin' about?'

'I want to see Gutteridge. Now! Is he in his office?'

Clive shrugged. 'He was the last time I looked. You know the way, don't you?'

'I'm not sure I do yet, but I think I'm just beginnin' to find it,' Woodend said enigmatically, stepping past him and striding down the aisle.

He flung open the door of Gutteridge's office without bothering to knock. The manager was sitting behind his desk, surrounded by his tatty stage props. Woodend's visit had obviously taken him by surprise, but he soon recovered enough to stand up and hold out his hand in welcome.

'Mr Woodend,' he said. 'What an unexpected pleasure to see you again so soon.'

'Sit down!' Woodend ordered him, ignoring the hand.

The manager slunk back behind his desk, and the chief inspector took the chair opposite.

'The last time I was here, you told me you'd had a bit of trouble, an' you'd had to call in the police,' Woodend said.

'That is quite correct.'

'You also told me you'd never heard of Detective Inspector Davies.'

'As, indeed, I hadn't, save for the references to him in the newspapers.'

'We have a technical name for fellers like you in the detectin' business,' Woodend said. 'We call them "lyin' toe-rags".'

'Now look here, my dear man—' Gutteridge protested.

'Shut up!' Woodend interrupted. 'You said that when you called the local bobbies, they sent round a uniformed sergeant an' a constable. So why is there no record of any such call bein' made?'

'Could it be that policemen, like thespians, are so often caught up in their performance that they overlook the minor technical details?' Gutteridge suggested hopefully.

'As I see it, there are two possible explanations,' Woodend continued, treating the remark with the contempt it deserved. 'Either you were just spinnin' me a line to cover the blunder you'd made when you said you thought everythin' had been *taken care of* – or the incident actually *did* occur, but the officer you called came round as a personal favour. Now which is it?'

'I think it would be unwise to make any further comment until I have consulted my legal advisor,' Gutteridge said, sticking out his jaw stubbornly.

Woodend lifted up his left leg and pointed at his shoe. 'See that?' he asked. 'That's a size nine brogue.'

'I fail to see how that could be relevant to—'

'If it had been my intention to wade around in the filthy little sewer you call a business, I'd have worn wellington boots. But, you see, I've got a double murder to investigate – so I'm not particularly interested in collarin' a nasty little pimp like you.'

'Are you saying that there is still a possibility of my avoiding the full rigour of the law?'

'Aye, there could be a way to squirm out of it if you come clean now,' Woodend agreed.

Gutteridge reached for a pencil and began to roll it around nervously between his fingers.

'How can I assist your investigation?' he asked.

'I want to know how a modestly paid detective inspector thought he could raise nearly a thousand quid a year to send his kid to a special school.'

Gutteridge continued to play with the pencil. 'You must appreciate that life is rarely like drama,' he said. 'Even if one begins with a script, one finds oneself improvising well before the end of the first act.'

'So you just drifted into bein' a pimp, did you?' Woodend asked, unsympathetically.

'Throughout the whole history of the theatre there have always been men who've hovered like besotted moths around the stage door, in the hope that the artistes would show them favour.'

Woodend groaned. 'You're making my head ache,' he said, 'an' if you don't stop pissin' about an' start talkin' in plain English, I'll find a way to make yours ache an' all.'

'Are you threatening me?' the manager asked nervously.

'Aye, that's about the long an' the short of it,' Woodend agreed.

'I always advised the performers to stay clear of such men,' Gutteridge said, making an effort to use the plain English Woodend had demanded. 'But then I discovered that one of my artistes had been taking payment in return for her favours and—'

'An' you saw it as a way of supplementin' your pension fund,' Woodend said. 'So now all the girls are *expected* to turn a trick when the opportunity arises, an' you just sit back an' collect your cut.'

'I am an impresario. I provide a showcase for their talents. It is only right that I should be recompensed.'

'How does Inspector Davies fit into all this?' Woodend asked – although he thought he already knew the answer.

'Mr Davies first came to see me about a year ago. He had photographs he wished to show me.'

'Photographs of what?'

'Of some of the artistes consorting with patrons just outside the stage door of the theatre. He accused me of running a disorderly house. He said that if they found out about it, the inland revenue would be very interested in my additional source of income – and that I might even be incarcerated.'

'An' then he offered you a deal?'

'He said that in return for ten per cent of what the artistes earned, he would assume the role of protector.'

'Was it Davies you called that night you had a bit of trouble with rowdy punters?'

Gutteridge hesitated. 'Yes, it was he.'

'You don't seem very sure.'

'Once a man is caught up in a web of deception, it is sometimes difficult to unravel what is true from what is not. But it was Mr Davies, our protector, who I called on to perform his duty, you can be assured of that.'

Chief Inspector Turner had been expecting trouble since he'd got the phone call from the constable on the beat, but even so it came as something of a shock to see just how angry the man who had just burst into his office unannounced really was. He'd always known that Woodend was big, but now the man in the hairy sports coat seemed to have swollen to giant size.

'Listen, Charlie—' Turner began.

'Don't you go callin' me Charlie!' Woodend exploded. 'That's what my mates call me – an' you're about as far from bein' one of them as an Eskimo is from bein' a bloody Hottentot.'

'Listen, *Chief Inspector*—' Turner said, beginning again.

'No, you listen!' Woodend told him. 'For the last three days, while I've been doin' my damnedest to find a murderer, you've been doin' all you could to steer me into a maze. You must have been delighted when the gypsy got herself topped, because that complicated things – an' the more complicated *they* were, the happier *you* were. An' what about these uniformed bobbies you've had followin' me all mornin'? What were they for? To stop me goin' where you didn't want me to go? Or to put the wind up me, so I'd go runnin' back to Whitebridge with my tail between my legs?'

'It was a mistake to use the uniforms,' Turner admitted, 'but I had to try anything which might have a chance of throwing you off balance. Why don't you sit down, Mr Woodend?'

'Because I'm particular whose chair I plant my arse on,' Woodend retorted. 'An' because I'm not here for a cosy chat – I'm here for some answers.'

Turner sighed. 'What do you want to know?'

'You could start by tellin' me how long *you've* known that Punch Davies was on the take.'

'We still don't know for certain that he *was*.'

'Don't you? Well, I bloody do. An' I've got witnesses to

prove it.' Woodend took his Capstan Full Strength out of his pocket, and lit one up. 'All right, let's play it your way,' he continued, when he'd taken a deep drag on his cigarette. 'How long have you *suspected* that Punch Davies was on the take?'

'The first indication was early on in the season, when we started getting anonymous letters,' Turner replied. 'They all said pretty much the same thing – that there was an officer in the Blackpool force who was open to taking bribes.'

'An' what did you do about them?'

'You know yourself that people are always trying to stir up trouble by complaining about the police,' Turner said. 'And you must also be aware of the fact that there's any number of complete nutters out there who will do anything to get attention.'

'In other words, you did bugger all.'

'We filed the letters. You can see them, if you like.'

Woodend dismissed the suggestion with an impatient gesture of his hand. 'What happened next?'

'The rumours started.'

'An' where did they come from?'

Turner shrugged. 'Who's to say where rumours start?'

'But they confirmed that there was a bent bobby on the force – an' that that bobby was Davies?'

'Yes.'

'Did Punch know the rumours were circulatin'?'

'No.'

'You're sure of that?'

'I had him in the office for a quiet word. He was astounded when I told him what people had been saying.'

'Let me get this straight,' Woodend said, incredulously. 'You suspected him of corruption – an' you had him in your office to let him *know* you suspected him?'

'I wouldn't put as crudely as that.'

'Put it how you like,' Woodend countered. 'It doesn't alter the facts. I've been in this business for a long time, an' I'd never let a villain know I was on to him. Unless –' he clicked his fingers as a sudden insight hit him with the force of a sledgehammer – 'unless you *didn't want* to catch him at all. Unless you only wanted to warn him off.'

From the look on the other man's face, he knew he had hit the nail squarely on the head.

'You've never worked on a provincial force before,' Turner said. 'If you had, you'd appreciate that catching criminals is only a part of our job. Another part is to make sure that ordinary people have confidence in the police. And it's also important – especially in a town like Blackpool – that there are no scandals to frighten visitors away.'

'So you were prepared to let Davies get away with what he'd done already as long as he called it quits?'

'Who had he actually hurt?' Turner asked. 'Only the people who'd bribed him. And since they wouldn't have had to pay the bribes if they hadn't been involved in something illegal, there are those who would argue that they only got what they deserved.'

'Maybe there are people who'd argue that way,' Woodend said. 'But I'm not one of them.'

'I'd like to offer you a word of advice,' Turner said quietly.

'*You'd* like to offer *me* a word of advice?' Woodend asked, astounded. 'An' what might that word be?'

'If you're going to come out of this investigation with any credit to your name, the wisest thing you could do would be to keep Punch Davies' shady dealings as much out of the public eye as possible.'

'You do realise that Davies was probably killed because of what you call his "shady dealin'"', don't you?' Woodend demanded.

'It's a possibility – though not one we're happy to contemplate,' Turner conceded.

'So what happens when I arrest the murderer? How the bloody hell are you goin' to bring him to trial without mentionin' *why* he killed Davies?'

'Grow up, Chief Inspector,' Turner said contemptuously. 'If you offer a man a choice of being charged with the murder of his crooked business partner, or with the manslaughter of a casual acquaintance during a bout of temper – which he regretted as soon as it was over – which one do you think he's going to go for?'

'DCS Ainsworth would never accept a deal like that,' Woodend said.

Turner shook his head, almost pityingly. 'You've no idea how things really work, have you?' he asked.

'Are you sayin' that Ainsworth knew Davies was bent all along?'

'Of course he didn't know,' Turner said exasperatedly. 'He didn't *want* to know. That's why people like *me* exist – to make sure people like *him* never get their hands dirty.'

Woodend gave Turner a look which was filled with disgust. 'Not half an hour ago, I was talkin' to a feller who I thought at the time lived on the bottom of the human slime pit,' he said. 'Now, it seems to me he wasn't even halfway down.'

It was that early point in the evening which fell between the end of the last boarding house meal and the beginning of the first house of the variety shows. Woodend walked along the nearly empty street, trying to fit everything he had learned in the previous couple of hours into a coherent whole. That Davies had been bent was easy to accept – bobbies were often subjected to temptation, and in his case it did not take a great brain to work out why he had succumbed. Turner's way of dealing with the problem – while being far from something Woodend would do himself – was also at least comprehensible. What *didn't* make sense was the way Davies had behaved after Turner had tipped him the wink about his being under suspicion. Most men would have taken the hint, and lain low for a while. Davies had chosen, instead, to act in quite the opposite manner and make his presence on the Golden Mile even more conspicuous. It was almost as if he had wanted to get caught.

Maybe that was it! Woodend thought. Perhaps Davies was so eaten up by guilt that there was a part of him which demanded he should be punished.

The sound of footsteps close behind him brought an end to

his train of speculation. Despite his showdown with Turner – despite the fact that he now knew everything the local DCI had sought to hide from him – he was still being followed. He came to an abrupt halt, and swung round so suddenly that the fresh-faced DC Eliot, who had been practically at his heel, almost cannoned into him.

'Let me give you a hint, constable,' Woodend said. 'If you're ever given the job followin' somebody again, try to keep at least half a dozen cars' distance between the two of you.'

Eliot blushed furiously. 'I wasn't exactly following you, sir.'

'Then just what were you doin'?'

'I suppose I was plucking up the nerve to approach you, sir.'

'An' why would you want to do that?'

'Because there's something I think you ought to know,' Eliot said earnestly.

Something he ought to know? Woodend glanced down the street. 'Oh look, there's a pub,' he said. 'What a happy coincidence. Come on, lad, I'll buy you a pint.'

Eliot asked for a shandy and Woodend ordered a pint of best bitter for himself. At that hour, they had their choice of tables, and the chief inspector chose one well away from the prying ears of the barman.

'So what's all this about, lad?' he asked, when they were sitting down.

'It hasn't been easy for me working on this case, sir,' Eliot said. 'You're the boss and I accept that, but –'

'But all the information I've been gettin' from you has been filtered through Sergeant Hanson and Mr Turner first?' Woodend suggested.

'That's right,' Eliot agreed. 'I don't think the Sarge is any happier about it than I am, but he's got his orders.' He took an almost birdlike sip of his shandy. 'The thing is, sir, I feel like I'm walking a tightrope, and I'm doing my best not to fall off.'

'We'd all like to come out of this investigation smellin' of roses,' Woodend told him, 'but in the end we have to do what we think's right. So why don't you tell what's on your mind?'

'The other day, I was talking to a street seller on the Golden Mile, and he said that he'd seen Tommy Bolton coming out of Gypsy Elizabeth Rose's booth looking really angry.'

'It's Tommy Bolton the comedian we're talkin' about here, is it?' Woodend asked.

'That's right, sir. Anyway, I reported it to Sergeant Hanson, and he said he'd have to take it upstairs. I saw him again a couple of hours later, and he told me that he'd mentioned it to Mr Turner.'

'An' what had Mr Turner told him?'

'According to Sergeant Hanson, Mr Turner decided it had nothing to do with the case, and he saw no point in bothering a big star like Mr Bolton unnecessarily.'

'So I never got to hear about it.'

'That's right, sir.'

'An' what's made you decide to tell me about it now?'

'This morning I was talking to one of the doormen at the Central Pier theatre. I asked him – just on the off chance – if he'd known Mr Davies, and he said he had. So I asked him when was the last time he'd seen the inspector, and he said it must have been some time in the last week.'

'On the Golden Mile?'

'Yes, sir. But a bit more specific than that.'

'Spit it out, lad.'

'He said he'd seen him in the actual theatre. He turned up between shows, and said he had to talk to somebody.'

'Tommy Bolton?' Woodend guessed.

'That's right, sir. Tommy Bolton.'

Twenty-Eight

Tommy 'Now Where Was I?' Bolton stood in the centre of the stage, bathed in spotlights. He was not alone. Next to him was a slack-mouthed man dressed in a loud check jacket and an even louder cloth cap.

'I asked my wife where she'd like to go for her holidays,' Tommy Bolton told the audience. 'She said she fancied somewhere she'd never been before, so I suggested she tried the kitchen. She didn't like that.' He shook his head wonderingly, as the audience giggled. 'My wife! I've been in love with the same woman for over twenty years – and if the missis ever finds out, she'll kill me.'

There was more laughter, but Woodend, standing at the back of the hall, leant over to his sergeant and whispered, 'That joke was creakin' with age when Adam was a lad.'

'Anyway, we decided on Spain,' Bolton continued. 'The Costa Packet. We went to book the tickets and my wife said, "You'd better buy three, because my mother'll want to come."' Bolton put his hand on his hip in an exaggerated gesture. 'Now don't get me wrong, ladies and gentlemen. She's a wonderful woman, my mother-in-law – it's just that you can tell when she's knocking on the front door, because all the mice throw themselves on the traps.' He paused to allow more laughter. 'I wouldn't say she's a big woman, but she collapsed right in front of a bus last week, and the driver said that while he'd got enough *room* to get round her, he wasn't sure he'd got enough *petrol*. Still, if I'm ever told that I've only got six months to live, I'll definitely move in with her – she'll make that six months seem like it's forever.'

He paused, and frowned, as if puzzled by something.

'Now where was I?' he asked his stooge, who had not moved an inch during the entire monologue

'You were talkin' about takin' your wife on holiday to Spain,' the stooge replied in a gormless manner.

'That's right,' Bolton agreed. 'Now the thing about Spain is, most people think it's just Blackpool with a bit more sun, but they couldn't be wronger . . .'

Woodend tapped his sergeant on the shoulder. 'Mr Bolton looks like a man who appreciates surprises,' he said. 'Let's arrange one for him in his dressin' room, shall we?'

The young blonde woman who was sitting on the armchair with her legs crossed was a rather a tasty dish, Tommy Bolton decided, but he didn't at all like the look of the big feller in the hairy sports coat leaning back on the sofa. And anyway, what were they doing in his dressing room? He'd see to it that somebody lost his job for this.

'I sign autographs outside,' he said abruptly.

'I'll bear that in mind,' Woodend said, producing his warrant card. 'In the meantime, Mr Bolton, we'd like to ask you some questions.'

'Now?'

'Now.'

'Look, I've got another show to do in an hour and a half,' Bolton protested. 'I need my rest.'

'We won't keep you long,' Woodend promised him. 'At least, not half as long as we would if we had to take you down to the station.'

Bolton slumped into the free armchair. 'What's this all about?'

'I'm not entirely sure myself,' Woodend admitted. 'It's just that your name keeps croppin' up in our investigation.'

'What investigation would that be?' Bolton demanded.

'What investigation do you think it *might* be?' Woodend countered.

'Inspector Davies' murder?'

'Aye, an' Gypsy Elizabeth Rose's death, an' all.'

'But you can't think I had anything to do with them.'

Woodend turned to Paniatowski. 'I don't think I suggested that, did I, Sergeant?' he asked. 'As I recall, all I said was that his name kept croppin' up. Isn't that right?'

'Perfectly correct, sir,' Paniatowski confirmed.

'For instance, you were at the Palace Hotel, Fleetwood, the night that poor old woman was knocked down, weren't you, Mr Bolton?'

'I left well before the accident occurred,' Bolton said hotly. 'You can check on that.'

'We can, an' you did,' Woodend said easily. 'Then there was the matter of you havin' your Rolls Royce nicked from right out of your own garage.'

'You can scarcely blame me for that. I was the victim.'

'True,' Woodend agreed. 'So let's put that aside for the moment, shall we? What really bothers me is that you seem to have been acquainted with both the murder victims.'

'Hardly acquainted,' the comedian said.

'Sergeant?' Woodend said.

'You were seen leaving Gypsy Elizabeth Rose's booth – by several witnesses,' Paniatowski lied.

'Does the fact that I'm a big star mean I can't visit a fortune-teller if I want to?'

'Again, accordin' to the witnesses, you didn't look very happy,' Woodend said. 'What were the exact words one of them used, Sergeant?'

'The witness said that he looked as if he wanted to kill somebody, sir.'

'So I was in a bad mood,' Bolton conceded. 'There's no law against that, is there?'

'Depends,' Woodend said. '*Why* were you in a bad mood?'

'Somebody had told me that this particular gypsy really could look into the future, but all she did was trot out the standard clichés about a long happy life and good health. I was furious with myself for having wasted so much time on her.'

'That's plausible, isn't it, Sergeant?' Woodend asked.

'It would be if that had been the first time he'd been to see her,' Paniatowski agreed. 'But there's a photograph of the two of them posing together on the outside of the booth which was taken on another occasion. In the picture, they look like the best of friends.'

'It's very unnerving when you talk about me as though I wasn't here,' Bolton said. 'I wish you'd stop it.'

'So what about the first time you visited her?' Woodend asked, ignoring Bolton's protest. 'Did she tell you anythin' interestin' then?'

'I didn't go for a consultation. I just posed for the picture. It's something that big stars do to help out the little people along the Golden Mile.'

'I'm sure that was very kind of you,' Woodend said dryly. 'And what about Inspector Davies' visit?'

'He . . . he came to ask me a favour.'

'What kind of favour?'

'He asked me to put on a show at his daughter's school. It's something else big stars are expected to do. It's called giving something back to the local community. Not that we haven't given enough back already. Do you really think so many people would come to Blackpool if big names like me weren't appearing here?'

'An' did you?' Woodend asked.

'Did I what?'

'Did you agree to put on a show at his daughter's school?'

'No. I . . . I've got rather a busy schedule this year.'

'Aye,' Woodend agreed. 'What with tellin' mother-in-law jokes twice a night an' comperin' mucky shows for a bunch of local bigwigs, you must be rushed off your feet.'

'I'm not sure I like your attitude,' Bolton said.

'I'm bloody sure I don't like yours,' Woodend told him. He climbed to his feet. 'It's time we're off, Sergeant. Tell Mr Bolton we've finished with him for the moment, but we'll probably be back.'

'We've finished with you for the moment, but we'll probably be back,' Paniatowski said, deadpan.

Woodend grinned. 'Not a bad stooge, is she?' he asked Bolton. 'An' I bet she comes a bloody sight cheaper than yours.'

*　　*　　*

Maudsley Tower – the weather vane in the Whitebridge joke – stood on the crown of a hill overlooking the town. The monument was reached by a steep dog-legged path which began where the tarmac road finally petered out, and as dusk fell it was being climbed by a young man with a lot of things on his mind.

Bob Rutter reached the top of the hill and turned to face the valley which now lay below him. It was good to get out of town, he thought – good to be somewhere you could be completely alone with your thoughts.

The abandoned mills and other signs of industrial decay were slowly being blacked out by the falling night, and lights were coming on all over Whitebridge. It wasn't a bad place to live, Rutter decided. It couldn't, of course, be compared with London, but there were compensations. For instance, he'd seen a couple of new housing estates where he was sure he and Maria could be very comfortable. And from what he'd heard around the station, he'd have the choice of several good primary schools to send the baby to once it had turned five.

But five years was a long time. Would he still be in Whitebridge when his child was old enough to carry a satchel full of pencils and colouring books? On present indications, the answer would probably be no. He wasn't getting anywhere with this case he'd been assigned – which was probably why DCS Ainsworth had given it to him. Two cars had been stolen in the previous three days and – to all intents and purposes – they had vanished into thin air. There were no new leads. And though he'd scrupulously revisited the ground covered by the officer who'd previously been on the case – including calling in at every garage within a fifteen-mile radius of Whitebridge – he'd seen nothing in the least suspicious. Which left him precisely nowhere – the smart ex-Scotland Yard whiz kid who couldn't even crack a simple car-theft ring in the unsophisticated North.

He lit up one of the cork-tipped cigarettes which Woodend never missed an opportunity to mock as unmanly, and wished he was back working with Cloggin'-it Charlie on a nice juicy murder.

The darkness had now covered the town, and he could see at least five or six illuminated petrol station signs. Did the answer to his problems lie in one of them? he wondered. It didn't seem likely.

He turned to walk back down to where he'd left his car. In the gloom, he was going to have to tread the path carefully, he thought, then he laughed out loud as he realised his whole career with the Central Lancs police was probably going to be a matter of treading carefully.

Paniatowski was experiencing a warm glow which had very little to do with the glass of vodka sitting in front of her. What a day it had been! She had learned that Woodend trusted her and decided to trust him in return. And it was all working out! They had been a real team in there with Tommy Bolton – understanding each other and taking cues without even needing to be signalled.

'So what do you make of our Mr Bolton?' Woodend asked.

'What do *you* think, sir?'

Woodend shook his head. 'Nay, lass, it doesn't work like that. I'm the boss, so I get to speak last. That way, if you say somethin' bright an' I agree with it, that just shows how good I am. Whereas if you say somethin' *stupid* an' I agree with it, you get the blame later for leadin' me astray.'

A couple of days earlier Paniatowski might have taken the statement at face value. Now, she merely grinned.

'I don't believe his story about going to Elizabeth Rose for a consultation,' she said. 'He's far too self-centred to be really spiritual.'

'Aye,' Woodend agreed. 'If he ever gets to heaven, his first question to Saint Peter will be why it's God who's got the star billin' instead of him. What about the visit from Mr Davies?'

'I don't believe him, but I'm not quite sure why,' Paniatowski confessed.

'Then let me explain it to you,' Woodend said. 'I've seen Susan Davies, an' I've been to her school. Not all the kids are quite as slow as she is, but I'm willin' to bet there's not one of them that could follow Tommy Bolton's act. No, if Davies had been lookin' for entertainment for her, he'd have gone an' asked one of the clowns at the Tower Circus to put on a performance.'

'Maybe Bolton got it wrong,' Paniatowski suggested. 'Perhaps Davies wanted him to put on a show at his *son's* school.'

'Same difference,' Woodend said. 'There were quite a lot of kids in the theatre tonight, but how many of them did you notice laughin' at his jokes?'

'I didn't notice the audience at all, sir.'

'Then you've broken Rule Number One in the *Workin' for Charlie Woodend Manual*, which clearly states that his sergeant will notice *everythin'*.'

'I'm sorry, sir,' Paniatowski said.

'Forget it. You're new an' you're only just startin' to learn the rules,' Woodend said generously. 'But if you're still makin' the same mistakes in six months, I'll come down on you like a ton of bricks.' He paused to light up a Capstan Full Strength. 'Anyway, since you didn't notice the kids yourself, I'll tell you about them,' he continued. 'There wasn't one of them who was the least bit amused by his patter. An' why should they have been? They don't have wives who make their lives a misery – they've got parents for that. An' they don't have mother-in-laws, either – only grannies who spoil them rotten. You'd have to be an idiot to think Tommy Bolton could keep a group of children amused, an' whatever else Punch Davies was, it doesn't strike me that he was thick.'

Paniatowski glanced down at her watch.

'It's the third time you've done that in ten minutes,' Woodend said. 'Have you got an appointment or somethin'?'

'I've arranged to meet somebody for drinks.'

'Oh aye? Sergeant Hanson, is it?'

'How did you know that?'

'I obey Rule One of my own manual,' Woodend said. 'I

notice everythin'.' He took a sip of his pint. 'So tell me, do you think this thing between you an' Hanson will turn out to be serious?'

'I'd rather not discuss my private affairs, sir,' Paniatowski said, as a sliver of her old self pricked the surface.

'You can please yourself, lass,' Woodend said. 'But you'll end up tellin' me your whole life story. My sergeants always do.'

Yes, Paniatowski thought. I can believe that.

Twenty-Nine

It was half-past nine the following morning when Edna Davies heard the knock on her front door, and opening it found herself looking at a cheery young man in a smart suit who she'd never seen before.

'Yes?' she said.

The young man smiled, displaying a set of brilliant white teeth. 'Mrs Davies?' he asked.

'Yes, that's me.'

'I was wondering if *Mr* Davies was at home. I've got something to give him. He's been expecting it.'

'Mr husband is dead,' Edna said flatly.

The young man's face fell. 'Oh my God! That's terrible. Was it a sudden illness?'

'He was murdered.'

The young man shook his head from side to side. 'Terrible, terrible,' he said, sounding genuinely upset. 'I'm not used to this.'

'Neither am I!'

The young man made an effort to pull himself together. 'You don't understand,' he told her. 'People are usually so pleased to see me. It's the part of my job I like most – the expression on their faces when they realise who I am. Of course, the best of all is when I can bring the photographers with me, but even when they've put an "X" in the box because they wish to remain anonymous, as your husband did—'

'Who sent you?' Edna Davies demanded. 'Are you from some sort of evangelical church organisation, because if you are you can just—'

209

'It's nothing like that,' the young man interrupted hastily. 'Didn't your husband tell you?'

'Tell me what?'

'Oh dear,' the young man worried. 'Perhaps if he *didn't* tell you, I shouldn't say anything myself.' He turned the matter over in his mind. 'You are Mr Davies' widow, aren't you?' he said finally.

'I've already told you I am.'

'And the heir to his estate?'

'He left everything to me in his will, yes.'

'Well, in that case, I suppose it rightfully belongs to you.'

'*What* rightfully belongs to me?'

'Your husband scooped a first dividend on Littlewood's Football Pools a week last Saturday. I have the cheque in my pocket – made out to him – to the value of twenty-five thousand six hundred and eleven pounds, five shillings and ninepence.'

Bob Rutter sat as his desk, flicking through his case notes. The sign on the outside of his door said 'Detective Inspector R. Rutter', and the first few times he'd seen it, he'd felt a thrill run through his entire body. But that sensation had soon passed. He was starting to realise what it was like to be working on his own – getting precisely nowhere – and he didn't feel much like a detective inspector any more.

The phone by his elbow rang shrilly. He picked it up. 'Inspector Rutter?' the switchboard operator asked. 'I've got a call for you from the Manchester police.'

'Inspector Sam Platt here,' said a new voice. 'I thought Jed Rowe was in charge of this stolen car business.'

'He was,' Rutter replied, 'but now it's been handed on to me.'

Dumped on me would be closer to the mark, he thought.

'So you're the man I have to talk to now, are you?' Platt asked.

'That's correct.'

'Righto. Well, it looks as if we might have got a break at last. We raided a used-car lot this morning, and found several vehicles which had been reported stolen, including two – I might say – from Whitebridge. They'd been done up, of course, resprayed a different colour, and so forth, but we've checked the chassis numbers and they've been nicked, all right.'

So we get a couple of cars back, Rutter thought. Put that on the scales at the opposite end to three or four we lose every week, and my track record still doesn't look good.

'Now we come on to the good bit – at least as far as you're concerned,' Platt said. 'The dealer we've arrested was eager to make a clean breast of it as long as we were prepared to let the judge know how co-operative he'd been. And one of the first things he's told us is that this car-theft ring offers a customised service.'

'Would you mind explaining that?'

'Simplicity itself, my old son. If our laddie had a customer who wanted a cream-coloured Ford Anglia, he'd just ask for it, and it would be delivered in two or three days. And he was guaranteed that wasn't the original colour of the car.'

'But that means that the thieves must have a stock to draw on,' Rutter said.

'Just what I thought.'

'And how did he contact the thieves to place his order?'

'He didn't. They rang *him* every two or three days.'

Rutter felt the faint ember of hope which had been ignited in his bosom start to cool and die. 'So you've no idea where the cars were coming from?'

'I didn't say that, exactly. It was usually a woman who rang our laddie. He's from Whitebridge originally, and he's prepared to swear this woman had a Whitebridge accent herself. So it's just possible the headquarters of the racket is somewhere in your area.'

Rutter thanked the Manchester man and replaced the receiver. So the ring could be operating out of Whitebridge, he thought. What would it need to work properly? Somewhere to store a fair number of stolen cars, for a start – a place where they wouldn't be noticed by passers-by or nosy bobbies. And then they would also need fairly easy access to the kinds

211

of equipment necessary to modify the cars, so that if, for example, they got an order for a cream Ford Anglia and only had a black one in stock, they could spray-paint it without too many problems.

Rutter felt a smile forming across his features. He had only been in Whitebridge for a few days, and he hadn't even been over half the patch – yet he'd seen enough to realise that if he were running that kind of racket, he'd know exactly where to situate it.

Woodend gazed gloomily at Paniatowski across the table in the police canteen. 'My workin' assumption was that Inspector Davies was so desperate to get special schoolin' for his daughter that he was prepared to do anythin' to lay his hands on the money,' he said. 'Well, that theory's gone right out the window, hasn't it?'

'Not necessarily,' Paniatowski countered. 'He didn't know he was going to win the football pools and he could have been trying other – illegal – ways to obtain the money before he did.'

Woodend shook his head. 'Nice try, lass, but if that had been the case, he'd have gone to see the principal of his daughter's school as soon as he read about the place in Switzerland. But he didn't – he waited until he'd scooped his first dividend.'

'But why lie about the money? Why say he'd inherited it?'

'I've been thinkin' about that. This school he wanted to send Susan to is not only expensive – it has to be exclusive as well. They might well have looked down their noses at somebody who'd won the pools – but bein' left the money in a will is a perfectly respectable way to get rich.'

'So where does that leave us?' Paniatowski asked, her despondency matching her boss's. 'Back at Square One?'

'Not quite. Davies might have been an honest man, but we know that somebody in the Blackpool police has to be bent.'

'Because of what the manager of the Gay Paree told you?'

'Exactly,' Woodend agreed. 'Only nutters admit to crimes they haven't committed, an' Gutteridge's no nutter. So if he says he was paying off a bobby to turn a blind eye to his pimpin', he has to be tellin' the truth. But why finger Punch Davies? Because that way he could protect the feller who's really been puttin' the squeeze on him.'

'But why should he do that?'

'Because he's bloody terrified. There's a strong possibility that whoever he's been payin' the kickback to has already killed twice. Even if he hasn't, I'm almost certain *Gutteridge* thinks he has – and he'd rather go to jail than risk bein' the third victim.'

'So shouldn't we go and see Gutteridge right now, and try to sweat the truth out of him?'

'No, that wouldn't work,' Woodend said. 'If he's goin' to crack at all, he's only goin' to do it when we can threaten him with somethin' which is almost as frightenin' as the hold his protector's got over him.'

'Like what?'

'Like the prospect of a long stretch in prison, rather than the few months he'd probably serve for what he's confessed to so far.'

'And how could we convince him that there's a real possibility he'll be sent down for a long time?'

'We need to connect him with another – more serious – crime.'

'For example?'

'I'm buggered if I know,' Woodend admitted.

Bob Rutter drove past the abandoned shell of the Calcutta Mill, and pulled on to the forecourt of Grimsdyke's Garage. He had expected the old man himself to appear when he ran over the bell-wire, but instead it was his granddaughter, Jenny, who came out of the office. And she was not dressed in her usual grease monkey's overalls that morning, but instead was wearing a sombre black skirt and sweater.

'We're closed,' she said – but without any of the fire in her voice Rutter had heard the last time they'd spoken.

'Your grandfather?' he asked gently.

The girl nodded. 'He died in his sleep last night. It was all very peaceful.'

Rutter got out of his car. 'I'm sorry,' he said. 'I liked him. He was a nice old man. But I've still got business here. You know that, don't you?'

The girl nodded again. 'The first time I saw you, I knew you were going to cause trouble. But it doesn't matter now. Not with Grandad dead.'

'Shall we go and look around the mill?' Rutter suggested.

Jenny Grimsdyke shrugged indifferently. 'Why not?'

She walked round the side of the garage, then turned towards the back of the mill. She came to a halt in front of a large up-and-over metal door. The paint was peeling from it, and it looked as if it had not been used for years, but when Jenny pressed the button the engine hummed smoothly and the door began to open without even a squeak.

'This was the loading bay in the days when the mill was still a going concern,' the girl said. 'Tons and tons of cotton used to be shipped out of here every day. Not any more.'

The motor had completed its operation, and the door now lay flat against the ceiling.

Jenny and Rutter stepped inside. The loading bay was huge, and even with the couple of dozen cars parked in it, there was plenty of space to spare.

'How did you get into this racket?' Rutter asked.

'A man approached me. He said his name was Jack. He asked me if I wanted to earn a bit of extra money. I knew it was a question of either accepting his offer or closing the garage down – and closing it down would have broken my grandfather's heart.'

'How much did he pay you?'

'Not as much as he offered at first. I wouldn't take it. I didn't want a lot of cash – just enough to keep the garage open.'

'Tell me how it worked,' Rutter said.

'I'd get a phone call to say a new car was being delivered. Once it arrived, I'd be here to hide it. Every few days I'd ring the car salesrooms in Manchester and Liverpool to see what they wanted. The cars had already been resprayed before they got here, but if the customer had a special request – say he wanted black when all we'd got was green – I'd change the colour for him.'

'But they'd *already* been resprayed?'

'That's right.'

'So there were other garages involved?'

'There's a chain of them throughout the North West. It's a very slick operation. The only reason they needed me to be part of it was because I was the one with the storage space.'

'Do you know the names of any of these garages?'

'A few.'

'And would you tell me the names? It might persuade the judge to go easy on you.'

The girl shrugged. 'Why not? There's no honour among thieves, so they say, and I don't owe them anything. They were using me just as much as I was using them.'

Rutter took a quick sideways glance at Jenny Grimsdyke. For all that she'd been involved in a car-theft ring, she was still little more than a kid. And she hadn't even done it through greed – she'd just wanted her grandfather's last days on earth to be happy ones. It was awful to think of her going to prison for that, and he found himself wondering what Charlie Woodend would have done in his situation.

'I think I may have found a way out for you,' he said.

The girl looked puzzled. 'A way out?'

'It's obvious that somebody from the garage was connected with this racket – but it doesn't have to have been you.'

'What are you suggesting?'

'Your grandfather's dead. The law can't touch him now.'

'Grandad would never have been involved in anything like this!'

No, Rutter thought, though the old man must have suspected something of what was going on, otherwise he'd never have said what he had when they'd met by accident in the pub. But there was no point in telling the girl that – no point in letting her know that her attempt to keep the old man in blissful ignorance had been at least a partial failure.

'I'm sure your grandfather wouldn't have become involved,'

he said, 'but who's to know that for sure, except the two of us?'

'I won't do it!' Jenny Grimsdyke said firmly. 'And I won't allow you to do it for me.'

'You'll go to jail then.'

'I don't care.'

'For God's sake, the old man's gone!' Rutter said exasperatedly. 'His reputation won't matter to him now, one way or the other.'

'I know it won't,' Jenny agreed. 'But it still matters to me.'

'Aye, well, it's your choice,' Rutter said, thinking, even as he spoke, that he'd only been in the North for a few days, but already, when he opened his mouth, the words which came out sounded like Charlie Woodend's.

It was just after two o'clock in the afternoon when Woodend marched – unannounced, as usual – into Chief Inspector Turner's office.

'I think my lad, Rutter, might have solved one of Punch Davies' cases for you,' he said, without preamble.

'The hit-and-run?'

'Talk sense! Bob's in Whitebridge, and the hit-an'-run took place in Fleetwood. He's a bloody good detective, but even he couldn't crack an investigation from that distance.'

'Then it must be the stolen car ring.'

'That's right,' Woodend agreed. 'A couple of hours ago he raided a garage in Whitebridge an' came up with the names of several other garages involved in the racket. One of them is right here in Blackpool. So what are you goin' to do about it? Raid the place – or sweep it under the carpet because it wouldn't be good for the town's image to expose some home-grown crime?'

Turner's face flushed with anger. 'That was uncalled for!' he said.

'That's only your opinion,' Woodend countered. 'Well, are you goin' to raid the place or not?'

Turner reached for the telephone. 'Yes, I'm going to raid it,' he said through clenched teeth.

'Well, if you don't mind, I think I'll come along for the ride,' Woodend told him.

'And what if I do mind?'

'I'll come along anyway.'

'You're here to investigate two murders, not a car-theft ring,' Turner reminded him. 'This is none of your business.'

'It was my lad who did all the footwork, an' I want to make sure that nothin' happens to take any of the credit away from him,' Woodend said.

Turner's face was bright red, and the veins on his forehead so prominent that they looked as if they might explode.

'Are you saying that you don't trust us?' he demanded.

'Funny you should mention it,' Woodend replied, calmly. 'That's exactly what I'm sayin'.'

Thirty

The Excelsior Garage and Used-Car Salesrooms was located on the edge of Blackpool, just beyond Boundary Park. It had a smart, freshly painted frontage and a plate-glass window which positively shone in the sunlight. A number of fairly new second-hand cars stood on the forecourt, all of them – Woodend was prepared to bet – legitimately acquired.

'I do like criminals who use their brains – they're a lot more fun to catch than the other sort,' the chief inspector said.

'I beg your pardon, sir?' said Monika Paniatowski, who was sitting behind the wheel of the unmarked police Humber.

'I like the ones who use their brains,' Woodend repeated. 'Look at this place. It seems to be a successful business in its own right, an' if you're involved in anythin' crooked, that's exactly how your business *should* seem. The best place to hide a piece of straw is in a haystack, an' the best place to hide a stolen car is in a busy garage.'

An innocent-looking black van appeared in the rear-view mirror. 'Here come the local lads,' Paniatowski said.

'Aye, let's hope they've enough sense to carry out a raid without trippin' over their own feet,' Woodend replied.

A second black van was making its way along the road behind the garage, which was parallel to the one they were parked on. Both vans stopped simultaneously and the back doors were flung open, disgorging a couple of dozen men in pointed blue helmets.

The second their feet touched the ground, the policemen broke into a run, heading for the garage. 'They're not makin' a bad job of it for local flatfeet,' Woodend admitted.

Some of the officers had already entered the front of the building. Woodend reached across and opened his door.

'Right then,' he said, 'let's go an' see what treasures Aladdin's cave has got to offer us.'

By the time the chief inspector and his sergeant had reached the building, the uniformed officers had fanned out. Some of them were already keeping a watchful eye on the half-dozen mechanics whose work they'd disturbed. The rest were scouring the area for anybody who might have gone into hiding.

Woodend surveyed the workshop. It was a big place, with several pits and a couple of hydraulic ramps. Three cars were in the process of being repaired, and another four were waiting to be dealt with. The whole establishment gave off the impression of being an efficient, well-organised business.

'Are you in charge here?' asked an angry voice to Woodend's left.

The chief inspector turned to find himself looking at a fat man in a shiny blue suit.

'I said, are you in charge?' the man repeated.

Woodend looked around for Chief Inspector Turner. 'I appear to be – for the moment,' he conceded.

'Well, I want to know what the bloody hell's goin' on,' the fat man said.

'That's easy. We have received information which leads us to believe that you are dealin' in stolen cars.'

'Stolen cars!' the fat man repeated incredulously.

'Cars which have been stolen,' Woodend amplified.

'All these cars were brought in by regular customers,' the fat man protested. 'I've got the paperwork to prove it.'

'Then I'd appreciate it if you'd show it to me,' said a fresh voice – that of the newly arrived Chief Inspector Turner.

'You'd better come to the office,' the fat man told him.

The 'office' was no more than a partitioned-off cubicle at the far end of the garage. Woodend watched as the fat man led Turner to it, and then rummaged though his desk drawer for the logbooks.

'I'm startin' to get a very bad feelin' about this,' Woodend said worriedly.

'So am I,' Paniatowski admitted.

'We should have waited until another car had gone missin', then raided the place in the middle of the night,' the chief inspector said. 'If we'd done it that way, we'd have caught them red-handed in the act of sprayin' the thing. But Turner wouldn't wait. Once he'd finally decided he was goin' to do the job he's paid for, he was all for goin' in mob-handed right away.'

'Maybe you shouldn't have told him anything about the ring until the moment when you wanted him to raid the garage,' Paniatowski suggested.

'Rule Number Two in the *Workin' for Woodend Manual*,' the chief inspector said. 'If I've made a mistake, you point it out to me in such a way as to suggest you don't even know you're doin' it.'

Paniatowski looked up at her boss, saw he was grinning, and grinned back. 'I'll remember that,' she promised.

Turner and the fat man had emerged from the office. Even from a distance, it was possible to see the look of perverse satisfaction on the local chief inspector's face.

Turner drew level with them, and came to a halt. 'So "your lad, Rutter" was convinced this garage was dealing in stolen cars, was he?' he asked.

'That's right,' Woodend agreed.

'Well, let me tell you something, Chief Inspector, the place is as clean as a whistle.'

Woodend scanned the garage. Maintenance pits, hydraulic lifts. Boxed-in office in one corner, pile of tyres in the other. But it was a bloody *big* pile of tyres, Woodend thought – enough for half the cars in Blackpool.

'I'd like a couple of your lads to shift them tyres for me,' he told Turner.

'What for?' the fat man in the shiny blue suit asked – and for the first time there was a suspicion of panic in his voice.

'What for?' Woodend repeated. 'Because I'd like to see what's underneath them.'

It required the removal of only a few of the tyres for it to be obvious that there was indeed something underneath them – and that the something was a car covered with a tarpaulin.

Not a small family car, either, Woodend thought. Whatever make it was, it was a big bugger.

'Leave the tyres that are stacked along the side alone for a minute,' he told the constables. 'Concentrate your efforts on clearin' the ones that are coverin' the bonnet.'

'You know what it is under there, don't you?' Paniatowski asked.

'I won't be certain until we've stripped back the tarpaulin,' Woodend told her. 'But I'd be lyin' if I said I didn't have a pretty good idea.'

The tyres had been lifted away. One of the constables took hold of the edge of the tarpaulin, and began to peel it carefully back. When he'd uncovered enough to make it worthwhile, Woodend stepped forward to examine it.

'Well, well, well,' he said. 'A Rolls Royce Silver Cloud. An' from the size of that dent on the wing, I'd say it's had a nasty bump.'

Tommy Bolton was sitting in his living-room when he saw the black Humber pull outside the bungalow.

It didn't *have* to be the police! he told himself. It didn't have to be them at all!

And then he saw the bulky man and blonde woman climb out of the car – and knew that it was.

Flight was his first thought – but how far would he get? No distance at all! And so, instead of making a dash for the back door, he walked over to the cocktail cabinet and poured himself a stiff whisky.

He had all but downed his drink when the bell rang. On shaky legs, he walked up the hallway and opened the door. He had hoped for a miracle – hoped that Woodend and Paniatowski were going elsewhere, and all he would be faced with was a door-to-door brush salesman. But it seemed that, for him at least, the age of miracles had finally passed.

'We'd like a word, Mr Bolton,' Woodend said gravely. 'Well, considerably more than *one* word, if the truth be told.'

'What if I don't want to talk to you?'

'That's your privilege, sir, but we'll search your house anyway.'

'Have you . . . have you got a warrant?' Bolton spluttered.

'Oh yes, indeed.' Woodend patted his inside pocket. 'Want to see it?'

Bolton shook his head. What would be the point? What was the point of *anything*, any more? His career would be in ruins whatever happened. He might just as well get the whole thing over with as soon as possible.

He led them into his expensively furnished lounge and offered them seats. Paniatowski took an armchair and Woodend the sofa, just as they had done the previous evening in his dressing room. Bolton himself had intended to remain standing, but when Woodend gestured him towards the other armchair, he couldn't find the courage to argue.

The comedian swallowed. 'Now, what's all this about?' he asked.

'We've found your car,' Woodend said.

'Where?'

'Where you – or one of your associates – left it. In the Excelsior Garage.' Woodend crossed his legs. 'The reason it was there was because it had a bit of a bump on it that needed fixin'. Of course, if it had been an ordinary car, the work would have been finished long ago. But it's not that simple with a Rolls. Everythin' about the car is quality. You can't just get spare parts an' paint for it from your local wholesaler. You have to order them from the manufacturer – an' that takes time.'

'My car was stolen,' Bolton said. 'Where it ended up is nothing to do with me.'

'That story might just have held water if you'd reported the car stolen *before* the hit-an'-run in Fleetwood,' Woodend said. 'But you didn't, did you? You waited till a couple of days *after* the accident. And why? Because until then you had nowhere to hide it.'

'It's not true!' Tommy Bolton gasped. 'None of it's true.'

'It's *all* true,' Woodend contradicted him. 'We know you knocked down that poor old woman, an' now we've got your

222

car it should be easy enough to prove. There'll be traces of hair an' fibre all over the front of the Rolls. Blood, as well, I should think. An' as if all that wasn't enough, there's a wound down the dead woman's back which should be a perfect match to the edge of the Spirit of Freedom ornament on your bonnet.' He reached in his pocket for his cigarettes. 'The game's up, Mr Bolton. Your best option now would be to try an' get us on your side by makin' a clean breast of it.'

Bolton nodded fatalistically. 'I was very nervous about making a good impression on the Golden Milers that night, and I must have had too much to drink,' he admitted. 'But it wasn't until we were getting into the car, at round about eleven o'clock, that I realised just how drunk I was. I knew it would be stupid to drive through Fleetwood in that condition, so I parked the car a little way along the promenade, and tried to sober up. I thought I *was* sober when I set out again, just after midnight. I swear I did. But I still didn't see the old woman on the crossing, and I slammed right into her.'

'You drove back here, an' parked the Rolls in your garage,' Woodend said. 'An' that's where it stayed for the next two or three days, with you goin' spare about what to do with it. Then somebody you trusted suggested he could get it fixed at the Excelsior Garage.'

'Somebody I trusted!' Bolton repeated, spitting out the words as though they were a curse.

'All right, let's say somebody you were *forced* to trust,' Woodend amended. 'Once the Rolls was safely in the Excelsior's hands, you reported it stolen – just in case your neighbours noticed that it was missin'. But your plan was always to have the bobbies find it again once the repairs had been done.'

'Yes, that's right,' Bolton admitted, defeatedly. 'Have we done now?'

'No, we haven't. Not by a long chalk. Tell us about Gypsy Elizabeth Rose.'

'I went to see her – but you already know that.'

'Yes, we do. But we'd like you to tell us *why* you went to see her.'

'Why? Because I'm bloody stupid, that's why.' Bolton

spread out his hands as if he were begging for their understanding. 'Look, I'd killed an old woman. It was an accident, but she was still dead. I felt terrible. I thought it would make things a bit easier to bear if I talked them through with someone else. You've seen that sign on Elizabeth Rose's booth yourselves, haven't you? "Are you looking for a real friend?" it says. "One to whom you can tell all your worries and problems?" Well, I needed a friend, so I went to see her.'

'An' told her all the details?'

'Of course I didn't tell her all the details,' Bolton said contemptuously. 'I was vague. I said I'd been involved in an accident a couple of years ago in which somebody had died – and I was feeling guilty about it.'

'But she wasn't fooled?'

'She couldn't have been, or the man wouldn't have come round to see me in my dressing room the next night.'

'What man?'

Bolton shook his head violently. 'I'm not going to tell you his name.'

'Why not?'

'Because I've got no proof that we ever met, so it's only his word against mine.'

'What's the real reason?' Woodend asked.

Bolton gulped. 'Because he terrifies me.'

'We can protect you,' Woodend said.

'No, you can't. Not from him. He'll find a way to get at me, wherever you put me.'

'Not if we arrest him too.'

'I'm not going to tell you who he is,' Bolton said firmly.

They could push him harder, Woodend thought, but then he would clam up and refuse to tell them the rest of his story. Better – far better – to get that story now, and return to the question of the mystery man later.

'What did this unnamed feller who came round to your dressin' room have to say for himself?' he asked.

'He said he knew that I'd knocked down the old woman, but he was prepared to help me. He had contacts who could fix the Rolls, and once that was done, I'd be safe.'

'What did he want in return?'

'He said he wasn't a greedy man. He'd be happy with ten per cent of my income.'

'An' you agreed?'

'What choice did I have?'

'Did you make the connection between him an' Gypsy Elizabeth Rose right away?' Woodend asked.

'No. I was so confused it took me quite a while to work it out, but the moment I did, I went straight round to see her.'

'She didn't deny it?'

'Far from it. She laughed in my face. And then she told me not to feel too bad about it – because I wasn't the only mug who'd fallen into the trap. Not by any means. There were half a dozen of us paying off her partner.'

'Tell us about the visit Inspector Davies paid on you. He didn't really want you to perform at his daughter's school, did he?'

'No. He said he knew that I was in trouble, and if I'd tell him everything I knew he'd help me in any way he could.'

'He didn't want anything else?'

'Like what?'

'He didn't ask you for money, for example?'

'No. He said his own reputation was in danger, and doing what he could to protect it was all he cared about.'

'Did you tell him what he wanted to know?'

'How could I? The man who was blackmailing me was a criminal. As long as I gave him what he wanted, I could trust him. But Davies struck me as an honest man, and there was no way *he* was going to completely overlook what I'd done.'

'Did you kill Gypsy Elizabeth Rose?' Woodend demanded.

'No!' Bolton gasped. 'I thought about it often enough but I . . . but I . . .'

'But you didn't have the balls for it?' Woodend supplied. 'I believe you. Knockin' down innocent old ladies when you're pissed out of your head is much more your style.' He paused, and allowed a comical, bemused expression to come to his face. 'Now where was I?' he asked Paniatowski.

'You were about to charge Mr Bolton with manslaughter,' the sergeant said.

'That's right,' Woodend agreed. 'Thomas Malcolm Bolton, I am chargin' you with the manslaughter of Ethel Phyllis Bainbridge. You are not obliged to say anythin', but anythin' you do say will be taken down an' may be used in evidence against you.'

It had just turned half-past nine in the evening when Woodend and Paniatowski left Blackpool central police station. They had been questioning Tommy Bolton, in relay, since they'd arrested him – and they both felt like wet rags.

'He'll have to break in the end,' Paniatowski said wearily. 'He'll have to give us the name of the man who was black-mailing him.'

'I'm not so sure of that,' Woodend replied. 'He's a bit like Gutteridge in that respect. As things stand, he won't do more than a few years in jail, an' that can seem a very attractive prospect to a man who's frightened that the only alternative is bein' murdered. An' he *is* frightened of bein' murdered. He's scared witless. Anyway, it doesn't matter – we probably won't need him.'

'Won't we?'

'I don't think so,' Woodend said. 'Everythin' I need to solve this crime is up there in my head. The only thing that's holdin' me back now is that the puzzle's still in separate pieces, an' my brain needs a bit of time to slot all them together.'

'It's as simple as that?' Paniatowski asked.

'Nay, lass, it's as *complicated* as that,' Woodend told her.

They had drawn level with a pub called the Green Man. Without saying another word, the chief inspector took his sergeant by the arm and steered her inside.

Woodend walked up to the bar. 'Do you sell wine?' he asked.

'Only by the bottle.'

'That'll suit us.' He turned back to Paniatowski. 'There's a phone over there. Ring Frank Hanson an' tell him you're very sorry but you can't see him tonight because you're out drinkin' with your boss.'

Paniatowski made the call, and then joined Woodend at the table. Though the sergeant tried to draw him out on the case, the chief inspector seemed reluctant to discuss it further, and they ended up talking about Woodend's experiences as a soldier in war-torn Europe, and Paniatowski's as a refugee.

The first bottle of wine was soon empty, and Woodend ordered a second. When they'd killed that, too, he signalled the waiter again and asked for two double scotches.

'I'd prefer vodka if they have any,' Paniatowski said.

'Is that what you drank the other night, when you were out with your boyfriend?' Woodend asked.

'No, we drank scotch then,' Paniatowski admitted.

'Then that's what we'll drink now,' Woodend said sharply.

For a while after his uncharacteristic outburst, the conversation was stilted and awkward, but by the time they were both halfway down their second glasses of whisky they were relaxed in each other's company again – and with the third they were laughing and joking like old friends.

It was only when Woodend ordered a fourth glass, just before closing time, that Paniatowski balked. 'I've had enough,' she said.

'One more won't do you any harm,' Woodend told her.

'Really, sir, I'd rather not.'

The waiter placed the two glasses on the table. Woodend looked from Paniatowski's face to the whisky, and then back again.

'Drink it, Sergeant!' he said. 'And that's an order!'

Paniatowski drifted hazily in and out of awareness. One moment she and Woodend were in the Green Man, the next they were walking along the promenade, with the chief inspector's arm around her waist to steady her. She was drunk, she thought in disgust. Disgracefully drunk. And it wasn't even her fault!

Another blink – another split second she hardly noticed – and they were climbing the stairs inside the Sea View Hotel.

'Have you got your key?' Woodend asked, in a voice which – to Paniatowski – seemed very loud and very hollow.

'My wha . . . ?'

'Your key. We're outside your door.'

Paniatowski fumbled in her handbag for what felt like an eternity, before eventually finding the key. She knew she wouldn't be able to slide it into the lock herself, and so she handed it to Woodend.

A sudden feeling of betrayal swept over her. She had forced herself to trust this man – it hadn't been easy, but she'd done it. And what was her reward for her efforts? He was about to revert to type – to act like every lecher she'd ever taken pains to keep at arm's length!

'So wha' happens now?' she slurred angrily. 'You shay . . . say you'll just tuck me up in bed, and then I don' remember anything else until I wake up in the morning and find you snoring next to me?'

'You're old enough to tuck yourself in bed, even if you are pissed,' Woodend told her. 'And if you think I'm the sort of man to take advantage of this situation, then you don't really know me.' He pushed the door open. 'There you are, lass. Set a straight course for your bed, and you should be all right.'

'Whash goin' on?' Paniatowski demanded. 'If you din' wan' to take me to bed, why did you get me drunk?'

'It was an experiment,' Woodend said.

'An ess . . . periment?'

'That's right. I had a theory that needed testin' out.' He patted her on the head in an avuncular fashion. 'Get a good night's sleep, lass, an' I'll see you in the mornin'. At eight o'clock, sharp, mind! Don't be late.'

'I won' be late,' Paniatowski said, as she tottered unsteadily in the general direction of her bed. 'I'm very reliable. Well kno' for it.'

The bed was closer than she'd calculated it was. Her left kneecap struck the edge of it, and she fell forward, sprawling on the counterpane.

'Shit!' she mumbled into her bedding.

Behind her there was a soft click, as Woodend, still standing in the passage, gently closed the door.

Thirty-One

A s Woodend tucked into his cooked breakfast, he found his mind turning to thoughts of Rutter. Bob had a strong stomach for most things, but after a night on the booze even the sight of *someone else's* fry-up was enough to make him look queasy. Paniatowski seemed to be made of sterner stuff, in this respect at least. Not only did his breakfast not repulse her, but she was making a fair stab at demolishing her own.

'How are you feelin'?' he asked.

'Fine,' Paniatowski replied, slicing with vigour into her thick pork sausage.

'No hangover?'

'I never have a hangover,' Paniatowski said – and then she frowned, because that was no longer quite true.

She looked out of the window, and then back at Woodend. There was something else which needed to said, she thought, and the sooner it was said, the better.

'About last night, sir –' she began.

'Yes?'

'I'm sorry I accused you of wanting to get into my knickers.'

'It was quite understandable, given the circumstances,' Woodend said. 'I'm sorry I had to get you drunk.'

'Why *did* you do that?'

'Like I said at the time, it was necessary research.'

'Necessary for what?'

'If I'm right about this case, that'll soon become self-evident. An' if I'm not, all it'll mean is that I've spent a couple of quid needlessly.' Woodend pushed his empty plate aside and lit a cigarette. 'As soon as you've finished eatin', we're off to Fleetwood.'

'Why Fleetwood?' Paniatowski asked.

'Because when we were in Tommy's Bolton's bungalow yesterday, he said somethin' which I considered was highly significant – an' which seems to have gone completely over your head.'

Paniatowski glanced up at Woodend's face to see if he was joking, and decided that he wasn't.

'What did I miss?' she asked.

'He was talkin' about havin' too much to drink that night at the Palace Hotel, an' his exact words were: "It wasn't until we were gettin' into the car that I realised just how drunk I was." That's why we're goin' to Fleetwood, Sergeant – to find out exactly who this "we" were.'

The Gay Paree Theatre had not closed its doors until nearly midnight, and after that Gutteridge had stayed behind – drinking neat gin and thinking gloomily about his future – so the loud hammering on his flat door at just before ten o'clock the following morning came as something of a shock to his system.

He slipped on his faded silk dressing gown and staggered up the hall. 'Who's there?' he moaned.

'Police!' said a voice from the other side.

'I have no wish to speak to you.'

'Open the door, or I'll kick it down,' Woodend threatened.

Reluctantly, Gutteridge slid back the bolt. The second he'd opened the door, Woodend and his sergeant barged past him and marched into the living-room as if they owned the place.

'This is an unforgivable intrusion,' Gutteridge protested weakly. 'I do have rights, you know.'

'Important people have rights,' Woodend told him, cuttingly. 'Doctors, businessmen – all the people who belong to the Golden Mile Association. But a seedy little filth merchant like you havin' rights? Don't make me laugh.'

'I'm an impresario,' Gutteridge whined.

'You're a pimp – which is how you got tangled up in this

whole bloody mess in the first place,' Woodend said. 'The Golden Mile Association wanted a bit of entertainment laid on for their "do". They asked Tommy Bolton if he'd provide it, an' because he was suckin' up to them in the hope they'd invite him to join, he agreed. But the thing was, they wanted a little bit more than mother-in-law jokes. They wanted some smut. An' where was Bolton to get it from? Why, from you!'

'We did nothing to contravene the law.'

Woodend glared at him. 'Did I give you permission to talk?'

'No, but—'

'Then don't! When I want you to say somethin', you'll be the first to know. Bolton came an' asked for your help, an', for a fee, you provided it. But that's not the really interestin' bit. While you were lyin' in your pit, we've been out at the Palace Hotel, talkin' to the staff. Some of their stories contradicted each other – well, you'll always get that – but one thing they're agreed on is that when Bolton left in that Rolls Royce of his, you were sittin' in the passenger seat.'

'I was born to own a Rolls Royce, but until that night I'd never even ridden in one,' Gutteridge said sadly.

'You're talkin' without permission again,' Woodend told him. 'I won't warn you a third time.' He made his Tommy Bolton face. 'Now where was I?'

'Bolton and Gutteridge left the Palace Hotel in Bolton's Rolls Royce,' Paniatowski prompted.

'That's right,' Woodend agreed. 'The same Rolls Royce which, just over an hour later, killed an old lady in the centre of Fleetwood.'

'What!' Gutteridge gasped.

'It's true enough,' Woodend said. 'The car's all the evidence we need. Tommy Bolton was arrested last night.'

'But we're not convinced he's the one we want to charge,' Paniatowski said.

Woodend shot her an angry look. 'That's enough, Sergeant,' he said.

The implication of Paniatowski's words sank in to Gutteridge's drink-befuddled brain. 'You're suggesting that *I* was behind the wheel?' he croaked.

'Bolton says you were,' Paniatowski lied.

'I've told you that's enough, Sergeant,' Woodend rasped.

'Can I . . . can I tell you what really happened?' Gutteridge pleaded.

Woodend nodded. 'Aye, go on.'

'It had been our intention to return to Blackpool immediately, but instead of turning right, Bolton turned left. I asked him what he imagined he was doing, and he replied that he was too intoxicated to drive at that moment, and would need some time to collect himself. He pulled into the side of the road, slumped over the steering wheel, and instantly fell into a drunken sleep.'

'And you couldn't resist the temptation to push him into the passenger seat, get behind the wheel yourself, and take the Rolls for a spin,' Paniatowski said.

'No, I—'

'I've told you before, Sergeant, we'll hear both sides of the story before we make up our minds,' Woodend said. 'Carry on, Mr Gutteridge.'

'I had no idea for how long he would be dead to the world, and I'd no intention of waiting to find out. I abandoned him to the dubious pleasure of his own company, and caught the last tram back to Blackpool.'

Paniatowski snorted her disbelief, and Woodend said, 'Have you got any witnesses to that?'

'Witnesses?' Gutteridge asked, feeling the panic inside him growing. 'The conductor! Perhaps the conductor will remember me.'

'Bound to,' Paniatowski agreed. 'After all, they only work about sixteen hours a day in the season, and they can't see more than a few thousand passengers during that time. I'm sure we'll have no difficulty in finding one who remembers bringing back a particular passenger on the last tram from Fleetwood – over a week ago.'

'Could you describe him for us?' Woodend suggested.

'I . . . I didn't really notice very much about him. He was

around thirty, I think. Possibly thirty-five. Or maybe even a little older.'

'Height?'

'I'm not sure.'

'You wouldn't like to make things a bit easier for us by admittin' straight away that you were the one who was drivin' the car when it hit the old lady, would you?' Woodend asked hopefully.

'I . . . I . . . I didn't even know Bolton's Rolls had been involved in the accident until you just told me.'

Woodend and Paniatowski exchanged sceptical looks. 'Well, maybe the conductor who brought you back to Blackpool will come forward, and we'll able to cross you off the list,' Woodend said, with a total lack of conviction. 'But in the meantime, don't even *think* of leavin' Blackpool without informin' us first.' He turned towards the door. 'Come on, Sergeant, we've got work to do.'

Paniatowski nodded, and followed him into the hallway.

Gutteridge listened to their retreating footsteps and the sound of his front door clicking closed behind them. Almost without realising he was doing it, he began pacing the floor.

Bolton says I was the one who killed the old woman! his mind screamed.

He'd denied it, and would continue to deny it. But who were the police likely to believe – one of the most popular entertainers in the country, or a man who ran a seedy strip show?

It seemed they had already made up their minds. And even if they hadn't yet, Tommy Bolton had the money to hire the most expensive lawyers in the country, whereas he . . .

Gutteridge walked over to the phone, and dialled a local number he'd been told to use only in times of emergency.

'Yes?' asked a gruff voice on the other end of the line.

'It is I. Gutteridge.'

'You're lucky to find me in. What do you want?'

'The police have just left me,' Gutteridge babbled. 'Chief Inspector Woodend, and his sergeant. Woodend more than implied that he's contemplating charging me with a hit-and-run accident I'm totally innocent of.'

'So what do you expect me to do?'

'If they do arrest me, I'll tell them about all the other things as well. I won't be able to help myself.'

'Stop beating about the bush, and tell me what it is you want.'

'Money,' Gutteridge said. 'If I am to escape from this dreadful place, I'll need cash. At least a couple of hundred pounds.'

'That shouldn't be any problem. Why don't I bring it round to your flat?'

'No!' Gutteridge gasped, remembering what had happened to Gypsy Elizabeth Rose. 'No, it will have to be somewhere public.'

'But not *too* public,' the other man cautioned. 'I don't want to be seen meeting you by somebody I know. Especially since you're about to do a disappearing act.' He fell silent for a few seconds. 'I've got it!' he continued. 'Why don't we meet at the top of the Tower? There'll be plenty of people around, but they'll all be holidaymakers, so they won't recognise either of us.'

That made sense, Gutteridge thought. 'When?' he asked.

'Say in half an hour. But don't you approach me. I'll make sure it's safe first, and then I'll come to you. Agreed?'

'Agreed,' Gutteridge said.

It was still too early in the day for the Tower to have attracted a lot of visitors, but Gutteridge was a little reassured by the fact that there were five other people with him in the lift which journeyed through the centre of the hollow cast-iron frame. Five witnesses at least, then, to his meeting with the man who made his bowels turn to water – and the chances were there were others already on the platform. He should be safe under their watchful eyes – and within an hour he would have left Blackpool forever!

The lift came to a slightly juddering halt, and Gutteridge heard the woman standing beside him let out a sigh of relief. She had nothing to be frightened of, he thought viciously. She didn't know what *real* fear was.

He stepped out on to the observation platform which circled the apex of the Tower. Ahead of him was the chest-high rail and, projecting out of that, the mesh fence which had been erected to prevent accidents and deter all but the most determined suicides.

Gutteridge counted the number of people he could see on the platform. Twelve. Still perfectly satisfactory.

He walked over to the rail, and looked down on the street, nearly five hundred feet below. From here the cars looked like no more than toys, and the bustling people smaller than the tiniest of ants. He checked his watch. It was nearly thirty-five minutes since he had made his appointment. His man should here by now.

The lift had reached the loading area again. The operator opened the gate, and the two families who had been waiting for it stepped forward. Suddenly a man in a smart blue suit was standing between them and the lift, waving what looked like an official card.

'Sorry, ladies and gentlemen,' he said, 'but the lift will be out of action for the next few minutes.'

'Here, who are you to go tellin' them that?' the lift operator complained. 'I'm in charge here. I say when the lift is or isn't workin'.'

The man in the blue suit swung round and showed the operator his warrant card.

'Police!' he said authoritatively. 'You've just taken a dangerous criminal up to the platform, and I don't want any of these innocent people going anywhere near him.'

'Dangerous criminal?' the operator repeated. 'Oh well, that's different.'

The man in the blue suit stepped into the lift. 'Take me up to the platform,' he said. 'If anybody, other than the man I'll point out to you, wants to come down, you're to bring them immediately. But under no circumstances are you to take anybody else *up* to the platform until I say it's safe. Have you got that?'

'Yes,' the lift operator told him. 'I've got it.'

Gutteridge heard the lift coming, and turned expectantly

when the gates clanked open. The man in the blue suit looked straight at him, then turned and said something into the lift operator's ear. The operator nodded. The man in the blue suit stepped on to the platform and walked around to the other side of the tower. A young couple, holding on to the hands of their two children tightly, took his place in the lift, and the operator slammed the gate closed. With a whirr from the engine, the lift began its descent.

Gutteridge glanced nervously around him. The man in the blue suit was still out of sight on the other side of the platform. But why should that matter? All he was doing was being cautious. Wasn't he? He'd said he'd bring the money, and the leather briefcase he'd had in his hand when he stepped out of the lift was proof that he'd kept his promise. It was all going according to plan. It was all . . . going . . . according to plan.

His breathing was coming harder and faster, his vision was beginning to blur slightly and his hands felt as if they had turned to ice. Gutteridge reached forward and grasped the rail for support.

The whole of Blackpool was spread out before him. He could see the miles of golden sands, stretching as far as Fleetwood in one direction and Lytham in the other. He could see the three piers projecting out into the sea, and the tramcars making their way along the promenade. He was a long way up, he realised – higher than anyone ever should be.

The man in the blue suit had appeared again, and was talking to a group of the sightseers.

Why was he talking to them? Gutteridge's panicked mind screamed. The whole point of the two of them meeting at the top of the Tower was so they wouldn't be noticed – and yet there he was making himself conspicuous!

The lift had returned, and there seemed to be a sudden rush for it. Gutteridge counted heads. Five adults and three children! Eight people! All his remaining witnesses!

As they entered the lift, he moved forwards it himself, but the operator held out his arm, barring the way.

'Sorry, mate. There's no room for any more.'

'But there's plenty of room!' Gutteridge protested. 'You could fit at least a dozen more people in there.'

'Have to follow regulations,' the operator said stubbornly. 'Can't take any more.'

He slid the door closed and turned the handle. The lift began to sink out of sight.

I should have forced my way in, Gutteridge thought. He'd have had let me in if I'd made trouble.

But it was too late for that now. The lift had gone, and he and the man in the blue suit were all alone on platform – no more than a few feet apart.

'G-give me the money,' he stuttered, reaching out for the briefcase. 'G-give me the money and I'll be out of your life for ever.'

The other man smiled, and took a step backward. 'If only it were as simple as that,' he said. 'If only I felt I could trust you.'

'You can trust me,' Gutteridge assured him.

'No, I can't. The police will catch up with you in the end, and when they do you'll tell them everything you know.'

'I won't. I promise I won't.'

The man in the blue suit glanced at wire. 'There's only one solution to the dilemma we're facing – and we both know what that is,' he said.

'No!' Gutteridge croaked.

'Yes,' the other man said firmly. 'Only one solution, but two ways of bringing it about. The easy way is for you climb up the wire and jump. It will all be over very, very quickly. The hard way is for you to resist. If you do that, then I'll knock you unconscious, pull you up the wire and throw you over. When they ask me what happened, I'll say I tried to stop you killing yourself, but I wasn't in time.'

'Nobody will believe you!'

'*Everybody* will believe me.'

'There'll be marks of the struggle on my body!'

'Do you really think they'll survive a five hundred foot drop?'

It was true, Gutteridge thought. It was all so horribly true.

He was going to die – and there was nothing he could do about it. And yet he still couldn't bring himself to climb over the netting.

He heard the lift start its ascent again, and felt a faint glimmer of hope. If he could scream – if he could just attract the operator's attention . . .

The man in the blue suit closed the gap between them at lightning speed, and struck Gutteridge hard at a pressure point on his forehead.

The theatre manager's knees buckled, and he fell to the ground, unconscious. His attacker was well aware that he did not have long for the next phase of the operation – but he didn't need long. He grabbed Gutteridge under the armpits and hauled him to his feet. A few seconds was all it would take. Half a minute at the most. He looked up at wire, assessing his task.

The lift gate creaked open, and Woodend stepped out. He turned and saw the two figures – one lifeless, the other manhandling him.

'It's over,' he said. 'Your best plan now would be to come quietly, Sergeant Hanson.'

Thirty-Two

It was rather early in the day to go on to the vodka, but when the waiter asked what they wanted, Paniatowski ordered a double anyway.

'I'm sorry it had to be Sergeant Hanson,' Woodend said.

Paniatowski shrugged. 'It was who it was,' she replied, hoping that the chief inspector would leave it there.

'If you ever want to come to terms with your feelin's, you'll have to learn to stop denyin' them in the first place,' Woodend told her.

Paniatowski felt anger start to bubble up inside her. 'He was a fling – that's all,' she said. 'He meant nothing to me. For God's sake, I hardly knew the man.'

'You gave him your trust,' Woodend said softly. 'An' that's not somethin' you hand out lightly.'

He was speaking the truth, Paniatowski thought. But he was saying more. He was saying: 'We're a team – and whatever else you do, don't lie to me.'

She took a slug of her vodka. 'I'll be more careful, next time,' she promised.

'But not *too* careful,' Woodend cautioned. 'If you spend all your time worryin' about gettin' your fingers burnt, you never find out what a great pleasure it is to warm your hands by the fire.'

Paniatowski grinned. 'What are you quoting from, sir?' she asked. 'The follow-up to the *Working for Woodend Manual – Uncle Charlie's Advice to the Lovelorn*?'

For a moment, she wondered if she had gone too far, then Woodend returned her grin and said, 'Somethin' of that nature,' he agreed. 'Shall we talk about the case now?'

239

'Yes, I think that would be a good idea,' Paniatowski said.

'An ambitious young sergeant finds himself workin' in a place where there's a lot of activity which, if it's not exactly criminal, in teeterin' on the edge of it,' Woodend said. 'An' he sees the opportunity to make a tidy sum for himself. A bit of protection money here, a percentage off an illegal gamblin' operation there, a deal with a stolen car ring somewhere else. An' of course, his masterpiece – his blackmailin' partnership with Gypsy Elizabeth Rose.'

'And then the anonymous letters started to arrive,' Paniatowski said.

'Exactly,' Woodend agreed.

'Where do you think they came from?'

'We'll never know for sure, but in all probability one of the people he was puttin' the squeeze on finally decided he'd had enough. Anyway, once the anonymous letters *did* start to arrive, Hanson had two options. One of them was to quit while he was ahead – but he was too greedy for that. The other was to make sure that when Chief Inspector Turner finally got off his arse an' started investigatin', there was somebody else already in place to take the fall. An' the somebody he chose was Punch Davies. I imagine it won't be long before we come across a few bank accounts which Hanson opened in Davies' name. They won't contain a lot of money – but there will be enough in them to incriminate him.'

'He'd arranged for a number of other people to implicate Davies as well, didn't he?' Paniatowski said.

'Aye,' Woodend agreed. 'People like Gutteridge. But they were what you might call a last line of defence. They were only to implicate Punch when it was plain they were goin' down themselves. But we're getting' ahead of ourselves. Hanson was settin' Davies up to take the fall, then Chief Inspector Turner – God bless him – completely buggered up his plans by tryin' to warn Davies off. An' that had an effect that neither Turner nor Hanson could have anticipated. Up until that point, Davies had had no idea he was under suspicion. Once he found out he was, he was determined to clear his name.'

'That's why he suddenly started putting in appearances on the Golden Mile.'

'Correct. An' he must have been a pretty good detective, because we know from the fact that he talked to Elizabeth Rose an' Bolton that he must have been gettin' close to at least part of Hanson's network. An' that, of course, is why he had to be killed.'

'And Gypsy Elizabeth Rose?'

'I don't think Hanson ever intended usin' her as part of his plan to run rings round Charlie Woodend, but then one of his team – possibly Stone, or maybe Eliot – must have come up with the information that Davies had been to see her. Now Hanson had two choices again – he could suppress the report an' run the risk of me findin' out later that he'd done it – or he could tell me about that meetin'. He decided in the end to tell me about it, because, in the meantime, he'd come up with a neat little refinement which he thought would only add to my confusion.'

'What neat little refinement?'

'I'll get back to that later,' Woodend promised. 'For the moment, let's stick to the main story. After I'd been to see the gypsy, Hanson started to wonder whether it might have been a mistake to let me talk to her. An' from there, it was only a short step to him seein' her as the weakest link in the chain. So she had to be got rid of.'

'What I don't see is how you came to suspect Fr— Hanson in the first place,' Paniatowski said.

'That wasn't hard – once we'd learned that Davies, instead of bein' a crook, was as pure as the driven snow,' Woodend told her. 'You see, the villain really had to be some kind of bobby.'

'Why?'

'Because the rumours about Davies emerged from police headquarters, which means that was where they must have been planted in the first place. And the only person who *could* have planted them was another bobby. Then there was my little talk with Gypsy Rose Elizabeth.'

'What about it?'

'She told me that the thing I had in common with Davies was that we both felt guilty about lettin' our daughters down. That rattled me – as it was intended to – because, you see, I was already subconsciously frettin' over movin' my Annie away from her school an' all her friends.'

'You've lost me,' Paniatowski confessed.

'Everythin' depends on whether you believe the gypsy's warnin' or not.'

'And did you?'

'For a while, I at least half-believed it,' Woodend confessed, 'but when I found out about the blackmail business I began to see her less as a mystic an' more as a con-man. So if she hadn't read my mind, just where had she got her information from?'

'Police records!'

'Spot on. She knew I'd been transferred from London. She knew I had a fifteen-year-old daughter who was still at school. An' bein' both a smart woman an' an amateur psychologist, she worked out I'd probably be worryin' about Annie. But the point is, she'd never have been able to get that information on her own – it had to come from a bobby.'

'Clever,' Paniatowski admitted.

'Me? Or Elizabeth Rose?'

'Both of you.'

'Hanson was clever, too,' Woodend said. 'He tried to bugger up my brain by the Annie thing, an' he tried to bugger up yours by encouragin' you to go on a wild goose chase over this hit-an'-run accident.'

True, Paniatowski thought bitterly. Hanson had known who'd knocked down the old lady, but he must also have known – given the stark facts as they stood – that it wouldn't be Bolton she suspected, but one of the last five Golden Milers to leave the hotel.

'I still don't why you homed in on Hanson, rather than anybody else on the local force,' she said.

'If you're goin' to fit somebody up, your best plan is to choose a feller you know well. That way, he's not likely to surprise you. The first time I met Hanson, he told me he'd worked very closely with Davies. In fact, he said that the only reason he wasn't workin' on any of Davies' current cases was because he'd been on leave when they were assigned. An' there was an added advantage in pickin' Davies rather than anybody else.'

'What was it?'

'Davies trusted him. It's more than possible that he kept Hanson informed about his attempts to clear his name.' Woodend paused to light up a Capstan Full Strength. 'Then there was the fact that Hanson seemed very interested in spendin' a lot of his time with you.'

'Are you saying he didn't find me attractive?' Paniatowski demanded – and the moment the words were out of her mouth she realised how ridiculous she must sound and felt herself starting to blush.

Woodend chuckled. 'Oh, he found you attractive, all right. But you were also an invaluable source of information from right in the middle of the enemy camp.'

'I've been a fool, haven't I?' Paniatowski asked.

'We're all entitled to one mistake, lass,' Woodend said. He grinned again. 'Just don't go makin' any more.'

'I'll do my best not to.'

'But the biggest clincher of all, as far as leadin' me to Hanson went, was that Gypsy Elizabeth Rose's body was buried in a shallow grave,' Woodend continued.

'What did that tell you?'

'That the killer needed to make it difficult to establish the exact time of death. An' why? Because though he had a rock-solid alibi for earlier in the evenin', the one he had for the time she was actually killed was shakier – an' certainly wouldn't stand close scrutiny.'

'Hold on a minute,' Paniatowski interrupted. 'I'm not disputing the fact that Hanson had Elizabeth Rose killed – but he couldn't have done it himself, because he was with me.'

'When you came into the dinin'-room the mornin' after your night of passion with Hanson, you looked a real mess. It wasn't just that you were wearin' the same clothes you'd had on the previous evenin' – a clear pointer that you hadn't been back to your own room – but from the look on your face I'm guessin'

that it must have felt as if you had the Halle Orchestra playin'
in your head. An' out of tune, at that!'

'I was feeling pretty rough,' Paniatowski admitted.

'Now the thing is, from what I'd seen of you earlier, I'd
gained the impression you were the kind of lass who could
hold her booze, an'—'

'Now I get it!' Paniatowski said.

'Get what?' Woodend asked innocently.

'Get why you insisted that I got drunk last night.'

'Do you?'

'Yes. You did it because you wanted to see what I'd look
like this morning.'

'An' you looked fine. From bein' virtually legless at midnight, you'd recovered enough to be ready for action by eight
o'clock in the mornin'. So I knew I'd been right about you
when I'd decided you could hold your booze. But it had
been an entirely different story after the night you spent with
Hanson.'

'We both had a last whisky just before we went to sleep.
He must have slipped a knock-out drop in mine.'

'Aye, he did,' Woodend agreed. 'An' while you were out
for the count, he drove down to the South Pier an' killed the
gypsy. When I saw you this mornin', I was finally sure that's
what must have happened, an' I knew that as well as puttin'
a tail on Gutteridge, we needed to put one on Hanson.'

'It's an education working with you, sir,' Paniatowski
told him.

That's just what Bob Rutter might have said, Woodend
thought, feeling inordinately pleased with himself.

'I suppose you're here because you're expecting me to pat
you on the back and bring out the cigars, are you?' Detective
Chief Superintendent Ainsworth asked, looking up from his
paperwork at the man in the hairy sports coat who was standing
in front of his desk.

'No, sir, I'm not here for that,' Woodend replied evenly.
'I'm here because you left instructions that I was to report to
you as soon as I got back to Whitebridge.'

'You've left Blackpool in a real mess.'

'Really. I thought I'd done a pretty good job.'

'A pretty good job!' Ainsworth repeated. 'You've arrested one of our own for a double murder, and you've got one of Blackpool's top attractions locked up on a hit-and-run charge.'

'They did do it,' Woodend pointed out.

'Of course they did it!' Ainsworth exploded. 'Nobody's disputing that. But there are ways to handle delicate matters of this nature – and ways *not* to handle them. And you seem unable to distinguish between the two.'

'Are you sayin' I shouldn't have arrested Tommy Bolton, sir?' Woodend asked.

'He had a bit too much to drink – as we all do on occasions – and accidentally killed an old woman who probably hadn't got much longer to live anyway. He'd never have repeated the mistake, and by locking him up you've done serious damage to Blackpool's tourist trade.'

'Are you sayin' I shouldn't have arrested him, sir?' Woodend repeated.

Ainsworth took a handkerchief out of his pocket, and mopped his brow. 'No! No, of course not.'

'That's all right, then. What about Frank Hanson? Should I have let him get away with it?'

'He had to be punished for his crimes, of course. But that might have been accomplished without the glare of publicity there'll be when he comes to trial.'

'You're sayin' I should have given him the same option he was givin' Gutteridge, an' let him jump off the Tower?'

'I can think of officers who would have done that,' Ainsworth said, noncommittally.

'Aye, well, I'm not one of them,' Woodend said. 'Besides, he'd never have taken that option. He's a real chancer. Even now, he probably still thinks he can find some way to wriggle out of the mess he's landed himself in.'

'But you didn't even try, did you? You didn't even test the water,' Ainsworth said. He turned his attention back to the paperwork on his desk. 'That's all, Chief Inspector. You can go now.'

'There is one more thing before I leave, sir,' Woodend said. 'Sergeant Paniatowski.'

'What about her?'

'I've nothin' against workin' with women, sir, but I find her a bit hard to take. I'd appreciate it if you could assign me another bagman for my next case.'

'Would you, indeed?!' Ainsworth demanded. 'Well, let me make one thing clear, Chief Inspector. I'm the one who decides who works with who in this county – and you're stuck with Paniatowski. Is that clear?'

'Yes, sir,' Woodend said, bowing his head.

And then he turned quickly to the door, before Ainsworth had a chance to see the grin which was starting to spread across his face.

Epilogue

His mother had forgotten to lock the box room again, and Peter Davies took the opportunity to sneak in. He closed the door quietly behind him and ran his eyes over all the toys – especially the dolls. They were as new and fresh as when they had first come out of their wrappers. They had never been played with – and never *would* be played with. Except by him.

He remembered the old days, the days when there had been just him, Mummy and Daddy. How he had snuggled up in bed with them. How he had been the centre of their world. And then Susan had come along, and spoiled it all.

He stood on tiptoe and took one of the dolls from the shelf – a bright pink one with a bald head and puckered lips. It had been one of Susan's favourites, back when she'd been a toddler. Back when she'd shown some interest in the world around her.

Holding the doll by its legs, he turned it upside down and told himself he was going to count slowly to ten.

'One,' he began. 'Two . . . three . . . four . . .'

There'd been a time when he had thought his daddy hadn't loved him as much as he loved Susan. But he'd been wrong. His daddy had loved him more – much more. And he'd proved it.

'Five . . . six . . . seven . . .'

He felt a tightening across his chest, and his small breaths were now coming quickly and irregularly. It was no good – he simply could not hold out any more.

He loosened his grip, and felt the doll slowly slip from his hands. He waited until he heard the sound of the impact before he opened his eyes again. The doll was lying on the floor, in just the position he'd expected it to be.

He experienced the moment of panic which always hit him at this point. What if he'd damaged it? What if there was even a thin, hairline crack on its skull? However would he explain that to his mother?

He picked up the doll and saw there was no evidence at all of its fall to the ground. He breathed a sigh of relief. He was safe – at least this time. But he knew there would be other times, because there always were.

He replaced the doll on the shelf, making sure it was in exactly the same position as he had found it. Then he opened the door again, listened carefully for his mother and stepped quickly into the corridor.

He sighed. Dropping *dolls* on their heads was a lot of fun, he thought – but it was nowhere near as good as doing the real thing.